FATES

OF

MIDGARD

An Inner Origins Book

ELLIS LOGAN

An Earth Lodge® Publication
Roxbury, Connecticut

Published in the U.S.A. by Earth Lodge®
Cover Design by Maya Cointreau

ISBN 978-1-944396-25-1

"Let silence, then, be granted,
While we sing the loss of thanes."

Snorri Sturlson
The Prose Edda

"His hair is black, his look draws love, his glance
shoots fire, and the hero-light gleams around him."

M.I. Ebbutt
The Legend of Cuchulain

Chapter 1

"Are you going to lie there all day?"

"Hold on, let me give it some thought." I closed my eyes and checked in with my body. "Maybe."

I stayed on the floor, the hard oak planks cool against my shoulder blades. It was a nice contrast to the warm, humid air in the room.

"Yeah, I think I might," I reaffirmed. "It's pretty comfy down here."

Laughter pealed around me, echoing in the large hall and making some of the silver shields hanging on the wall ring in sympathy. I opened my eyes and gazed at my tormentor.

Amber Slaight stood peering down at me, amusement clear in her eyes. Her dark hair was wound in several small braided buns atop her head, which only served to accent her pixie-like appearance. Well, that, and a plethora of rave-worthy glitter eyeshadow and long fake lashes. I swear, only Amber could get decked out for training and not chip a nail.

I grinned up at my friend who only moments before had handily flipped me over her shoulder onto my back.

"But, then again, maybe I won't," I said, kipping up and landing lightly on my feet in one smooth movement.

"Good. You know, I think you've really got the hang of the glima now. Let's try it again." She came at me head on, grappling with me as she attempted to flip me again.

"Not this time," I vowed, and pushed back, pulling her arm down across my waist, twisting my body to push her to her knees. Quickly, before she could sprite her way out of it, I put one knee into her back, forcing her to the ground and pulling her arm behind her to apply more pressure. "Yield."

More laughter tinkled out of her and she nodded. "I yield."

I grinned and let her up, lending her a hand for support. Amber had been training me in the ancient Viking style of hand-to-hand combat, glima, for the last two months. Despite the fact that I was several inches taller and had years of training in martial arts, including Krav Maga and Capoeira, today was one of the few times I had outmaneuvered her. Amber Slaight was a fae warrior, part of the elite Light Guard, and one of my best friends.

When I'd found out I was fae just a few short months ago, it had all come as a shock to me. My mother had raised me to be a normal human girl. Well, as regular as you could be when you held several black belts and moved to a new town every six to twelve months for your mother's work. At the start of my senior year of high school we'd settled in Bennington, Vermont, and everything had been picture-book perfect. I'd quickly fallen in with a great group of people, and even found a serious boyfriend. It was the first place I'd ever lived where I'd really felt home.

Unfortunately, before the month was out I'd I discovered my boyfriend's parents were sinister Dark fae, my mother was a Light fae who worked hard to protect the world of humans, and I had special powers. My mother had been kidnapped, tortured and drugged in an attempt to lure me to the dark side. (Hey evil people, here's a tip, don't mess with my family if you want me to work with you.) Then, to top it all off, my boyfriend dumped me.

Don't get me wrong, it hadn't been all bad. I'd met Amber and some other really nice Light fae when I journeyed to their homeland of Valhalla in Aeden, a hidden underground realm of the fae, nestled deep in the hollow core of the earth. I'd even gotten to know my father, Bran Le Fay, who turned to be the commander of the Light Guard and a really good guy. The dad I had never known had immediately arranged a rescue team to retrieve my mom from the Shade Council, the leaders of the Dark fae. Mom was still unconscious in a form of suspended animation, suffering the effects of a Light anti-serum that we had yet to find the antidote to, but at least she was safe here in the fae sanatorium with several other Shade victims.

"You know, I think we may make a Lasrach warrior out of you yet," Amber winked at me, bringing me out of my thoughts.

"Really?" I quipped. "Because in the two months I've been here, we have yet to go over any lasair moves."

Lasair was a specialized form of fae martial arts that integrated dancelike moves and acrobatics in a way that made Brazilian capoeira look positively remedial. The word itself meant "flash of light," which is exactly what the swift, graceful moves brought to mind – if your brain could process what was happening before you were taken down.

"Patience, young grasshopper. Glima may look clunky compared to lasair, but it is essential to learn how to move flawlessly and slowly before you can flash. Besides, with all your other training, I think you will pick it up even faster than the glima."

"I thought all my moves were slow, compared to yours?" I asked wryly.

"Slow for a Light Guard, but you know you're a better fighter than most. Save the false modesty for the men-folk – we must be gentle with their fragile egos."

I laughed, and Amber joined in, linking arms with me.

"Come on, let's go grab some food."

"Alright," I agreed, letting her drag me out of the training room. "Speaking of men-folk, have you had any news from Ewan?"

Amber's boyfriend was also in the Light Guard. He was leading one of the three teams tracking down research firms with ties to the Dark, searching for an antidote to the anti-serum. So far, there had been several promising leads, but the labs kept turning up empty or wiped clean of any useful information. With every day that passed, I felt more and more frustrated. Since Amber hadn't seen her boyfriend in all that time, I knew she was getting just as antsy as I was for some concrete results.

"Ugh, no," she growled. "I am so sick of the Dark. Your father says he can't understand how they are always two steps ahead of us. He thinks it must have something to do with the Morrigan's visions."

I shivered at the mention of the vilest man I'd never met. Mikael Morrigan was the leader of the American Shade council, and was just about as dark as they come. Even worse, he was a powerful Earth fae with a penchant for igniting natural disasters. As a descendent of Verdandi, one of the three "fates" or seers known as Norns, he had an awesome tendency to see deeply into the present moment, which apparently meant he could see our plans even as they hatched. Even more disturbing, as least for me, he was able to tap into other people's visions as they were having them.

Why did this bother me? Because, lucky me, I had Norn ancestry, too, and had inherited my paternal grandmother Kalila Norna's ability to see events before they happened. Mikael had been torturing me for months through my visions, threatening my family and friends if I didn't join the Dark and help them take over the world. I didn't have a handle yet on what that would entail, but I knew helping the Dark wasn't an option for me.

The Dark had a long history of using humans for their own evil purposes. Pretty much every corrupt corporation you could think of that abused the earth, caused pollution or took advantage of the downtrodden had a fae on its board pulling the strings.

Ever since I'd tuned into my own abilities as an earth fae, I couldn't begin to imagine harming the planet in any way. I could feel the light and the energy that flowed through everything on a quantum level, and the idea of poisoning that beauty of being had become especially disturbing to me. Not that I was running out and buying hippie skirts and flower garlands anytime soon. But, the sentiment was there.

We rode the moving staircase in a spiral down from the tower's training arena, each of us silent and captive to our own thoughts. When we arrived at the bottom, I forced myself not to think about the Morrigan – not only was it unproductive, but just thinking about him could have the unpleasant side effect of inviting him in with another forced vision and psychic visitation. It had happened enough times over the last few months that I knew better than to leave any opening, no matter how small. I turned my mind back to what Amber had said about the lasair training as we exited the golden tower that housed all the defense, intelligence and military training facilities of Aeden's capital city, Valhalla.

"So, great teacher, when do I get to start the lasair training, anyway?" I asked, smirking at her.

"Actually, I think we can start tomorrow."

"Seriously?" I whooped. I wasn't a woo-girl, but sue me, I was excited. "Yes! Finally."

Amber laughed.

"If I'd known this was all it would take to get you out of your funk, I would have started the training weeks ago," she teased.

"Yeah, well, I'm just excited that I get to learn the key to defeating a Light Guard," I laughed, hip checking her as we walked. "Once I know lasair, I'll be able to kick Alec's butt, assuming he ever comes back here."

Even though I'd started off joking, the old irritation crept up, and I couldn't help the angry promise that colored my words.

"Now Siri, you know he's doing the best he can. He's been working around the clock under Ewan and Mitch, following every lead they get to find an antidote for your mom."

"Hmpf." I made a face. "Yes, he's been very dedicated to his work. Yet somehow, I can't help noticing that while you get regular updates from Ewan, Mitch, and Bran, Alec has not bothered to contact me once. Not. Once." My voice rose in volume as I spoke, and Amber glanced around with wide, amused eyes, raising a finger to her lips to shush me. We'd just entered our favorite café at the bottom of Tower Six, which also housed a vast indoor, multi-level marketplace, and I could see that I'd drawn the attention of the other diners.

"Fine," I muttered, bowing my head close to hers. "But I mean it. The next time I see him, he's going down."

Out of all the fae I'd come across, Alec was the one who had affected me the most. So much, in fact, that whenever we were near each other I'd felt this massive pull towards him, an amazing flow of energy that lit up every aspect of my being. Amber called it "the surge", and it was the type of romantic connection that all fae tweens dreamed about. It was rare, it was powerful, and it had filled us both with a longing too intense to ignore. I thought we had come to an understanding, and started something together. And then he'd left.

At first, I'd told myself to have faith, but as the bloom of love wore off and the weeks went by, I couldn't help feeling abandoned. Alec had said he thought my family wouldn't accept him, that I was destined to be matched with a more impressive family bloodline. I'd scoffed at that notion with the typical disbelief of any red-blooded, freedom-loving, American girl, but maybe he'd meant it. I suspected now that he was trying to give me room so I could meet someone more suitable, someone with less mixed-human DNA and more fae power and clout.

As if I needed or wanted any more of either. According to ancient Druid prophecy, I was the girl who combined the three necessary bloodlines needed to end the war between the Dark and the Light, either returning peace above and below, or bringing about an era of world slavery and domination by the Dark. I mean, honestly, didn't I have enough to deal with? I figured the least I deserved was to choose my own boyfriend. Too bad he didn't entirely agree.

For all his cockiness, apparently Alec still had some self-esteem issues. His mom was human, and he was sure that the faes-that-be would all be chomping at the bit to hook me up with their prodigals. If he'd bothered to check in with me, he'd know that wasn't the case at all. I'd barely met anyone besides Amber, Bran and a couple other guards since we'd arrived, sticking almost entirely to training and eating during my waking hours. No one had tried to introduce me to their eligible sons. No one had tried to seduce me. But, he hadn't bothered to check, leaving me to become more and more annoyed with his absence.

"I don't care if he is trying to help us and find the antidote for the anti-serum. He could easily have passed on a message or contacted me by now. He's just being a jerk. As usual," I hissed in Amber's ear.

To my surprise, she giggled, her tinkling peal of laughter gaining us even more attention. "Oh, Siri, you are the best, really you are. Of course he's a jerk. He's a guy. But he is totally your jerk. He's not great at opening up, Odin knows, but trust me – even the great Alec Ward can't outrun the surge."

"He can if he's never around to feel it," I muttered.

"Stop worrying so much. Come on, let's eat."

CHAPTER 2

Amber dragged me to the counter where we ordered some raw fruit wraps and cheesy vegetable soufflés. Animal protein was strictly off the menu down in Aeden, although fae did indulge from time to time when they were among humans. Vegetable food sources fueled our fae DNA, sustaining our immune systems in ways that meat never could, and the closer it was to its natural state, the purer the energy rush. We grabbed a couple waters, too, another sought-after source of regeneration for fae. In my head, I'd taken to calling the water here my "happy juice." The waterways that flowed through Aeden were all supercharged by ions from the underground central sun, giving us an energy boost whenever we drank or bathed in them. I'd learned the hard way not to drink any water right before bed, since it tended to affect me a lot like coffee.

I followed Amber to the outdoor seating area, where we had a great view of the seven golden spires circling the source of everyone and everything on earth, the Tree of Life. The tree stood almost 1000 feet tall, and its trunk measured a massive 144 feet in diameter. Fae legend said that the tree had created the earth itself, anchored in orbit by the seven spires which were really part of a vast space ship that had brought the Ancients to our solar system. I wasn't sure how much of the story I really believed, but it was certainly pretty awesome to look at.

That, and the gorgeous red sun that shone directly above, never moving, never setting. When I'd first arrived in Aeden, I'd learned that the Tree of Life anchored the small cold fusion star above me, fueling the particles that are needed to sustain life on this planet. Without it, life on earth would cease to exist. I was sure the human scientists above ground would have a field day with that idea. In fact, my father assured me that was one reason why the Light fae had always kept Aeden a secret, knowing that the humans would fear the life-sustaining powers of the tree, and seek to claim the protection of Valhalla for their own power and gain.

I stared morosely at the tree, part of me wishing I'd never learned about its existence, never learned I was fae. Never had visions, never met Alec.

"Earth to Siri, come in, Earth to Siri." Amber waved her hand in front of my face.

"What?" I yawned and started in on one of the fruit wraps.

"I asked, how have your studies with Mialloch Airron been going? Is he as boring as he seems?"

"Nah, he's not so bad. He's kind of sweet actually. I get the feeling that he hasn't been able to hang out with too many other young fae over the years."

"I should say not! The great Mialloch Airron, consorting with commoners? Who would allow such a thing?" She laughed. "No, Mialloch has been kept apart most of his life, getting special schooling, only attending official court events and spending the rest of his time being groomed to serve on the high council, like his father. You knew that, right?"

"No, I had no idea. He doesn't talk much about himself. My dad only said he was to "tutor me in the ways of the fae" and left it at that."

"What do you guys study, then?"

"The laws of the land, folklore, legends, history. Stuff like that mostly. Aeden in general, you know, plants, animals, geography, the people, that sort of thing."

"Ah, a nice proper crash course in all things fae, I take it?"

"Exactly."

"Sounds riveting."

"It's not too bad. Actually, I think I would like it if I could get past the feeling that I am in summer school and the teacher thinks I'm 'special.'" I used my fingers to make air quotes and Amber snickered.

"What's summer school?" A dry tenor voice sounded behind me, and muscled arms clad in multiple bangles of heavy silver and gold gently placed a tray of food next to mine.

I would have known those bracelets anywhere.

"Hello, Mialloch," Amber smiled at the young fae beside me. Mialloch Airron, fae tutor and apparently heir to a council seat, was tall and attractive, as most fae seemed to be. He was several years older than I, but still coming into his fae powers as an air elemental.

I watched as he carefully lined up his silverware on his tray and laid his napkin fastidiously across his lap, tidily straightening the corners. In my months of study with Mialloch, I'd noticed that he was nothing if not precise. Every morning at eight on the dot he would knock on my chamber door. Once we had exchanged pleasantries and seated ourselves on the sofas across from each other, he would proceed to grill me on the details of our lessons from the day before, followed by another hour of histories, legends, and laws. The material was interesting enough, but the delivery system was less than stellar. If I hadn't been the studious type, I was sure I would have been bored to tears.

But, the lessons seemed important to my father, so I kept up with them. I think Bran felt bad that he hadn't been there for me growing up, not that it was his fault. It's hard to be there for your daughter when you don't even know you have one. Mom had met him on a black ops mission – she'd been commanding a US army team, and he had been with a British Special Forces unit. They'd met, fallen hard and fast for each other, conceiving me in the process. Unfortunately, after the mission ended they'd only had each other's code names and Mom had never been able to track him down to let him know he had a child.

Now Bran was trying to make up for lost time, making sure I had the full fae education I should have had, complete with Guard training. We often had dinner together at my mother's bedside, exchanging the many memories we'd never shared. He was a good man, and I was thankful for this chance to get to know him. I held the image of my mother's recovery foremost in my head at all times, looking forward to the day when she'd wake up and get her first look at him. The look that'd be on her face? Priceless. Even though my cell phone didn't have reception down here in Aeden, I was keeping it charged and at my side at all times, just for that moment.

I smiled to myself, lifting my face to the sun shining above us, allowing myself to be comforted by its warm rays. The temperature in Aeden was a near constant 85F with regular tropical-style downpours and subsequent rainbows. The sun never set, and it never rose. Everything stayed the same. It was a far cry from my life "above below" on Earth, or Midgard as the Valhallan fae liked to call it.

"So, Siri, have you thought more about what you would like to study next?" Mialloch broke into my reverie.

"Well, as exciting as the genesis of Earth and the history of the Ancients before Earth times has been, I was thinking maybe we could start going over fae science, beginning with medicines, plants and herbs. Maybe we will hit on something useful to counteract the anti-serum."

"Isn't that a long shot?" Amber asked.

"Well, yeah, but-"

"Amber is right, Siri," Mialloch interrupted me in that annoying all-knowing way he had. "If there was a fae remedy that could help, I am sure our scientists would have tried it by now."

"I suppose," I reluctantly agreed, chewing my lip. "Still, science has always been one of my favorite subjects. And it can't hurt to know more about the local biology, can it?"

Mialloch looked me over slowly, smiling. I'd never felt any sort of attraction to him beyond the regular comfort and warmth that the touch of Light fae would always bring, but something about the way he was looking at me made me notice him as a man for the first time, not just my teacher. The notion took me off-guard and left me regretting my choice of words.

"I think an understanding of fae biology and plant sciences is a fine avenue to explore, yes. We can start tomorrow. I will leave you now, and acquire some reference materials that I think you will find stimulating. Good day, Siri, Amber." He nodded at us both, taking his tray and sauntering away.

"Mmm, stimulating, indeed," Amber leered over my shoulder. "Who knew the young oak had it in him?"

"Young oak?"

"Oh, just faeling slang for someone who is destined to act old before their time, unyielding, boring, you know. But that. Well, well, well. Looks like someone has their eye on you."

"Oh please, let's not go there. I don't feel even the slightest bit of attraction for him, no surge, no nothing. Besides, he's never given me the slightest hint that he sees me as anything other than his pupil."

"Well, he just did. That was a serious checking out he gave you. Besides, his kind don't care about the surge."

"His kind?"

"Fae elite. Someday he'll be on the Light Council. That boy will mate for power and position – probably have an arranged marriage."

I thought back to what Alec had said the last time he saw me, how he was sure my father would try to set me up with someone more important than him, someone with purer fae blood that his half-human self. If he was right, if my father was trying to set me up with Mialloch...

"I think I need to talk to my father," I growled, gathering up my trash and starting to stand.

"Why, what's up?" Amber looked at me with concern. "Have you had another vision?"

"Only of me using my new glima moves on my dad. I just remembered something Alec said the night he left. I think the whole tutoring thing might be a ruse to get me together with Mialloch."

Amber's dark eyes widened. "Oh, seriously? I hadn't thought of that. But it does make sense. Oh wow! If not your dad, Mialloch's own father could totally have engineered it. He's been trying to get Mialloch to date for a couple years now, but Mialloch is all books and no play, if you know what I mean. Oh, they're good. What a perfect plan."

"Um, hello? Already taken here? I don't need to be set up, I have Alec." Or, at least, I thought I did. "I may not have seen him in forever, but I'm not ready to hook up with every fae boy I meet."

"Does your dad know that?"

I gaped at her and she raised her hands in defense.

"Hey now, I didn't mean it that way. I'm sure your dad doesn't think you're a loose woman. No, I meant, does your dad know you are taken?"

I blushed. "No, I haven't talked to him about Alec at all. I think he suspects, maybe, because one time we had a conversation about the surge, and he looked surprised that I knew anything about it. But no, I haven't mentioned Alec."

"Well, then cut your dad some slack. Parents always want to see their kids settled with someone suitable. They just don't always have the best idea what would actually suit us," She winked at me.

"I'm still going to go talk to him. No way will I have him parading boys past me at some fae cotillion or anything. But I guess I'll leave the fighting gloves at the door."

"Probably a good idea," Amber agreed.

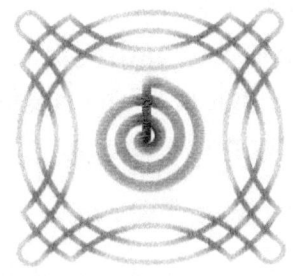

CHAPTER 3

Ten minutes later, I was facing off with two Light Guards outside my father's office. The door was locked, so I knew he must be inside, but they weren't responding to any of my threats to open up.

"Look, Dorian, I know you can hear me." I stood toe to toe with the unresponsive guard, poking him in the chest with my finger as he ignored me and continued to stare straight ahead. "I want to see my father. Now."

"Commander Le Fay is in a meeting, but I am sure that he will see you in a few minutes, if you'll just wait patiently." The voice behind me would normally have been soothing, after all, Mireia served as the ambassador of Valhalla, but today it simply made me want to ruffle her feathers.

"Commander Le Fay has some explaining to do," I said, crossing my arms over my chest and glaring at her. "What's he doing in there, anyway?"

"If you must know, your father is talking with some of the operatives above below. They reached a water station and checked in twenty minutes ago."

Hope flared in my chest. "Any news about the antidote?"

"I don't know. Like you, I was told to wait." The barest hint of annoyance lent a slight blush to her dark cheeks. "Shall we?"

She pointed to the set of golden doors on the other side of the landing, these ones etched with a bisected spiral indicating the search for order – the ambassadorial offices. My father's doors had a plus sign engraved upon them, setting forth the ideals of equal justice, balance and harmony.

This was the first time I had been in Mireia's offices, and I was struck by how different they were from the ones across the hall. My father's command center held a massive round table surrounded by chairs where he conducted most of his meetings, and an extensive view of the homes and farms outside the city. Two small rooms off to the sides held his private office and a secure holding cell. I'd been told that infractions and treason among the Light were rare, but when they did occur they were taken seriously.

Mireia's rooms, on the other hand, were luxuriously appointed, in stark contrast to most of the décor I had seen in Aeden. Works of art from all over the world adorned every shelf, including strange pieces whose origins I couldn't begin to guess. Tapestries lined the walls depicting the origins of the fae, their original planet, their travel through space, and the genesis of Earth from the Tree of Life. The ancient woven cloths brought the stories to life in a magical way that Mialloch had never managed during our forays into the fae histories.

"Make yourself at home," Mireia said, indicating some hand carved wooden chairs by the windows. The room looked out over the central plaza, its view dominated by the great redwood outside.

"Wow, this is amazing. It's like you have a front seat to the center of the world." I walked over to the window.

"Indeed," she said, joining me at the glass. "These rooms remind me that we are all one. We all come from the same place, you, me, humans, the dark, the light. We all came from an origin steeped in hope. Our ancestors lost everything before they journeyed here, but they never gave up. And look where we are now."

"Yeah right, look at us, stuck in the middle of a fae war, with the threat of Dark domination looming over all our heads."

"No. Look. Really look where we are. Standing next to the source of all life. Standing next to a dream. This world is nothing, if not a possibility. We are immeasurably blessed. Every moment of life we have is borrowed. A blessing. Keep that knowledge in your heart, and you can never go wrong. It is only when we start to doubt the blessing, to feel disconnected from the oneness of life, that fear sets in and darkness overshadows our true nature. Everyone's true nature is one of light. Remember that."

Her words stunned me.

19

"I've never thought about it that way. But you're right, I guess I've always known that on some level."

I thought about Rowan, Cooper and Holly. All darklings, young fae with family ties to the Dark who hadn't chosen a side yet. Despite other people's warnings that I shouldn't trust them, I still felt the good in the darklings. But someone like the Morrigan, or Rowan's father Sullivan Carey? Just thinking about them gave me the creeps, and I shuddered.

"Are you cold?" Mireia asked, ever the good hostess.

"No, I just...I can't help thinking about people like Mikael Morrigan, and the other Shade leaders. What about them? I don't feel anything good when I am near them. The Dark, their touch is so cold and shattering. How can you find the light in them?"

"Sometimes, it's just a matter of trust. You have to hold the knowledge deep in your core. You have to hold the light for them, so they can find their way back." Her eyes looked sad and removed, like she was viewing something in the distance. "To do anything else is to deny the true nature of who and what we are."

"You sound like you have personal experience in this."

"I do. My brother used to work for Bran, until he was captured by the Shades a long time ago. He was very young, inexperienced. By the time our people were able to get to him, he had already undergone months of brainwashing by the Dark. He renounced the Light and became a Shade agent. I haven't seen him in twenty years, although I understand he leads an elite fighting team for their Council."

"Oh wow, I am so sorry. I didn't know that could happen, that you could switch sides. I mean, I thought once you had your Choosing Ceremony, that was it."

"We thought so, too. But the Dark have devoted much of their time and resources to finding ways to break their tie to the Light, and our own. Their methods are very effective. You have seen how they raise their own young, subtly influencing them against the Light, not really showing them the truth of the Dark until they have been fully drawn in."

"Yes, Miko told me as much. It's terrible." I wanted so badly to save Rowan from that fate, but the longer I went without seeing him, the more I feared that wouldn't be possible. Since he'd dumped me two months ago, he'd refused to talk to me directly, although he was still feeding Vala helpful information about his father's dealings with the Shades whenever he could.

"Ah, Mikowa. How is your little friend enjoying his stay here?"

"He loves it. I barely see him anymore, he spends all his time in the tree there. He says he's doing his own reconnaissance, but I think it's so safe here, he just doesn't feel he's needed."

"He's probably right. And, being in the life tree does give him a unique vantage point."

When I'd first come into my powers, I'd unknowingly saved the squirrel from becoming roadkill using my fledgling healing abilities. He'd followed me home and helped me escape when the Dark first attacked my mother and me at home. He was the first animal I'd ever communicated with, but not the last. The first time he'd spoken to me, I'd been floored. Apparently squirrels had an honor code, and if you saved a life you were owed a year of service in return. Miko was just how you'd expect a squirrel to be – feisty, fast, and always hungry. He'd been a lot of help to me in those early days, running from the Shades. I didn't begrudge him the fun he was having here in Aeden.

The slight hissing sound of the pneumatic doors sliding open alerted us to a new visitor.

"The Commander will see you know, faeling Le Fay."

I bristled at Dorian's reference, resenting his implication that I was still a child, simply because I hadn't reached eighteen and chosen sides yet.

"Careful, Dorian. I can return to mock you all day while you're on duty."

"I'm not worried. I will just set out some blocks and coloring books for you by my feet, I am sure that will keep you distracted," he taunted me.

I was ready to say something witty back, I'm sure, but Mireia beat me to it.

"Claffsson, thank you for letting us know Commander Le Fay is ready to meet with his daughter. You may go now."

Mireia knew how to put someone in their place without lowering herself to their level. I totally needed to learn that skill. Dorian left without another word and I thanked Mireia for our talk. Heading back across the landing to my father's doors, where a new set of guards was now installed keeping watch for the hour, I squared my shoulders and took a deep breath before raising my hand to open the door panels.

I reminded myself to see the light in my father, no matter how annoyed I was with him for what I now suspected was a thinly veiled attempt at matchmaking.

Striding confidently into the room, I took in the scene. Where the table was usually bare and clean, sheets of paper and open scrolls littered its surface. My father, usually as resplendent and brawny as a blonde mid-life version of Thor, looked haggard. Dark circles under his eyes hinted at his level of weariness, and his long hair was wild and unbrushed. I'd never seen him look so ragged. The fight went out of me, replaced by concern.

"Dad, are you okay? You don't look well."

He looked up at me and smiled. "I'm alright, child. One of our teams was captured last night, and I have been trying to figure out what went wrong."

Instantly, I thought of Alec and Ewan. I felt the blood drain from my face.

"What happened?" I asked, afraid to know, but needing the full story.

"We lost contact with Kuan Fu and her people after they went into a research facility in Yanxi. We don't know what happened exactly, but we've received confirmation that the Shades have them."

Relief flooded me. Not Alec, then. A moment later, guilt hit me, too. Surely there were people who would miss these team members. More light fae suffering at the hands of the Dark. I shuddered, remembering what Mireia had said about reconditioning prisoners, and hoped that these people wouldn't suffer the same fate as her brother or the anti-serum test subjects in the Sanatorium.

"That's terrible. But how can these old scrolls help us?"

"Some of these scrolls hold old prophecies from our ancestors, and some have descriptions of places we haven't searched yet. I am hoping I can find something new. Any information that we might have missed." He dragged a hand through his hair, and I began to understand why it was looking the way it did.

"But, why are you here? You had something you want to discuss?"

Suddenly, my love life didn't seem so important. Still, I supposed that if I could offer him some sort of distraction from the day's events, some mundane family interaction, it might actually be good for him.

"It's about my studies. Actually, it's about Mialloch, in particular."

"Oh?"

The way my father perked up suddenly with interest did not escape me.

"Yes. It has come to my attention that some people might get the wrong idea about us, that a family like his might think you were, um, trying to play matchmaker?"

"Ah, I see." He rubbed the week-old scruff on his chin and peered at me intently. "And that would be a problem?"

Warning bells went off in my head and I reminded myself to stay cool.

"Well, yes," I responded lightly. "Since you've only just met me, and you know I am in the middle of a crisis now, I wouldn't want anyone to think you were being presumptuous and trying to set me up with someone I barely know."

He laughed at me then. "Ah, but now you are getting to know him. He is a nice young man, is he not?"

"Well, yeah, sure, he's nice, but—"

"His father is a fine man, a good friend of mine and an asset to the Council, as Mialloch will one day be. Is it not good to align yourself with people who can be helpful to you, and to get to know the people who matter to me?"

Irritation began to set in.

"Look, he is a good teacher, if a little boring, but I'm not interested in dating anyone new." My father's eyes flared at my words. "If you want me to meet people, fine, but don't go around trying to set me up with anyone else without asking me first, okay? Where I come from, girls don't do arranged marriages anymore. We marry for love."

"Ha, love. Next thing, you'll be talking about the surge to me."

"And would that be so wrong? I know you felt it for my mother. You know it's not just some fairy tale," I accused, standing over him. "It's not like you ever married another woman after Mom. So why would you expect me to toss something like that away in exchange for 'an asset'?"

"Toss it away?" He stood up and gripped me by the shoulders, looking at me intensely. "Are you trying to tell me that you have experienced the surge with someone? Someone here? Who?"

I couldn't tell if he was upset, worried or just excited. "Yeah, someone from here. But he's not here now."

"What do you mean he's not here now? No one has traveled lately from Aeden outside of the Guard. Are you telling me you have been seeing one of my men behind my back?"

Okay, so definitely not excited, I thought. I knocked his hands off my shoulders and took a step back.

"Gee, dad, how do you know it's a guy? Maybe I like girls, huh?"

"Siri, you're trying my patience. Who is this person?"

"You should know. You sent him to me, after all." He just glared at me, and I relented, deciding to cut him some slack. "Alec? Alec Ward? Remember him, one of your top fighters?"

Realization dawned across his features, and he sank back into his chair, gesturing for me to do the same. He leaned back and gazed at the ceiling as if searching for answers, before finally returning his gaze to me.

"Okay. So, Alec, is it? He is a fine young man. Not one I would have chosen for you, given his background and his lifestyle, but yes, he is a good man."

"His background?" Alec's worries sprang to mind, and I bristled at the thought that he might have been right. "Do you mean his human mother?"

"No." My father sighed, sounding twice as exhausted as he had when I'd first entered. "I mean the losses he has suffered. He was hurt badly as a child by the Dark, and has much anger and sadness in him still. I would have chosen someone more stable, more protected, for you than Alec."

"You don't think Alec can protect me? What makes you think I even need protecting?

"No, that isn't quite what I meant. The connection of the surge is intense. Sometimes, I wish I had never felt it. It makes all other interactions seem...pale. I know Alec can protect you from the Dark. But who will protect you from Alec?"

"Oh, Dad." I leaned forward and hugged him. "Don't worry so much. Everything is going to work out fine."

He exhaled shakily into my hair, and chuckled. "I wish I'd known you as a child. Have you always been this wise?"

"Of course," I winked. "Tyr-wise, and Tyr-brave, just like Mom."

He embraced me tightly and then set me back in my chair.

"Hmm, so, Alec Ward, eh? Just wait till Flynn gets news of this, he's going to be bursting with excitement."

"Flynn?"

"Alec's father. He's been investigating Shade activities in Virginia."

"Oh. Well, don't go telling him anything yet. Alec and I barely got a chance to discuss the situation before he left in October, and we haven't talked since. I think he's been worried about how you'd react. He warned me that you would want me to meet people from the ruling families."

"Siri, I'm not going to deny that I think that would have led to an easier life for you in many ways. But you're right, I can't deny you a chance at this sort of a connection. Every princess deserves a fairy tale, right, isn't that what the humans say?" he asked with a smile. Even tired and disheveled, my dad remained a handsome charmer.

"Yes, dad. Every girl. Let's just hope my fairy tale wasn't written by the Grimm brothers. I think I'd like to keep all my toes."

CHAPTER 4

We were buried in scrolls when the call came.

The crystalline bowl of water that always sat on the table shimmered and rippled, ringing gently like a Tibetan singing bowl. The surface smoothed out, and a face appeared in the water. Bran rushed to the bowl, cupping it gently with both hands.

"Ah, hello there, young priestess. You have more news for us?"

I peered over his shoulder. I couldn't hear the whole conversation, since the words of whoever was on the other end could only be heard in the mind. Water fae could communicate through any water source – the rest of us relied on Valhallan water to connect with sacred or consecrated waters above in Midgard.

I caught sight of the face in the bowl and gasped. Without thinking, I elbowed my father out of the way and grabbed the bowl from him, sloshing a bit of water as I collapsed into my chair.

"Rose! I can't believe it! Where are you calling from?" Rose had become a close friend almost immediately when I'd arrived in Vermont. In all the places I'd lived, she was one of the only people I'd ever considered a "best" friend. I'd missed her terribly since I'd come to Aeden, despite Amber's great company. She wasn't fae, though, so I hadn't held high hopes of seeing her any time soon.

I've been apprenticing with Vala as a Druid priestess for the last two years in my spare time. My mom never had the knack for it, but you know how I love plants and being on the mountain, so I was totally up for it. I didn't find out about what was going on with you guys, though, until a couple weeks ago. Vala finally told me, although she's worried it might put me in danger. She looked at someone next to her and stuck out her tongue. Same silly Rose. God, I'd missed her.

"That is amazing. I can't tell you how much I've missed you! This is so great. So, you're a Druid?"

Yeah, and you're a fae. Who knew? We both laughed. *Listen, so here's the thing. I'd really love to spend more time catching up, but first I have to tell you why I called. I think I might have an idea about where we can find an antidote to the anti-serum. I talked with Vala about it, and she agreed to finally let me call you guys. We are still researching it, but I think I'm really on to something. Can you meet me at the safe house in Montreal? Bring your passport, too.*

"Why? Where are we going?" My father looked at me tensely, not able to hear the other side of the conversation.

Ireland, baby. We need to see Airmed, this super reclusive fae healer who I think has what we need. The legends are spotty, but I've got a good feeling about this.

"Wait, Airmed, I know that name. Her name came up in my studies of the Ancient genealogies."

Really? See if you can find out how to get on her good side, because from what Vala says, Airmed does not like visitors. Not at all.

"Ugh, that doesn't sound good. I'll see what I can do. Hey, so, um, how is everybody else?"

You mean everybody, like the whole school, or everybody like Rowan? She smirked at me.

"Jerk. Like Rowan. Is he okay?"

He's not the same as he was before. I think he misses you. He doesn't talk much in school anymore, even Cooper has a hard time making him laugh. The only one he really smiles for anymore is Holly. What happened with you guys?

I glanced at my dad, who was taking in every word. "I can't really talk about it right now. Just, keep an eye on him, okay?"

Definitely. So, tomorrow in Montreal?

"Oh yeah baby, you, me, Montreal! I can't wait! Hey, and do you think you can bring me a Gio's calzone? I miss that place."

Got it, calzones all around. See you soon!

She shimmered out and I leaned back, beaming. My father didn't look nearly as enthused.

"Montreal?"

Okay, so maybe I should have cleared my plan with the Commander of the Light Guard. I swallowed and laid out the conversation for him, watching as his face went from excited to concerned.

"So, you and your friend, who is just a priestess-in-training, have decided that this is a great time to go traipsing off to Ireland in search of some unknown remedy. All by yourselves?"

"Um, well, when you put it that way...I mean, I did assume that Amber would come with, too."

"Right. Great. Because you assumed that I would be perfectly comfortable letting my only daughter, whom I have only just now gotten back in my life, voyage virtually unescorted through Midgard while her mother lies sleeping in the Sanatorium?"

He paused. If looks could burn, I would have been lasered in half.

"Fine. Perfect," he said angrily. "I know you won't be happy unless you go. But I will have a team in place to meet you in Montreal, and you will behave and listen to their team leader at every moment of the mission. Every. Single. Moment. Do you understand me, Siri? I will not have you thinking you can fight these Dark operatives on your own. If any danger presents itself, you are to hang back and let the Light Guard handle it."

"But, Dad, my glima has gotten really good, and Amber was going to start training me in lasair tomorrow."

"I repeat, you will let the Light Guard handle it, and you will defer to the team leader in all decisions. Am I understood?"

"Fine," I ground out.

"Good." Despite the worry etching his forehead, his eyes twinkled. "You know, you really are just like your mother. Now, why don't you go pay her a visit and pack a bag for tomorrow while I make some calls. You and Amber will leave in the morning."

CHAPTER 5

My eyes widened in surprise when I entered my mother's private room at the clinic to find a visitor already sleeping beside her, sharing her bed.

I padded quietly across the room, and took a seat in the chair next to the bed, watching the sleeping pair as their bodies rose and fell in unison, breathing in, and breathing out. The small, black squirrel's tail curled around his body like a blanket while he snored. My mother breathed soundlessly.

"Miko," I whispered gently, stroking his head with one finger. "Wake up."

His eyes opened slowly and came into focus.

"Siri? What are you doing here?"

"I could ask you the same thing," I smiled.

He yawned, daintily stretching his arms.

"I like visiting your mother. She has nice dreams, and it's quiet here. Sometimes those birds outside don't know when to quit chattering. Even when they aren't singing, they are still gossiping, you know what I mean."

"It certainly is quiet here. But I didn't know you visited my mom on your own. Wait a minute, what do you mean she has nice dreams. You can hear her thoughts, too, even when she's sleeping?"

"Sure, kid. You, her, anyone. I told you before, all we animals communicate telepathically. We make sounds, too, but we don't need to. We understand the thoughts before the sounds. As long as they are true dreams and the soul is still linked to the body, I can hear it."

"True dreams?"

"Well, yeah. When you astral travel or have visions that actually take you out of your body, that's a whole different thing. Then you are thinking and processing with your soul, not your brain, not your subconscious. So then, of course I can't hear you."

"Wow, you could be a spy," I teased.

"Yep, fears, desires, we know them all. That's why we are so relaxed, really. We know that everyone is the same. It makes it easier to forgive and co-exist peacefully."

"So, um, is my mom happy? Are her dreams ok? She looks peaceful, but..." I trailed off, thinking of how traumatized she must have been in the days leading up to her infection with the anti-serum, the torture she must have endured. "She must have been so worried, not knowing where I was or if I even got away."

"Don't sweat it kid. She knows you are alright. She actually astral travels quite a bit and some of that knowledge stays with you when you come back to regular dreaming. She knows you're both in Aeden, she knows Bran is trying to help her. She is very peaceful. Like I said, it's quiet here."

"I've heard of astral travel, but I thought it was just something yogis in India did. You're saying we all do it when we sleep?"

"Pretty much, yeah. The body is just a vessel for the piece of Light, or soul, that inhabits it. Your soul can, if it wants to, travel or wander while you are sleeping, visiting other people and places. Even different times, to some degree, since the soul itself isn't bound by physical space-time reality the way the body is."

"Can animals astral travel?"

Miko preened himself, pretending to be offended. "Of course we can, we have souls, don't we?"

"Okay, yeah, sorry! So, she's okay? It's safe for her to travel?"

"Oh, sure. The soul always returns if the body needs it. Of course, her body doesn't really have much need for it right now. And she won't remember much of her travels when she wakes up, since the brain doesn't process that non-physical information very well. But, at least she is at peace."

I sighed, leaning my head on her shoulder. I wished she would wake up, more than anything. During the first few weeks in Aeden, I had tried night after night to heal my mother the way I had healed Miko, opening my body as a channel for the Light, holding her in my arms and sending love and warmth into her body. It hadn't made any difference. According to the doctors, the anti-serum hindered the flow of our Light enough to force us into a state of suspended animation. After infection, only the barest trickle of Light continued flowing through the afflicted, just enough to allow the body to sustain life processes, but not enough to maintain consciousness.

"Can she hear you?"

"No more or less than she can hear you. Don't worry, she knows you have been visiting, and is proud of everything you have been learning here. She almost never dreams of her time with the Dark."

"That's something, I guess. Thank you Miko, for sharing all this with me."

"Anytime, kid. I guess I should have told you sooner, I just didn't think of it. I still forget that this is all new to you."

"That's alright."

Miko brushed a stray hair out of my forehead with his tail. I sighed and closed my eyes, pretending that my mother was simply sleeping, that we'd fallen asleep watching a movie together in bed, and that this was all just a dream. Some days, I missed her so badly it hurt.

I hoped that Rose was on the right track, that whatever she had uncovered would really work to help bring my mother back. That it would bring all the afflicted back from their deep sleep. Out of body traveling or not, I was sure they were all wanting to return to their daily lives, and I knew, watching the hollow eyes of their visitors week after week, that they each had families who missed them terribly.

Rose. I couldn't wait to see her. And as wonderful as Aeden was, I was looking forward to being above below again, too. Eating regular human food, breathing regular earth air, seeing green trees and a starry sky.

"Green trees? Regular food? What aren't you telling me? Are we going back topside?"

I raised my head to look at Miko. The excitement in his eyes was unmistakable.

"Bored much?" I shook my head. "No, don't answer that. Amber and I are leaving in the morning to meet up with my friend Rose, and a team. Rose thinks she has an idea of how to cure mom."

"What, and you were going to leave me behind?" He looked about as offended as any squirrel could.

I laughed. "I wasn't sure I'd be able to drag you away from the Tree. But now that I know where you really spend all your free time...are you sure you want to come? If you want to stay here with my mom, I wouldn't mind. I like the thought of someone being with her who can hear her."

"I get that, kid, really I do. But what kind of squirrel would I be if I let you go into the world alone, when I'm supposed to be protecting you for a year?"

"I won't exactly be alone, you know," I smirked.

"Yeah. Light Guard. That's great and all, but they can't hear the truth behind people's words the way I can. No offense, but I'll feel better knowing I'm with you."

"Okay." I smiled into the little squirrel's big eyes. "Honestly? I'm glad you're coming. I think you've helped me more than anyone, adjusting to everything. Thanks, Miko."

"Anytime, kid. It's been an honor to know you, to have felt your light first hand. Now, if you don't mind, I want to let some of my new friends know I'm going away for a while. I'll meet you later in your room."

He ran over to the door and it opened automatically, letting him back out into the main hall. The doors quietly slid shut behind him and left me alone in the room with my mom. I laid my head back down on her shoulder and closed my eyes, breathing in her scent. Even with the Aeden toiletries keeping her clean, my mother still had its own special scent, unique and instantly comforting. More than that, her skin was still satiny smooth. I breathed deeply, relaxing into her energy. Letting the darkness behind my eyes take me.

It was so very dark, so very quiet. The ground was cold, hard, covered with a thin layer of frost. Lights from a car above me on a hill illuminated the deep woods, and I wondered where I was. I could hear shouts up above.

I started forward in the direction of the shouting. The woods thinned, the undergrowth becoming more sparse. I was almost on the edge of the forest when I practically stumbled over someone crying.

In the dim light, I could see that a dark-haired girl lay propped up against a large pine tree with her eyes closed. Another girl sat next to her near my feet, crying with her back to me. They both looked so familiar. I took another step forward, and gasped in horror as I got a clearer look at Holly, blood matting her hair and spattering her white down jacket.

"Oh no, no, no, no." I shook my head, taking several steps back into the shadows. This, I did not want to see. Why did it have to be Holly? I didn't want to see her die. I may have only known Rowan's sister for a short time, but she had been my friend. Always friendly, always happy.

"What's wrong, Siri?" A harsh voice jeered in my ear.

"You!" I whirled around to face the Morrigan in fury. "You leave my friends alone, do you hear me?"

"Now, now, Siri," Mikael laughed. "I don't know why you would blame this on me." He stood deep in the shadows, his face hidden from view as always. Even in my clearest visions, he hid himself from me.

"Do you think you can threaten me with this, you coward?" I gestured angrily behind me. "How can you think this will convince me to join you? Get a grip, and stay away from my friends!"

His body sank back into the shadows as he retreated, but his laughter echoed all around me. "Either way, Siri, either way. I will have you. Join us, it's your only option."

I screamed in anger – and opened my eyes.

"Scumbag," I muttered.

I had so had it with Mikael and his threats, not to mention his creepy-ass laughter. Most of my visions lately seemed to end with someone close to me dying and I was almost starting to miss the old days. Mudslides. Earthquakes. You know, happy visions.

Vala continued to follow up on each one and ensure that it did not come to pass. By this time, I think my friends at home all had more protection charms on them than anyone should need in a lifetime. Vala had hinted there might be more to it, something in the visions we were missing, but I didn't know what.

What I did know was that the Morrigan was a piece of trash. There was absolutely no way I would ever serve the agenda of the Dark, not after the visions he'd been haunting me with for the past two months and what they had done to my mom. They really should have re-thought their tactics, because right now being a Shade held about as much appeal as listening to a Beiber album. None. At. All.

Vala was careful to remind me that each of my visions simply showed a possible future that I accessed on my own, a special talent I had thanks to my Norn ancestry. She was insistent that Mikael was not actually sending me the visions, just sharing them. Mikael, also descended from a Norn, could only have visions of the present – this also gave him the creepy talent of entering any vision of the past or future while someone else was having it. For the hundredth time, I thanked my great-great-great-grandmother Skuld for her awesome gift. Not.

I sighed and sat up, brushing the hair away from my mom's face.

"I'm sorry, mom. I'm trying to get a handle on my visions the way you taught me, but it doesn't seem to be doing me any good. But I promise, I'll keep trying. And I'll be back soon, okay?"

Of course, she didn't answer me. Every day, I wished she would open her eyes and tease me about my cheesy taste in movies, say anything, but it never happened.

I leaned down and kissed her cheek, breathing in her scent one last time before I left. Who knew when I would be back, how long I would be topside.

"I love you," I whispered, and gave her one last hug.

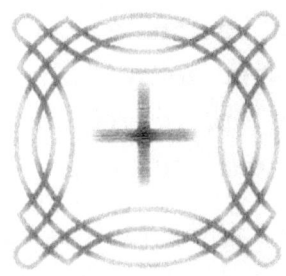

CHAPTER 6

The next morning I was awoken by a sliver of light cascading across my face. I opened my eyes and saw Auroreis standing by the window in my bedroom, pressing the button that retracted golden shutters to let in the ever-present sunlight of Aeden. The inner world of Earth had clouds and rain, just like Midgard, or Earth as I knew it, so the rays could be dimmed, but night never fell.

The fae had long ago found that the best way to avoid insomnia and what Alaskans fondly call "Summer Mania" was to provide lightproof rooms so that the pineal gland could properly recharge and maintain the body's hormonal system during sleep. Of course, that didn't change the fact that the sun never set, and that the fae had no visual way of marking time down in Aeden. Those who lived in the cities kept to a loose work schedule based on Greenwich Mean Time and the twenty-four-hour earth day, but those who lived apart slept, ate, played and worked whenever they felt moved to do so. I hadn't done much in the two months I'd been here other than train with Amber and study with Mialloch, but I could imagine that life on one of the many fae homesteads must be pretty idyllic. The fae had a fairly socialist system set up, wherein basic provisions were provided for and shared by all.

"Amber stopped by a few minutes ago, miss. She said to meet her on the gravicycle deck in half an hour."

I jumped out of bed. "Oh no! But I haven't even packed!" I'd gone straight to bed the night before, totally worn out after my visit to the Sanatorium.

"No worries. I've already started a bath for you. I'll pack your bag with essentials, Amber said to make sure to bring a jacket, and wear layers, but not to worry about bringing too many clothes since they have a full wardrobe in Montreal. She told me it is very cold where you are going. I can't imagine it, actually being cold." The young faeling who served as my personal maid held up a cropped black jacket Amber had lent me back in Montreal, looking at it in wonder. "What's it like?"

"Not as great as being warm, trust me. But, you can't have snow without cold weather, and you can't snowboard without snow, so it's pretty awesome in my book."

"Snow! You've seen snow? I've heard of it, the fluffy ice that covers whole mountains in some realms above."

"Yeah," I laughed as I headed into the bath. "Snow is pretty cool."

I gestured at the wall plate, shutting the golden door behind me for privacy. Mireia had arranged for Auroreis to be my personal maid when I'd first arrived in Valhalla, and I still hadn't quite gotten used to her ever-presence. I mean, okay, I admit it, it was nice having someone launder my clothes and pick up after me. But I drew the line at helping me bathe. Auroreis was a sweet young girl who'd grown up on a farm, and lucky her, I was her first introduction to life in the big capital city. She thought I was a foreign wonder, and I thought she was easy to get along with. All in all, we'd both adapted pretty well and evolved into a relaxed companionship.

I would have liked to have taken my time getting ready, enjoyed the bath a little longer. After all, who knew how long we'd be topside, and when I would get to enjoy the restorative qualities of Aeden bathwater again. Unfortunately, Amber wasn't one to wait patiently, so I ducked under the water and washed up quickly with some fresh-scented floral soap, using the liquid to clean my hair and body. I rinsed and dried off, brushing my unruly wheaten hair and securing it up in a high ponytail off my face. If I didn't do something to tame it right away who knew what sort of tangle it would get into by the end of the day. Looking in the mirror, I eyed myself critically. Maybe I should braid it instead, I thought. I tilted my head, considering, and decided not to waste any more time. I rubbed some cream on my face and added a touch of mascara to my pale lashes, completing my daily vanity routine.

I cinched my robe around my waist and back out to the bedroom. Auroreis had already left, leaving a tray of hot tea made from the leaves of a local tree steaming on my bed. A few small energy bars decorated a plate next to the cup, made with dried fruits and protein-rich nuts. Miko had beaten me to breakfast, already sitting next to the tray daintily nibbling on a large hunk of one of the bars.

"Morning, Miko."

"Morning, kid. Hurry up and put on your fur, it's time to hit the road. Amber's already waiting for us up on deck."

"Yeah, yeah."

I swiped an untouched rectangle off the tray and stuffed it in my mouth as I picked out my travel outfit. It had been so long since I had worn anything other than the light, loose linen capris and armless shirts that made up most of my Valhallan wardrobe. And shoes. I hadn't worn shoes since my first day here.

No one here wore shoes, because regular traffic would damage the cala, a soft, durable grass native to Aeden that was used through most buildings instead of carpeting. Besides, cala was especially beneficial to fae bodies, enhancing biosynthesis and grounding our light so that our immune systems were boosted whenever we walked on it. It was another reason the fae in Aeden had longer lifespans, because it encouraged our cells to replicate flawlessly at a faster rate. Without it, we still lived a long time, but it had some seriously enhancing effects on our biology. Apparently, it had traveled with us from the stars, an integral part of the ship's life support system. Legend said it had made our trip from the stars possible.

See? I had been paying attention to Mialloch's sermons after all. I grinned and reached into the back of the closet, pulling out my folded gray skinny jeans and favorite pair of silver Sk8-hi Vans and kissed them like old friends. I'd gotten used to the comfort of the fitted tank tops here, though – I mean, come on, they had built in bras and they made my arms look great. They were a little shorter than most tops I usually wore, revealing a strip of stomach above my low-cut jeans, but with all the working out I'd been doing with Amber, I knew it looked great without even glancing in a mirror.

I grabbed the black jacket and stuffed it into my backpack, noting that Auroreis had added several pairs of underwear and another pair of jeans. I threw in some extra socks and my toothbrush and slung my messenger bag over my shoulder, along with the pack. I opened up the flap of the messenger bag and gestured for Miko to climb in as I pulled on my ancient blue hoodie.

"Come along, old man, your chariot awaits."

Miko grabbed another piece of food off the plate and hopped into the bag, curling up happily inside. I folded the bag closed and held my sneaks in one hand, munching on the last of the power bars as I left the room.

"Okay, Auroreis, I'm outta here!" I called out. She came rushing from her room on the other side of the living room and barreled into me, hugging me tightly.

"Whoa there!" I giggled, making sure the bag holding Miko was out of the way. "I can't breathe!"

She hugged me tighter and whispered up at me, "Are you really coming back?"

I stared down at this fourteen-year old girl, just a few years younger than me and yet so much more sheltered than I could ever remember being, and smiled. "Yeah, of course I'll be back." I winked and ruffled her hair, hugging her quickly before I set her back from me.

"Now, you make sure you give Dorian a hard time for me every time you see him, and I promise I will bring you back some fancy Midgard candies, okay?"

"And maybe some pants, like yours?" She eyed my outfit with envy.

"Really?" I was already sweating in the humid Aeden air. I probably should have packed the sweatshirt, too. "Okay, deal. See you soon, with some tween jeans."

We hugged again and I made my way through the halls to the gravicycle deck on our floor. It had been weeks since I'd gotten on one of the golden machines, blazingly fast snowmobile-like contraptions with hover capabilities. I couldn't wait to do it again. Maybe Amber would even let me drive one this time.

Excited, I rushed to the doors marked with the rune for speed, or horse, depending on the context. It looked like a big M – perfect for a motorcycle mnemonic, the fastest steeds around. Yeah, yeah, the fae called them gravicycles, but in my mind, it worked. I burst through the doors and stopped.

"You have got to be kidding me," I exclaimed. Already straddling two of the cycles were Amber and Mialloch. "Mialloch? What the hell are you doing here? Amber?"

"It's a pleasure to see you, too, Siri. As always." Mialloch smiled warmly at me, oblivious to my mood, as usual. Didn't the guy ever rise above a flatline?

"Amber," I growled as dropped to the ground and pulled on my sneakers. "Why is he here?"

Amber rolled her eyes and gestured behind her, indicating the giant duffel bag secured as her second passenger. "Your dad has me bringing a ton of new gadgets topside, so you'll have to ride with Mialloch. And no – don't even ask. Today is not the day you get to ride solo. Not a chance. Anyhow, your dad seemed to think it was time for Mialloch to learn more about the world above. He wants him to come with us as an observer, meet his first Druid, get a taste of the world. That sort of thing."

"Isn't that dangerous?"

"For who?" Amber asked. "Me? I live for danger."

"No, smartass, I mean for him."

"Oh, please. You can take care of yourself pretty well, and we'll have other Guards with us. Babysitting is part of a Guard's job, I don't mind."

I glanced at Mialloch. His face hadn't changed expression once during our conversation. Apparently he wasn't offended at all by two girls discussing his lack of martial prowess. Bringing him up to Midgard felt rife with danger. I imagined his innocent, sheltered soul at any American high-school. It would be like taking a lamb to slaughter.

"Fine." His face lit up as I stalked over to him.

"Can I assist you?" He started to get up, and I stopped him.

"Just sit tight, I got it." I climbed onto the bike behind him, strapping myself into the harness efficiently and loosely wrapping my arms around Mialloch's torso. "Alright, let's rock."

Amber whooped and took off, while we followed her at a safe distance.

It was soon evident that our early morning departure had been sorely needed. The access point to the tunnels north of Montreal was over an hour away from Valhalla. I'd always thought the cycles had only one speed – breakneck. Mialloch's careful driving forced Amber to recalibrate her driving habits. At this rate, we wouldn't even reach the tunnels until afternoon.

Don't get me wrong, we were still travelling at a respectable highway speed, hundreds of feet above the ground, but we weren't coming close to approaching the 200mph rides that Amber liked to take me on. I wondered if Mialloch always rode like this, or if it was simply for my benefit.

Either way, I couldn't help remembering my first gravicycle experience, the thrill of riding with Amber, and the adrenaline rush I'd experienced watching Alec stand atop his cycle, arms spread wide with reckless abandonment. The excitement that day had been contagious. Just thinking about it brought a smile to my lips and caused my heart to beat faster.

As if in response, Mialloch placed a hand on my thigh, giving it a gentle squeeze and sped up, catching up with Amber. Maybe he had been driving slowly for my benefit, after all. Amber caught sight of us and grinned, gunning her engine to match Mialloch's new speed and we rocketed onwards.

Despite our slow start, we made it to the slightly chillier mountainous region of Niflhelf. According to my lessons, the vast mountain range held several entrances to Midgard – two in Eastern Canada and one in Greenland. It was the entrance in Greenland that had given rise to the Norse legends of the otherworldly realm of Niflheim.

Amber weaved around several mountain peaks, steering us towards a crooked, barren crag. Half-way up its sheer face, an opening gaped at us as if in surprise. She slowed down, and we glided silently into the cave, the dim UV lights on the cycles switching on automatically as Amber adjusted her speed to accommodate the smaller space and flew into a large tunnel. The first time I had flown these twisting tunnels with Amber, we had raced downward so quickly that the brilliant greens, whites and purples of the luminescent rock walls had streaked by like the laser lights in Space Mountain. This time, we went more slowly, Amber constantly turning around to make sure Mialloch was keeping pace, adjusting her speed so that we approached each turn of the corridor with care. After an hour or more, the tunnels seemed to begin to ascend, heading out of the mountains and up towards the lands I knew.

Finally, we entered a huge cavern and slowed down to a stop, hovering high above the floor for a few moments before each gravicycle gently dropped to the ground, parking in line with several other golden bikes.

"This is it? Have we arrived in Midgard?" Mialloch asked, sounding disappointed.

"Not quite. But we are getting close. Don't worry, it only gets better from here on out," Amber smiled.

"Yeah, wait till you see the chocolate fountains and yellow brick road," I joked. Both fae turned to me with confused looks on their faces. Ok, so note to self, no Willy Wonka or Land of Oz jokes. "Never mind, stupid joke," I sighed.

"Another movie reference?" Amber asked.

"Yup." We'd done this more than once over the months. So far, we had about thirty movies on the "must-see" list. We each got off our cycle, Mialloch reaching to carry the huge duffle of supplies before Amber could beat him to it. She looked like she was likely to argue, as she usually did, but staring up at the fae man towering over her she seemed to think better of it. Mialloch may not be a honed fighting machine, but he was certainly strong enough to shoulder a girl's bag. She reached down and grabbed his small pack, handing us each a small LED flashlight as I shouldered my own bag.

"Okay, time to walk. Mialloch, if you need a break from the heavy lifting, let us know. We've got a bit of a trek ahead of us."

We began walking upwards through the mountain passage in single file, the dark path illuminated by the small cool beams of light from our torches. For a while, no one spoke, each of us seemingly lost in our own thoughts as we traveled.

This time, when I felt the wall of heat that signaled a breach of the barrier between the realms of above and below, I barely paused, following Amber with long, sure strides. A moment later, a slight cough grabbed my attention.

"Erm, ladies? Are you sure we should proceed?"

Amber turned around and rolled her eyes at me while I stifled a laugh. Really, sometimes Mialloch was such a stiff.

"It's okay, Mialloch. I promise. What you're feeling is just the barrier between the worlds. I'm sure you've heard about it?"

"Ah, yes, the barrier." He reached both hands out before him, gently testing the heated energy of the magical force field. "How interesting. No one ever mentioned that it would feel so warm."

Miko poked his head out of the bag at my side. *Is he always like this?*

I snorted, thinking, yes, yes, he is.

"Yeah, well, just imagine how it would feel if you were a Shade, or a plain old human," Amber commented.

"Yes, I have heard that humans can't even see past the barrier, that it literally looks like part of the cavern wall to them, and that they are overcome with the most pressing urge to return from whence they came, no matter what lies on the other side. And I've heard that for a dark fae it as if their skin is pieced with a thousand needles all at once, and that they hear the screams of each innocent they have ever caused harm. The pain of it is said to drive them to their knees, senseless, where they will lie until someone returns them to the surface."

"Well, that sounds like fun. Is that true, Amber?"

"It depends how persistent they are. Most dark can't even approach the tunnels that house barrier access points. But if they do get as far as the barrier, they generally turn back at first contact. If they don't...If they try to walk through, then, yeah. The strain always proves too much for them. They fall to the ground from the exertion and the pain. Every ten years or so we find one who has been lying there a couple days or weeks, and return them to the surface to be cared for by their own kind. Eventually they recover."

"Wow. Cheery," I drawled.

"It's better than how they would treat one of us, if they ever found us helpless on the floor. Anyone at their mercy would either be reconditioned and brainwashed to serve the Shades, or subjected to torture and testing, like your mother. Or they'd just kill us."

I growled. I couldn't help it. Thinking of what they had done to my mom brought out my best side, what can I say?

"Mialloch, you ready yet? Come on, it's time to 'break on through to the other side.'" I sang out, paying lip service to my favorite Doors song.

"Siri, you are the most confounding woman," he laughed and shook his head. "But yes, I suppose it is time we moved forward." He put a strange emphasis on the word "we."

He locked eyes with me and stepped through. The moment he was on our side, Amber and I turned and began walking again, both of us feeling the pull of the sky waiting above. Even Miko was excited, having jumped out of my bag and scampering ahead of us at a light run. Apparently, he didn't need any help from our flashlights. Just another thirty or forty minutes and we would all be topside.

Soon, Amber and I had locked arms and were giggling, planning what human foods we would indulge in first, and what we would wear that night when we went out. Because, of course, we were going out. The night was calling and there were songs to be sung, dances to be danced.

At one point, Amber looked over her shoulder, noting Mialloch trailing us far behind, slowed, no doubt, by the massive duffle he still carried.

"So, what's up with you and Mialloch? What was all that talk about moving forward? And his hand on your leg on the bike? Is he putting the moves on you?"

"What? Are you serious? Come on, this is Mialloch we are talking about. I don't think he could ever conceive of a move, much less put it on someone."

"I don't know. I've known Mialloch a long time, he's always been serious, but I swear, around you, he acts practically..."

"Yes?"

"Male."

I barked out a laugh. "You have got to be kidding me. I can't imagine him being more serious. Wow. That would be interesting. Wow. Well, anyways, I can't imagine I'm at all his type. I'm sure he's just excited to be going on this little field trip."

"If you say so. But you haven't seen the way he looks at you when you aren't paying attention."

"Like a bug?"

"No. Like an exotic dessert he can't wait to sample."

"Whatever. You're crazy. As if Mialloch even eats dessert. I think he's on a low-carb, low-sugar, low-fun diet." I decided to change the subject. "So, how are we getting back to Montreal, anyway? Is someone picking us up?"

When I'd come to Aeden, we'd driven Ewan's 1966 Scout to a Guard-owned sanctuary deep in the Canadian woods, and hidden it behind a crumbling old camp building. But Alec had returned top-side before us, and I could only assume our ride was long-gone.

"Someone should be meeting us. Bran said he has a team on the way already."

"Ewan and Alec?"

"I don't know," Amber answered, chewing her lip. "Last I heard, they were on different missions. Bran's been pretty cagey lately with the updates, apparently my dad and Uncle Mitch both had talks with him about Ewan and I. Bran was pretty mad, since Guards aren't supposed to date anyone, never mind each other. But, it's too late for them to actually stop us, like I told you before, you can't fight the surge. So, the most they can do is torture us by trying to keep us apart."

"Oh. So, are you in really big trouble?" I thought of Alec, and how I'd already told my dad how I felt about him. He'd acted like he was okay with my choice, but would he punish Alec for breaking Guard regulations? What if he wasn't allowed to see me again? Suddenly, my feet felt like lead weights and I found it a little hard to breathe. My father had acted like he wouldn't stand in our way, but could I really trust him? Could I trust a man I'd only just met to hold my best interests at heart the way a father should? My faith started to crumble under these new doubts like the Great Wall of China during tourist season.

"Nah, we'll be fine. Long life spans, remember? Eventually they'll get over it. I'm sure they just want to teach us a little lesson, so they don't look bad in front of the other Guards. I mean, hey, if they'd let us fall in love without any punishment at all, then all the Guards might start dating. Can't have that, right?" she chuckled.

"Right, that would lead to love anarchy. Fae making out everywhere. Where would that leave Aeden?"

"Totally defenseless!" We both burst out laughing, imagining it. And then I thought about it a little more. Without the Guards, Aeden's only defense against the Shades were the barrier crossings. Somehow, I didn't think that was really enough to defend the numerous innocents who dwelled below. Plus, the Guards were needed above to help protect humans from the power plays of the dark. No. We needed the Guards. The world wasn't really safe without them, even with the light guardians who lived as humans. The more people fighting on the side of the light, the better. Maybe my dad was right. Love was great and all, but for now, we needed to stay focused.

It was a sobering thought.

Before I could dwell on it, I discerned a glow ahead in the tunnel, brighter than our torchlight. A few steps closer, and I could see the light expanding.

"Turn off your light!" I exclaimed.

"What, why?" She turned it off without waiting for an answer. "Woo hoo, we're here!"

We both grinned at each other and took off running towards the light, literally at the end of the tunnel.

"Come on, Mialloch, last one there's a rotten egg!" I yelled over my shoulder.

I could hear him chuckling behind us. "I think I've already lost," he called. "I'll meet you there."

And I ran.

Chapter 7

Coming out of the darkness of the tunnel, the light was practically blinding. Running hadn't exactly given my eyes time to adjust, and I shielded them, standing and straining to see who was waiting for us.

Amber was still running, barreling into a tall figure laughing in the distance. The man lifted her up and swung her around, exclaiming "Och girl, you'll be the death of me, you will!"

I laughed, too, recognizing the big voice, even if my eyes were still acclimating to the bright yellow sun. Ewan. Apparently their separation period was over, at least for a little while.

I looked away from the happy couple, not wanting to intrude on their moment, and that's when I saw him. Just standing there, lounging against a tree a few feet away, as if he didn't have a care in the world.

"Alec!?" His eyes were hidden in the deep recesses of the dark green hooded military coat he wore, but I saw the slight quirk of his lips as he tried not to smile, and I knew he was just as glad to see me as I was to see him. "Alec!"

I rushed into his arms and hugged him for all I was worth, just relieved to see him again. My face found his neck within the hood and I burrowed closer, warming the tip of my nose against his skin and inhaling deeply. With Alec, you never quite knew where the forest ended and he began, the scent of pine and coriander followed him everywhere, always reeling me in like a warm cup of cocoa.

"God, I missed you. I wasn't sure I'd see you here, Bran didn't tell us which team he was sending to meet us." I felt the warm rush of the surge spreading through me, flowing from my nose to my toes, telling me with every pulse of my blood that yes, this boy was my match in every way, mentally, spiritually, physically.

His arms tightened around me, but he didn't get a chance to answer.

"Is this some sort of family reunion Bran forgot to warn me about? Because otherwise it would seem that I should have brought a date." Mialloch's voice, tinged with what surely could not have been sarcasm, echoed behind me from the mouth of the tunnel.

"Mialloch," Alec deadpanned, his arms dropping to his sides. "So nice to see you. Bran forgot to mention we'd be babysitting."

"A pleasure, as well. You must finally have learned how to follow orders, if Bran thinks you are capable enough to serve on my team."

"Your team?" Alec started forward, clearly intent on inflicting some bodily harm.

I stepped in front of them.

"Alec, Mialloch, you guys know each other?"

"You could say that," Alec muttered.

"Yes, we shared classes together at the Academy, at least, until we entered separate tracks."

"Separate tracks?"

"Guards focus on history, tactics, languages, training. Kids like Mialloch focus on...well, I don't know, what exactly do you learn besides how to dance?" Alec asked with a sneer.

"Why, I-" Mialloch took a step forward as if he meant to threaten Alec, which couldn't lead anywhere good.

"Boys, boys." I stepped forward, putting myself between them. "I get it. You don't like each other. But you are both here for a reason." I looked at Alec and placed a hand on his chest, whispering, "Alec, please."

I raised my voice again. "You both need to calm down."

"Why is he here?" Alec spoke only to me.

"He's been acting as my fae tutor for the last couple of months, they thought he might have some insight into the old Druid legends Rose wants to discuss with us. Plus, apparently both our fathers thought this would be a good opportunity for him to see a bit of the world, part of his Council training."

"Bran planned this? He wanted you to travel together?"

"Well, yes." My eyes widened. "But not like that! He's just here as a, you know, an attaché! An observer. That's all, Alec, I swear."

I could practically see the gears turning as the walls slid back into place, Alec safely hiding behind them. Whatever ground we'd gained before he left, we'd just lost it. Alec still believed my father would think he wasn't good enough for me. I wanted to talk to him, to tell him about my conversation with my dad, but now wasn't really the time.

Right around this time, Amber finally climbed down off of Ewan, coming up for air.

"What's going on, guys?" she sauntered over to us, beaming from ear to ear as she swatted Alec's butt. "Are you happy to see us or what?"

Alec turned and grinned at her, grabbing her in a hug. "You? Always. Now, who's ready for some donuts?"

Alec took my backpack and then walked by Mialloch to grab the duffel near his feet, slinging it over his back before he started heading away into the woods.

"Donuts?" Mialloch asked me.

"Yeah, you know," Alec smirked over his shoulder, "big soft squishy things with no hard edges, basically just disguising a big hole? Sweet on the outside, dull on the inside? You're going to love them. They kind of remind me of you."

Totally oblivious to the social discomfort on the scene, Ewan wrapped an arm around Amber, pulling her close as they walked. "Yeah, we have a whole box of them in the Scout. Alec said we should pick up right where we left off last time we were all together, made me buy two dozen from Chez Boris this morning."

The last thing we had done in Montreal before I left for Aeden was get donuts. Well, okay, buy donuts and then fend off an inept attack from a couple of Shade wannabes. Ewan hadn't actually been there, so the fact that Alec had remembered made me feel all warm and glow-ey inside. Now all I had to do was convince Alec that nothing was going on with Mialloch, and convince him to mind his manners.

Chapter 8

Okay, so, easier said than done.

Mialloch and Alec seriously despised each other. Seriously.

Two hours, seventeen donuts later, the battle lines had been drawn.

Amber and Ewan had been no help at all. They'd spent the entire ride back to Montreal cuddling together in the front seat, forcing me to fight the urge to vomit several times. And I don't get car sick.

Normally, I would have been happy to spend so much time in the back seat with Alec. I mean, honestly. It was basically all I'd been fantasizing about for the last two months, in between kicking Amber's butt. Well, okay. Fine. Getting my butt kicked. Whatever.

Stay on point.

I would have loved to spend time with Alec like this, really, I would.

But all my fantasizing, it had never involved me crammed up next to both Alec and Mialloch. I had not imagined myself squished between two pairs of knees. One pair muscled and unyielding, sending sparks up and down my spine. The other set, stiffly pressing against my own and making me wish this vehicle had a third row of seats to dive into.

Miko was curled up in my lap, snoring peacefully. His last words, before he dozed off, were "be kind." Like, wow, really? Be kind? To whom? Mialloch or Alec? Besides, where was my kindness? Who was going to ever so kindly rescue me from this agony of anxiety?

Every conversation was a dead end. Alec kept his hood up the whole time, and Mialloch spent most of the ride looking out the window, most likely staring in awe at the novelty of green foliage, a yellow sun and blue skies.

Both boys (because clearly, they did not deserve to be called men, even if they were in their twenties) had a strange hearing impairment, wherein they could only hear me, not each other. This led to scintillating conversation, with no awkward pauses. None. At. All. No, none. Really.

Yeah, the ride was that great. When we finally arrived at the safe house in Montreal, everybody scrambled out of the car in relief. Even Ewan and Amber seemed anxious to get out of the Scout. I assumed that meant they weren't as oblivious as I thought, until they raced each other up the stairs to Ewan's room and I realized their relief was simply at having a private, empty room nearby. Couples. I guess they were due some alone time.

That left me and the wonder twins. I can't say how excited I was about that. Really. I can't. My mother taught me never to use certain kinds of language in polite company.

Alec went to the back of the Scout and dragged the bags out of the car, tromping up the stairs to the flat without a backward glance.

"Charming, as always," Mialloch grumbled.

"What is your deal?" I whirled on him, lowering my voice so Alec wouldn't hear us. "Why can't you two get along?"

"What do you mean?"

"I mean, you. Alec. Unable to have a civil conversation. It's like you two hate each other."

"Well, maybe it's because we do. That man has spent the better part of the last ten years showing off how great he thinks he is at everything. It's aggravating. He has no understanding of the finer realities of fae history. He doesn't know what it really means to serve your people. He doesn't understand sacrifice, or honor, or dedication-"

"Okay, hold up." I stuck my hand in his face. "I can get how watching Alec be awesome at things could be annoying. I've been there. But you're wrong. Alec is totally dedicated, and always honorable. It's what he does."

Mialloch glared at me. "I wouldn't expect you to understand."

"What is that supposed to mean?"

"Never mind." Mialloch waved his hand, as if brushing away a fly, and shouldered his way past me. It was the first time he'd ever been rude to me, and I was flummoxed.

Miko climbed up my leg and sat on my shoulder, staring after him with me.

"Did you see that?"

"Yep. You've got yourself a couple of complicated males in that nest."

"Do you know what is bugging them so much?"

"Yep, they both-"

"Siri, you coming?" Alec yelled down the stairs, interrupting whatever Miko was going to say.

"Coming," I called up, then whispered to Miko, "Well, go on, they both what?"

I started walking upstairs, paying more attention to Miko than where I was going.

"They both have some serious resentment issues towards each other. Old stuff, from when they were just young kits. And, of course, they both want to take you to mate."

"What?!" I had just reached the top of the stairs and glanced down at Miko, missing the last step and flying forward.

Long arms reached out to save me, pulling me towards a chest.

"Oh, sorry!" I looked up, taking in Mialloch's serious face. "I, um, tripped over Miko."

Nice save, kid. Thanks a lot.

"Anytime, Siri." Mialloch didn't let me go, looking like he wanted to say something. "I'm sorry if I offended you downstairs. Alec and I have just never seen eye to eye on anything."

"Oh, well, I wouldn't say never. I remember a time when we saw eye to eye on most things. And you seem to be getting an eyeful of something I like very much, right this moment." Alec's voice came from behind Mialloch, managing to sound both amused and impatient at the same time. I untangled myself from Mialloch's arms and smiled.

"Thanks, Mialloch, you totally saved my face." I edged around him and stepped into the apartment. Alec wrapped his arm around me and drawled, "Yeah, thanks, Loch. Follow me and I'll show you to your rooms."

He pulled me along with him while Miko hopped away towards the kitchen area, presumably to find some food. I found Alec's proprietary display a bit maddening, but I decided to go along with it for the moment.

We paused at a door just off the kitchen and Alec nodded over his shoulder. "This is your room, Mialloch. The bathroom is down the hall on the right. Rose should be here soon, so if you want to clean up or get some rest now's the time. Amber has big plans for us all tonight."

"Wonderful, Vye, I can't wait." Mialloch turned into his room and shut the door in our faces.

"Still a ball of laughs, that one." Alec huffed, turning us back around and leading me down the hall to the room I had stayed in last time.

He opened the door with his free hand and drew me in, kicking the door shut behind us. When I'd stayed here before, Alec had put me in here and slept out on the couch. I hadn't realized it at the time, but this was his room. His forest-rich scent had been all over the sheets, but I had assumed it was just the laundry detergent they all used. (For the record, it wasn't. They used unscented generic stuff in the wash. That fresh pine and coriander mix that drove me wild? Pure Alec.)

Yeah. So. That was last time. This time, I barely had time to breathe before Alec pulled me to him and pressed his lips against mine. It was the first time we'd had skin-to-skin contact since the woods by the tunnel, and this was so much better. I moaned and pushed the hood back off his face, running my fingers through his disheveled black hair.

Everything I'd been feeling, the annoyance at Alec's petty jealousy, the nervousness of separation, it all disappeared in an instant. This wasn't just hormones talking. This was the surge, and it plunged through me full-force, hitting me like a sledgehammer.

Anytime one light fae touches another light fae, it feels warm and comforting. It's just a side-effect of the light within us recognizing the light in them. The dark fae have rejected the light of Aeden, turned off the spigot so to speak, and physical contact accompanied by that kind of a disconnect made me feel nauseous and sick whenever I touched a dark fae. Even with Rowan, who was just a darkling, and hadn't officially chosen a side yet.

The surge? It wasn't like either of those things. The surge was a tidal wave of happy emotions crashing through you all at once, touching every nerve ending and setting it off in pure bliss. The surge was more than just physical ecstasy, it completely tapped you in to the other person's heart so that you experienced every single thing they were feeling, every ounce of love, desire, everything. It was almost like reading their thoughts, except it was more primal than that, more about emotions. I liked to think of it as telempathy, and Amber had taken to calling it that, too.

Right now, I was reveling in the feel of Alec's hands as they reached up under my shirt to create more skin-to-skin contact at my waist. Leaning back and tilting my head so he could trail his lips along my neck, I knew everything he was trying to tell me. I knew he would tell me later, again, in his own words, but I already sensed how much he'd missed me. I knew how slowly the days had passed. I understood that even as he feared I would be taken from him, he already considered me his. There would never be another woman for him, and he'd already spent countless hours imagining the sorts of solitary duties he would request, far from Valhalla, if I ever chose someone other than him.

I knew all this, because I felt each moment of emotion pass through me as if it had been my own. When he slowly walked me backwards toward the bed, I collapsed into the quilts wrapped in the purity of his love, and the weight of his insecurities. I had grand plans to explain how I felt to him, to help him release his worries, but when he cradled my face in his palms and stared into my eyes, kissing me again and again, I realized I didn't really have to. Oh, I would. Of course I would, because we all need to hear things aloud, it helps tame the beast inside us.

But he already knew.

He'd heard me. The surge was a two-way street, and he had felt my answering heartsong just as I had been reveling in his.

The surge filled us both, nourishing every aspect of our beings. I felt rejuvenated, enlivened. It never went away, and apparently never would, but it did settle down eventually, allowing my pulse to slow and our kisses to grow less frantic, becoming more like the caresses of a gentle summer breeze.

Finally, I lay on my back and Alec rested his head on my stomach looking up at me as he traced his fingers up and down my arm. Somehow, we'd made it all the way on to the huge bed, the dark indigo canopy above us masquerading as the night sky. For a moment, I thought of Rowan, and his indigo eyes, and prayed he was finding happiness wherever he was. I played with Alec's hair, trying to tame the inky wildness around his face. Myself, I couldn't have been happier at that moment.

"So, you really missed me, huh?" he grinned.

"A little bit," I teased.

"Tell me about your time down under. What have you been doing?"

"Mostly just training with Amber all day. She's been teaching me glima, says I am a master at it now, and she was actually about to start on the basics of lasair before Rose called and we came here instead."

"Disappointed?"

"To be here? With you? Not a chance. But if you can see your way to working in a little training with me each day, I will be the happiest girl on the planet."

"Yeah, I think I can play Obi-Wan to your Padawan."

I hummed happily. "Can't wait."

"So, what else have you been doing? Did you meet a lot more fae?"

"Not really. Amber's kept me pretty busy. We spent all our waking hours together when she wasn't on duty, and I've been studying with Mialloch almost every day, too."

"Whose idea was that?"

"My dad's. He thought Mialloch could give me a good foundation in fae culture. I certainly know every legend in Aeden now, plus most of the plants, history, customs, blah, blah, blah. You know. What really interests me is fae science, but we didn't really get into that."

"No, that isn't Loch's area of expertise," Alec muttered.

"Loch? You act like you hate each other, but you have nicknames – I noticed he called you Vye earlier. Did you used to hang out?"

"When we were kids we were pretty close. Loch is short for Mialloch, obviously. He used to call me by my last name, Ward, it was sort of an inside joke, since Ward means protector and I saved him from getting bullied a couple times when my Dad and I first moved down to Aeden. That's how we became friends. But then we had to split tracks in school, and his parents made it pretty clear they thought I was too human, too common, to hang out with

72

Mialloch outside of school. He started hanging out with the other council kids, and I threw myself into my training. That's when he started calling me Vye." Alec sighed. "Do we really have to talk about this?"

"I'd like to, yeah. I understand you, in here, I really do." I touched a hand to my heart. "But I'd like to actually know more about who you are, where you are coming from. You know?"

"Yeah, I know." He rubbed a hand over his face and sat up. "Okay, so here's the thing. You've probably noticed the purple ring around my pupils?"

"It's kind of hard to miss," I shrugged.

"Okay, well, when a fae has kids with a full-blooded human, even if the fae already has human ancestry, weird things can happen. Most of the inter-breeding took place years ago. These days, fae marry fae. We just don't mix as much as we used to, whether we live above or below. Some people blame the divide between the light and the dark on our human ancestry. So it's frowned on, you know?"

I nodded, understanding what he was saying, but also surprised that light fae would feel this way. I guess they weren't all as high-minded as I had thought.

"Right. So weird traits. Some kids get pointed ears, or folded lobes. Some kids have webbed feet or hands if their parent is a water fae. A lot of the modern conceptions of what a fairy looks like come from over a thousand years ago when there were more fae living above below and intermarrying. There were a lot more first-gen offspring out in the world then. Some first-gens just have severe mood swings or major ADHD – that's especially true with the fire-related families. Anything can happen, though, really. Earth fae children tend to have great eyesight underground, and in first-gens, like me, it can be so good that our eyes change color, or reflect light in strange ways, sometimes even looking like animals."

"So, your purple ring, does that mean you can see in the dark?"

"Yeah. I can even read heat signatures if it's dark enough. Loch's new friends started calling me Violet one day, saying I was cute for a mutt, that maybe he should keep me as a pet. He laughed, and I punched him. He's been calling me Vye ever since."

"And you've hated him, and all the council kids, ever since?"

"Pretty much. There were some other incidents. Other kids. Other names. But you get the idea."

"Alec, I am so sorry. I know how it feels to be the odd man out, really, I do."

I told him about the years I had spent traveling the country, seeing the world with my mom, changing schools every six to twelve months. Some places had been nice. But there always seemed to be a clique of mean girls to contend with, or some rich kids who thought they ruled the world.

"I didn't know it was so hard for you. I figured you had an easy life above below, like I did, before the Dark ruined everything. The day they killed my mom and sister, my world ended. I thought I'd found a real friend in Loch, but two years later that was over, too. Joining the Guard has meant everything to me. My dad is almost never home.

We're not close anymore the way you and your mom are. Seeing me...I think I remind him of my sister too much, I can see how much it hurts him sometimes. I don't want to give up my work with the Guard. I like being part of a team. And I don't think that will be good enough for you, or your dad."

"You're wrong, Alec." I hugged him, and leaned back again, before I could get distracted. "I already talked to my dad about us. He admitted he'd had some hopes that I would hit it off with Mialloch when he assigned him as my tutor, but he didn't have any idea that I'd already connected with you. When he found out I'd experienced the surge, he kind of freaked out, but when I told him it was with you, he was relieved. He likes you Alec. He respects you. Do you really think he would have sent you and Ewan to meet us if he didn't approve?"

"I guess not. But then why did he send Mialloch?"

"I told you. They think he might be helpful, since he knows so many legends. And maybe his dad is still hoping we'll hit it off, I don't know." I threw my hands up, frustrated. "Who cares? It doesn't matter." I poked him in the chest, punctuating my words with my finger. "I. Choose. You."

He grunted and grabbed my hand, making a face. I laughed, and he kissed my fingertip. The rest of the hour passed in a blur as we snuggled and caught each other up on what we'd been doing. He told me about the false leads and run-ins with Shades he'd had; I showed off some of my best new glima tricks. Eventually we just lay there, watching the sun as its rays dipped between the buildings outside, tinting the world with splashes of pink and lavender. I'd missed the beauty of an orbited star setting in the sky.

Someone rapped on the door.

"The Druid girl is here, she just called asking us where she should park." Ewan's voice rumbled through the heavy wooden door, and I jumped up.

"Rose's here!" I exclaimed.

"Yeah," Alec chuckled. "I heard."

I yanked him off the bed and pulled him out into the hallway, practically running to the living room. I heard Mialloch's door opening as we passed, but I didn't slow down.

"Rose!" She had just stepped inside the door and was shaking hands with Amber. "You're here!"

We hugged and I stepped back, smiling. "God, I missed you! Have you met Amber? This is Amber Slaight, and Ewan Patterson over there. And this is Alec. Alec, this is Rose David."

Rose's eyes twinkled up at him from under her long bangs. As usual, she wore her naturally bright red hair in pigtails, and she had added a few light pink streaks. She was dressed in her favorite rainbow-patched jeans, a yellow sweater and a vintage striped vest.

"Nice to meet you, Alec. I've heard a lot about you." She glanced meaningfully down at Alec's hand, which was clasped in mine again. Amber reached to close the door and Rose stopped her. "Um, I wouldn't close it just yet. I kind of brought dinner, too."

"Dinner?" I questioned, peering around her. I could hear footsteps on the shadowed porch, and laughter.

"Yeah, well. You'll see in a minute." She looked at me apologetically and shrugged. Just then, a dark head of hair came into view, and I recognized Holly Carey.

"Surprise!" Holly rushed forward through the door and embraced me as she gushed, "I hope you don't mind. Rose told us she was coming to see you, and I was just so excited to come and meet more light fae, I talked her into bringing us. But look, we brought calzone's from Gio's! Of course, they'll need to be heated up."

"Calzones?" I opened my eyes to look behind her. She started talking about how they would need to be heated up in the oven, but her words faded away as I saw Rowan standing there quietly in the doorway.

"Hey, Siri." He ran a hand nervously through his hair, making the blue-tipped blonde spikes stand up on end. "Nice to see you," he nodded. "Alec."

"Ah, Rob Carey, was it?"

"Rowan, like the tree."

"Right, sorry. Well. Welcome to Montreal. And you are?" Alec looked meaningfully at Holly.

I made introductions all around, ignoring the surprise on most of the other fae's faces when they shook hands and realized that Rowan and his sister were both darklings. While the darklings would feel the touch of a light fae the same way we experienced it, the touch of a darkling would cause light queasiness in us. When I'd been dating Rowan,

I'd been totally clueless about my fae side and chalked it up to nerves.

Mialloch attempted not to stare, but only succeeded in watching Holly like a beautiful butterfly he would like to experiment on. I guessed it wasn't often that Light fae got to meet any darklings, or heard of one deciding to become a Light fae. According to what everyone told me, the Dark raised their children to believe that the Light cared nothing for humanity, that they had selfishly thrown the Dark out of Aeden and that the Dark wanted nothing more than to help humans. Of course, it wasn't until after their official choosing ceremony that newbie Dark fae were shipped off to Shade training centers where they were brainwashed into believing that any sort of joy or kindness was weakness. I was glad Rowan had talked Holly and their friend Cooper into joining the Light with him.

"Well, come on in, don't everyone just stand there." Amber closed the front door and ushered the newcomers into the ultra-modern living room. She took the boxes of calzones from Rowan and set them on the kitchen island nearby, while she pre-heated the oven. "Go on you guys, sit, take a load off."

Alec pulled me over to one of the white couches with him, and Rose followed, sitting next to me. Holly and Rowan sat across from us, while Ewan and Mialloch sat in a couple arm chairs. Holly grabbed one of the grass green pillows off the couch and hugged it to her.

"Oh, this is unbelievable! Rowan's caught me up on everything that's been going on, and Rose and I have been hanging out all the time. Emilie is kind of mad, actually, she thinks I've gone off the deep end."

Rose laughed and Holly smiled at me warmly. "I'm so glad you moved to town, if we hadn't met you, all this never would have happened. And Montreal! I've never been to Canada, before, I don't think I ever realized just how close it was!"

Alec squeezed my hand and I could practically read his thoughts, his amusement telegraphed so strongly through my hand. I squeezed back, hoping he would continue to be kind. Alec had no love for the Shades, and I knew how hard it was for him to extend his trust to a darkling, even if they were innocent.

"I know, right? Sometimes we forget how small this whole world really is." Amber said to Holly as she rejoined us, carrying a tray of hot herbal tea, water and natural sodas. "Okay, the food should be ready in ten minutes. Help yourselves to some drinks, please."

We all reached forward, grabbing cups and cans. I saw the nervous look Mialloch gave Holly when his hand brushed hers, and hoped she hadn't noticed. Rowan and I reached for the same cup of tea, but he stopped, gesturing for me to take it. His eyes burned into me, and I knew he wasn't over our breakup. It didn't matter that he was the one who had dumped me. He hadn't gotten along with Alec from the moment they'd met, and I could only imagine what he was thinking now.

"So..." Rose began, tucking her legs up under her and blowing on her tea. "Like Holly said, we thought it would be good for Rowan and her to meet more Light fae. Plus, of course, we all missed you."

"Actually," Holly interrupted, "our Choosing is coming up in few days, and I was hoping that maybe some of you could come down for that, if you're back from Ireland in time."

"I'd love to go," I volunteered. "I've never been to a Choosing before and mine isn't for another month, so it'll be great to see what one's like. Your parents will be okay with us coming? They aren't upset you're going Light?"

"Um, actually..."

"We haven't told them," Rowan said flatly. "I'm pretty sure that is not going to go over well at all. My dad has gotten one hundred times worse since you left. He's almost never home, and when he is all he does is talk on the phone with the Council or walk through the house yelling at us."

"We're going to do the ceremony at Vala's, where it can't be interrupted," explained Rose.

"You think your parents would try to stop it?" Mialloch seemed shocked.

"I think it wouldn't cross their minds not to," Rowan answered, looking at me.

"He's right," I agreed. "They're both totally Type-A personalities. Deviations from the plan are not acceptable. Their mom might hear them out, but definitely not Sullivan."

"Right, so," Holly broke in with forced cheer, "we'd love to have as many Light fae there as possible. To celebrate. Plus, we are probably going to need some help afterward. I'm not sure we'll be able to go home right away."

"No," Alec interjected. "That is definitely not an option. Once you are Light, it won't matter if you were family. They would send you to a facility for reprogramming, or worse."

I put my tea down and placed a hand on his knee, knowing he was thinking about the fate of his own family. We locked eyes and he placed his hand over mine. When I looked back at the group, I noticed the flicker of pain that washed across Rowan's face before he transformed his face into an impassive mask.

"So, that's it then?" Rowan asked sarcastically. "We go home, get our stuff, go to Vala's and leave everything behind? And trust that the Light will take us in?"

"Like Vala already told you," Rose explained patiently, "A team is going to arrive and take you to Aeden the day after your choosing. She discussed it with Bran and Mireia and everybody thinks it's best if you go underground, literally, for a while. Hopefully all this will blow over quickly and you'll be able to return to the surface. Or, you might decide not to return. In the end, it's up to you. But with everything going on, you will be safest as new Lights without any guardians if you go to Aeden."

"She's right," Amber agreed. "And hey, if we are back from Ireland in time, we can be the team to bring you back. Either way, I promise you are going to love it. Siri and I will be your tour guides."

"And I would be honored to tutor you both in the history and culture of Aeden," Mialloch offered Holly with a slight bow of his head.

"Wow, thanks, that will be great!" Holly blushed.

"Don't be so sure," I muttered under my breath, and Rose nudged me with my elbow, pressing her lips together in an effort not to laugh. No one else seemed to have heard.

The timer on the oven dinged and Amber stood up. "Okay kids, grub's on! I don't think I've ever actually had a calzone before, this is gonna be great."

While everybody made to follow her, I turned to Alec and gave him a quick kiss.

"Thanks."

"What for?" he asked.

"For not being a jerk to Rowan and his sister. For being you. And, of course, for all that dancing you're going to do with me later tonight."

He groaned and let out a long "No!" with lots of moaning thrown in for dramatic effect.

"Yes," I laughed, and gave him another kiss before I dragged him off the couch with me. "Now, come on. We need to carb load for later."

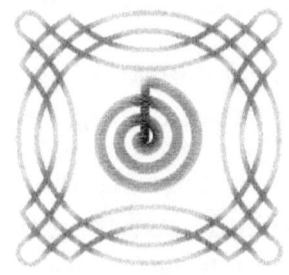

Chapter 9

After sharing a meal the group had reached an easy rhythm of banter. As usual, Gio's food had healing powers, raising blood sugar and encouraging endorphin releases that put everyone at ease, even the guys. No one was glaring at anyone or using demeaning nicknames.

Finally, Rose cleared her throat.

"So, I think it's time we talked about what really brought us all here," she started.

"Hold on." Amber held up her hand. "I think this is going to call for some additional chocolate and sugar coated goodness."

She got up, walked to the kitchen, and returned with the box of donuts the guys had brought us earlier, cutting up the remaining donuts into quarters so that everyone could partake. She stuffed a huge piece of vanilla and raspberry drizzled beignet in her mouth and waved at Rose to begin.

"Okay, go on, I think we're ready now," she winked.

"Okay," Rose laughed. She grabbed a piece of cinnamon chocolate fusion and began talking.

"So, you know I've been training with Vala. As a beginner, I have to spend most of my time reading over old Druid legends, some of them written on parchment that is practically crumbling away. Everybody says that the Druids didn't write down any of their stories, that it was all oral history, but that's actually not true. A few Druids did write the stories down, but of course they only passed from Druid to Druid."

She paused to take another bite of her donut.

"A few days ago Vala had me transcribing a really old parchment. She'd never read it herself, having only just inherited it from another Druid in Wales the month before. The parchment tells the tale of Airmed, an Ancient fae healer, and records her legendary healing incantation. The thing is, this parchment had it written down differently than what I learned as a child. I think it holds the key to healing anything – including the anti-serum."

"What key?" I asked.

"The clue is in the words. The incantation every good Druid knows goes like this:"

> *Bone to bone*
>
> *Vein to vein*
>
> *Balm to balm*

Sap to sap

Skin to skin

Tissue to tissue

Blood to blood

Flesh to flesh

Sinew to sinew

Marrow to marrow

Pith to pith

Fat to fat

Membrane to membrane

Fibre to fibre

Moisture to moisture

"But the one on the parchment had extra lines:"

Water to water

Flower to flower

Combine the two

At light's last hour.

"I don't get it, what does it mean?" Holly asked.

"I'm hoping it means that Airmed has a special tea that she makes when nothing else will work." She looked around us meaningfully. "Nothing has worked to cure the effects of the anti-serum. Maybe nothing does. Maybe the Shades aren't worried about counteracting the effects. But this tea,

Airmed's most powerful solution, if I'm right, it's worth checking out."

"I do think you are right," Mialloch answered slowly. Rose looked at him in surprise.

"You do?"

"Yes, the last lines are just the sort of word puzzle my grandmother has always delighted in playing when she visits me. 'Light's last hour.' If the Dark is trying to end the Light once and for all, maybe this is the last hour the passage refers to. And I'd bet the antidote isn't a tea."

"It isn't?" Rose sounded surprised.

"Airmed always carries a flask with her that is filled with a powerful healing flower essence. It is made with the sacred waters that flow near her home in Ireland, and a hybridized lotus that she cultivated specially to grow only in that pond."

"How do you know that? I thought this is your first time out of Aeden?" She quirked an eyebrow at him in question.

"It is." Alec answered for him. "But his grandmother is Airmed."

Mialloch inclined his head as the rest of us tried to absorb this new piece of information. "Exactly so."

"So wait, you are telling me that an Ancient fae healer is walking around with a magical healing elixir strapped to her belt and no one has thought to contact her yet?" My voice rose incredulously.

"It's not exactly common knowledge," Mialloch scoffed.

"But, you knew about it?"

"Like you, I assumed the scientists had contacted her already. Are you sure they haven't?" he asked Rose.

"Yes, I'm sure. I had Vala contact her before I left. She said she hasn't talked to anyone about any anti-serum. In fact, she said she hasn't talked to anyone in months."

"No, she doesn't have many friends or visitors," Mialloch mused.

"Well, she told us she would be willing to meet with us. She wasn't willing to talk about the incantation or the ingredients except face to face."

Mialloch pursed his lips. "No, she wouldn't be. Grandmother never surrenders any information until she is sure the recipient is worthy. She would want to test the person first."

"Test me?" Rose stood and planted her hands on her hips. "Seriously? Haven't I done enough? I found the incantation. I translated it. I figured it out."

"Actually, you thought it was a tea," I pointed out.

"Shush, you," she answered, pointing a menacing finger at me.

"Look, you have me." I was sure Mialloch was trying to sound reassuring, but it came off a bit pompous, instead. "Now I understand why Bran really wanted me along. He knew you might need a friendly face."

"What am I, chopped liver?" Alec asked.

"Chopped what?" Mialloch's face scrunched up in distaste.

"Never mind, it's a human thing. I meant, what about me? Your grandmother loves me."

"Just because she gave you extra cookies once, it hardly means she loves you," Mialloch huffed.

"Oh, but she did. She loved me." Alec leaned over and whispered loudly in my ear, "Grandmothers and mothers love me, you know. I am irresistible."

"Oh, I already know that," I chuckled back at him while Mialloch and Rowan both looked on scowling. I coughed and changed the subject back to the task at hand.

"Okay, so what's the plan then, exactly?" I looked back at Rose.

"Well, I can't go with you to Ireland, I have to help Vala get ready for their Choosing, plus I have school." She made a face.

Amber stood next to Rose, placing a hand on her shoulder. "Right you are. Mitch already arranged us seats on a flight out to Ireland, I talked to him while you guys were, uh, napping earlier. We're on a private red-eye that leaves at 1:55 a.m. Ewan will stay behind to hold down the fort, while Siri, Mialloch, Alec and I go to see Grandma. Which means," she said, waggling her eyebrows, "that we have plenty of time now to get dressed, pack our bags, and kill a couple hours at Zora's, Montreal's hottest fae-friendly nightclub."

Some of us, like me, laughed. The rest looked confounded. She clapped her hands

"Chop, chop, everyone. Get up and get yourselves beautified! Bring your bags with you and we'll pack the cars up before we go. Rose, you, Rowan and Holly can all come and see us off at the airport and then come back here with Ewan and stay the night. Okay, everybody? I want you guys back here in twenty. You, too, Miko!"

Miko grunted from his food coma by the box of donuts. *What, I'm not pretty enough already?*

You're gorgeous, I thought, answering him silently. *I think she means you need to come with us to the club, or at least wait in the car until we head to the airport.*

Ah. Well in that case. He headed over to my messenger bag and crawled inside, apparently gearing up for another nap.

"Come on Rose, Holly, I'll show you the room you'll be sharing. Rowan, you can bunk with Mialloch or you can take the couch," Amber continued, gesturing as she left the room.

"I'll take the couch, thanks." Rowan kicked back and relaxed on the sofa, watching me get up with hooded eyes. "And you? Where do you sleep?"

I blushed, but refused to give him any ground. "I don't. Remember – me, Ireland, hot date?" I instantly regretted my choice of words.

"How could I forget?" he drawled. He slouched down and closed his eyes, folding his arms behind his head. "Do you mind? I think I'm going to catch a quick nap before we head out."

Chapter 10

It took me ten minutes to get Alec out of the room so I could get ready. He'd exchanged his holey gray sweater for a dark green tee and black jeans, along with his usual black combat-style jacket and lace up boots. Then, he'd tried very hard to convince me to let him stay while I changed, but I shooed him out of the room.

Peering into my bag, I realized there weren't too many choices and shrugged. Gray skinny jeans and silver Sk8-hi's it was. I pulled out an ancient but girly black and silver concert tee and was just pulling it over my head when Amber, Holly and Rose barged in.

"Finally, I thought he'd never leave!" Amber flopped down on the bed, tossing a pile of clothes before her. "Dig in, people! I got club clothes here for everyone!"

Holly stepped over without hesitation, picking up a lacy blue mini-dress. "Wow, I don't think I've ever even tried on something this short. My mom would totally kill me." Her eyes lit up, and she started stripping down, giggling.

Rose laughed and headed to the pile. She had already changed into a short red a-line miniskirt with thick tights, chunky purple Fluevogs, and a short sleeve t-shirt sporting Rainbow Dash. She grabbed a pair of rainbow fingerless gloves and a dark purple leather jacket. "Oh, yeah, this will do."

Amber's eyes went wide with appreciation.

"Girl, you have a special kind of style all your own. I dig it." Amber herself had donned a pair of metallic pink Demonia platform boots with lime green laces, dark skinny jeans and a pale pink cashmere ballet-style wrap sweater. The boots added several inches to her petite frame, along with her dark hair that was whipped up into a sophisticated updo set off by a delicate set of pearl earrings. When she caught me staring, she patted her hair. "You like? I figured I should wear something travel appropriate. Now, what are we going to do about you?"

All three girls looked me over from head to toe. "Me?" I squeaked.

"Are you seriously wearing those pants? Don't you wear those, like, every day?" Holly said, turning from side to side as she studied herself in the full-length mirror. The blue dress brought out her eyes and made her legs go on about a thousand miles.

"Not every day," I said defensively. "And not at all since I've been in Aeden."

"Only because they're too warm to spar in," Amber retorted.

Actually, I'd grown to love the relaxed loose-fitting linen pants that I'd acquired in Valhalla, but I didn't say anything, thinking that the girls would probably approve even less of those than the jeans and sneakers.

"Okay, look, I only brought one pair of shoes, and I love these jeans. I've missed these jeans. They're, like, my soul mate. But, I will happily give up this old concert tee for something pretty and sparkly."

"Fine," Amber huffed, starting to sort through the pile.

"Oh, and can you make it green?" Green was Alec's color.

"Hmm, no can do. The green top you wore last time is in the wash, and green's not really my color, you know? But I have this!" She pulled out a slinky off-the shoulder, powder blue tee that had silvery strands of thread running through the fabric.

"Oooh, shiny!" Rose and I murmured at the same time, and burst out laughing. I snatched it from Amber's hands. "Okay, sold!"

I pulled off my concert tee, stowing it back in my pack, and put on the new shirt. I had to admit, it was a definite improvement. Amber gave me some long dangling silver earrings to wear that had tiny blue crystals hanging from them. Holly took over next, brushing out my thick hair and pinning it back on the sides with a couple small rhinestone barrettes from her purse. We spent a few minutes putting on some makeup and making faces in the mirror until Amber played den mother and hurried us all out of the room. I grabbed my bags and one of Amber's sleek black jackets before I followed everyone to the living room.

Amber split us into two groups of four, with the girls heading out to Rose's car on the sidewalk and the boys taking the luggage and following us to the club in the old Scout.

"Maybe they'll warm up to each other in the car," Amber winked at me. I looked behind me one last time as we left, hoping that was true. The boys were a decidedly frostier group than us girls, although they seemed to be bearing it with typical male stoicism.

After driving a short distance, we pulled up in front of a non-descript commercial building with dark windows. Amber parked and bounded out of the car, the rest of us in tow.

"Are you sure this is a nightclub?" Rose whispered to me, looking around the dead quiet street nervously.

I smiled, remembering I'd had the same reaction when I first came here, too. "Yep, just wait until we get inside.

The soundproofing the landlord had invested in really paid off. The muted beats of a DJ spinning heavy house music barely registered, even within the entrance of the club. A long line of would-be dancers waited in the corridor by a heavy iron door. Amber took all our jackets, leaving them at the coat check, and flounced up to the bouncer.

The huge man smiled down at her, swinging her up in a hug before setting her down.

"You're a sight for sore eyes, Amber! You in town for a while?" The bouncer was the same one that had been here the last time. Like most of the other club employees, he was fae.

"No, just a quick trip above below. We're only in town for the night. These are my friends, Siri, Rose, Holly. Ewan and Alec are on their way with a couple more friends."

"Okay, no problem, there's always room for you guys. Head on in. Nimh is spinning tonight."

"Sweet! Thanks, Ron." She leaned up and gave him a big hug.

Holly held out her hand to say hello but Amber rushed her through the door before she could shake Ron's hand. I wondered if maybe Ron wasn't fond of darklings, and hoped that Alec and Ewan would spare Rowan any awkwardness.

We entered the club, the raging bass flooding through me, the lights flickering across us like starlight. Amber made a beeline for a large empty table near the bar.

"Drinks are on me. What's your poison?"

"Um, Coke, I guess? We're not twenty-one," Holly sulked.

"Montreal, remember? Legal drinking age here is eighteen."

"Oh, okay, well I'm good then," Rose beamed. "Get me whatever's local, I guess?"

"Well, we're both still seventeen," Holly pointed at the two of us.

"You're cute. If you're in here, you're legal," Amber winked. "House rules are fae rules."

"Okay," Holly beamed, "make it a hard cider, then."

I nodded. "One for me, too."

"Okay, four Mystiques coming up." She bounded away to the bar, entering into an animated reunion with the bartender. We each took a seat, watching the sea of dancers on the floor. I was itching to join the crowd, and tapped my foot impatiently. I couldn't help wondering what was taking the boys so long.

Amber returned quickly with a tray of drinks, four glowing bottles of Mystique hard cider and four glasses of tawny liquid on ice.

"Those are pretty big shots, Amb," I smirked, reaching for one to smell.

"Hands off," she swatted at me, "those are for the men-folk. I have a feeling they'll be needing some liquid support."

"Ah." I nodded. "Unfortunately, I think you may be right."

"Yeah," Holly agreed. "Even my parents have noticed that something is off with Rowan. That's actually part of how he's been able to keep in touch with Vala so much. Mom thinks she's counseling him, and Vala keeps up the pretense by sending him home with herbs after every visit."

"Between you and me," Rose leaned in, "those teas aren't just for show. Vala told him they are just mint to help him in his studies, but they actually have stuff in them to help him release feelings. Vala says the sadness is blocking his chi."

"Sadness?" I asked.

"Well, you know." She pointed with her chin over my shoulder and I turned to see Alec just entering the room.

"Ah. Right. Sadness." I took a deep breath and gazed into my bottle, swirling it gently before I took a swig. "Well, a toast then? To friends, old and new?"

"To friends!" We all giggled and clinked our bottles. We were still laughing when the boys surrounded us at the table.

CHAPTER 11

"You girls going on a bender?" Ewan asked, disapproval in his gaze as he scanned the array of glasses and bottles on the table.

Ewan looked twenty five, but he was actually thirty four, a full fifteen years older than Amber, and sometimes he acted like it. Her Uncle Mitch, who happened to be their boss, had made sure Ewan didn't take his tolerance for granted. Even though age differences didn't mean much among the fae, since everyone aged much more slowly than your average human once they hit their early twenties, Amber had only been with the Guard for a little over a year. Dating within the Guard was discouraged, and Mitch had made it clear that if anything ever happened to Amber it would be considered Ewan's fault.

"Oh, sweetie, never. I got these for you guys." She used her arms to pull herself up towards his ear and stage-whispered, "I thought you might be in need."

He grimaced, and reached out, taking a gulp of the scotch. "You got that right."

"Come on, boys," Amber smiled, holding up the glasses. "To the Light!"

"And the night!" I shouted.

"The night!" Everyone else cheered and touched glasses and took their sips. I glanced around, drinking in the scene at the same time. The DJ was spinning a magical web of beats and heady lyrical samples, all underpinned by a foot stomping Skrillex vibe. I started to move, enjoying the feel of music pumping up through the soles of my sneakers.

The song rose in crescendo and everyone on the floor began jumping. Amber raised her arms and screamed joyously. I laughed, loving every ounce of crazy woo-girl that was confined in her diminutive fae body. Rose giggled and Holly laughed, too, and joined in with Amber's roof-raising. Holly grabbed both their hands and dragged them out onto the dance floor, Rose reaching over and grabbing my hand at the last minute so that we all made a chain, snaking through the crowd like water.

We found a spot and made it bigger. The dancing made it so. Everything receded, the questions I had for Airmed, the nervousness I felt about our mission, the many "what-ifs" that seemed to taunt me from day to day. The dancing made all those concerns smaller, and pumped up my heart, made me feel bigger, more alive.

Under the blacklights, I noticed that Amber's neon bootlaces and buckles shone brightly, reflecting green off the polished flooring. My earth fae night vision kicked up a notch and I could see the light emanating off my friends' bodies, what my yoga teacher had called "auras." A lot of people thought auras were silly, but we'd learned in science class that the human cellular structure, aka our bodies, actually emits measurable quantities of photons at all times. In other words? We make light. Now, with my fae abilities amped up, I could actually see it. Everyone on the floor glowed a little. The people who were fae, or magical like Rose, glowed even more.

I'd been told about the fae, how they were actually filled with Light, how it helped them live so long, how it gave them their abilities, how it was the life-sustaining energy that fueled them. But now I really got it. I could see it. Hell, I could practically touch it.

I threw my head back and laughed, heady with the vision. When I opened my eyes, I instinctively shielded my eyes from the light. Alec stood in front of me, and his light was so bright, so much more brilliant than the others. It curled towards me with a twirl of mint and aqua, mingling with mine to become tinged with streaks of silver, pink and gold, drawing it towards him even as mine pulled his towards me.

"We..." I gazed at him in wonder. "Can you see it?"

"See what?" He asked, with just a hint of his usual dimple playing by his lips.

"The lights," I whispered as he drew me to him.

"Always. Well, most of the time. Especially when it's dark like this, or if people are feeling happy."

"It's amazing."

He gazed around, looking bored. "They're okay." He looked back at me, searing me with the intensity in his eyes. "But they can't hold a candle to you."

"Mmm," I murmured, swaying with him more slowly than the music demanded. "So, did you come out here to dance?"

"I don't dance. I came out here because I saw the way you were responding to the lights. I thought you might have questions. But, now that you mention it, maybe I do dance. I think it's time for you to watch, and learn."

He walked over to Amber and whispered in her ear. Her eyes got wide and she grinned, apparently agreeing to whatever he'd said. She whispered something in Rose and Holly's ears and they began to clear a larger space on the floor, about six feet wide.

She and Alec faced off, and then she darted in gracefully, dancing around him and behind, kicking up and hooking one leg over his shoulder in an impossible move. His spine curved easily under her weight, like he was melting over backwards, immediately touching the floor with his hands and vaulting over her as she spun away. The space grew larger. They continued their dance and I slowly recognized their dance as lasair, the highest martial art of the fae. I had never seen two Lasrach warriors face off; I had only seen Guards use it against Shade operatives, who had a heavier, more aggressive style of fighting. This was beautiful.

As the song changed tempo, slowing down, Amber melted in to the crowd and Alec slid around me. "I did promise to teach you some lasair on this trip, didn't I? Come on, let's dance."

He gave me a little nudge, and I went with it, doing a tight undoff into the space. Many of the people around us slipped off to the bar to get refills on their drinks. The stools were now hidden within a sea of people three and four bodies deep. Apparently the slow tempo had been a signal that the DJ was between sets. I'd been so enraptured that I hadn't really noticed.

"Bring it on, Oberon."

"Really," he said, spinning into a low crouch. "You're going to compare me to the king of the dawn, the sun himself? Remind me to tell his real story sometime."

He held himself in a position that should have looked uncomfortable, or at least awkward, like a breakdancer frozen in mid-stream. On him? He beckoned me closer, and it just looked hot as hell.

"Now. Tonight is just about experiencing the spirit of Lasair, not learning real techniques. I want you to dance, Siri. Harness those capoeira moves you know. Mix in some tai chi and acrobatics. And dance. Flow with it, be one with the dance itself."

He moved and spun and whirled, touching me lightly in places as he passed behind me, around me, below me, letting me know without words each place that could have been a crippling attack.

"The secret of Lasair," he whispered into my ear from behind, "is that you never think of the fight or of your next attack. You need to fall in love with the dance itself, with the flow of the movement, and with your partner. You need to adore their every move. Your attacks are nothing more than an intense yearning to complete the dance, to make contact with the object of your affection, to touch your desire." His breath sent shivers down my spine. "Can you do that?"

"I think so," I nodded.

"Then let's dance."

And so it began. We danced and sparred for an hour, through the break and deep into the next set. And it was like he said. We pushed and pulled, one would give as the other took, back and forth, like two people in love. Every move was an act of wanting. It was a breathtaking form of martial art, unlike anything I had experienced before. I wondered how it had come about in the first place, who had thought to translate this depth of emotion and connection to a fighting form, something that by every right definition should have been the very embodiment of disconnection.

When I finally called it quits, we'd both worked up a good thirst. I leaned on the bar and begged for water, and was rewarded with an icy pitcher and two glasses. Alec carried them over to the table and we sat down, joining Mialloch and Ewan.

"That was pretty impressive," Ewan said. "I don't think I've ever seen someone pick up the feel of Lasair so quickly. You'll learn the actual forms quickly enough, you're a natural."

"It helps to have a good teacher," I grinned, pounding my water.

"Aye, I imagine it does. Amber learned quite quickly as well, I wonder if it has something to do with the surge."

"What do you mean?" Mialloch asked, eyes narrowing.

"Well, I was the one to do most of Amber's training. Even when she was sixteen, the surge was present between us, although back then it was fainter, easier to discount."

"You mean the surge can start off weak, and get stronger?" I asked, perplexed. "I thought it was just something that hits, like lightning."

"Or a sledgehammer," Alec said ruefully.

I punched him in the arm and looked at Ewan. "Well?"

"In older fae, it hits hard and fast, yes. Faelings are believed to be immune to the surge, for the most part."

"Oh, so does that mean that the surge is triggered by the rise in hormones in the body – like you can't experience it unless you are physically ready?" I interrupted.

"I think that's the idea, probably. Evolution at its finest, makin' sure we don't have child brides and tween mothers."

"Not to seem dense, but what does that have to do with Siri's learning quickly?" Mialloch pressed.

"Well, that should be obvious," Ewan shrugged. "I'm thinkin' that the flow of lasair, which harness the intuitive connectivity of love, can be better experienced and taught between two fae who are paired with the surge."

"The surge?" Mialloch sputtered. "Are you trying to tell me that you think believing in some fairy tale love legend will make you a better fighter? Come on, that is ridiculous. Almost as ridiculous as the idea that she would have the surge with someone like him." He glared and waved disdainfully at Alec.

"What," Alec's voice rumbled, "you think she's going to feel it with a stale book like you? Not likely."

"Shh," I soothed him, holding his hand. I looked at Mialloch. "It's true. I've seen the light we generate for each other. No one else can match it. I'm sorry if our parents led you to expect something from me. Even Bran didn't know until yesterday, but he is happy for us."

I heard a sharp intake of breath behind me and turned around. Rowan stood there, even paler than usual, and he looked heartbroken. The expression only lasted a moment but I knew what I had seen.

"Rowan, I...I'm so sorry. I didn't mean for you to find out that way." I moved forward to hug him and apologize, but he stepped away, evading my touch.

"Hey, how could I compete with that?" He grimaced, "at least now I know our breakup wasn't just about the fact that my dark side made you physically sick to your stomach."

"Rowan—"

"Whatever. Save it, Serious." He spun around and stalked off.

I started to get up, but Ewan stopped me. "Leave it. Sometimes a guy just needs time to himself. He'll be alright, you'll see. His heart's in the right place."

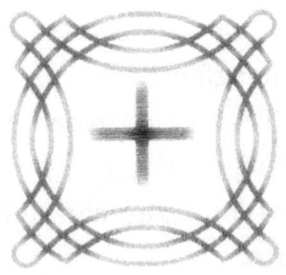

CHAPTER 12

Just like in Cinderella, all nights come to an end. This time, at least, no one had to leave the party at midnight. Or without their shoes.

We all left the club together, the girls chatting excitedly about the upcoming Choosing at Vala's. Mialloch had found Rowan at some point and they were presenting a united cold front towards Alec and me. We split up into two groups, Holly and Rose coming with us in Rose's car, Ewan following behind us with Amber, Mialloch, and Rowan in the Scout.

I sat up front with a very sober Alec as he drove, staring into the darkness along the highway and smiling as I listened to Holly rave about Zora's to Amber. In the mirror, I saw a pair of yellow aftermarket headlights approaching. I turned and watched as a massive black SUV passed us on the deserted road. Suddenly Alec slammed on the brakes, just missing the SUV that had braked hard as it swerved into our lane, forcing our vehicles to veer and avoid a collision.

Ewan managed to safely pull over on the median, but we were not so lucky. The world turned over, again and again, accompanied by the discordant song of glass breaking, metal crunching. Finally, the car righted itself and I was able to breathe again.

"Quick, out of the car, we don't know if any fuel lines ruptured." Alec sounded remarkably level-headed as he reached over and unclipped me from my seat. "Are you okay?"

His eyes glowed as he peered into mine, and I nodded numbly.

"Good, help the others out and then wait for me by the treeline over there. I'm going to go check on everyone else. I don't think this was an accident."

He was out of the car in a flash, running up the hillside back towards the highway. My door wouldn't open so I crawled out through his, taking in the rumpled, rough appearance of Rose's car. Oh, she was not going to be happy about this. Looking at the damage, I was glad that Miko had been riding in the Scout with the guys.

Wait. Alec's words to help the others came back to me. Where were Rose and Holly? I ran to the back of the car and saw Rose in the back, still struggling to get out of her seatbelt.

"Rose! Let me help you." I ran around to her side and helped her unclip the belt through the broken window. Miraculously, her door worked and she was able to get out.

"I'm so glad you are okay!" I hugged her, even as a feeling of dread started to pour over me. "Rose, where is Holly?"

"I'm not sure. I don't think she was wearing her seatbelt. I don't usually wear one in the back seat, either, something just made me put it on when we left the club. Oh, gods! Holly!"

We both started calling Holly's name, fanning out in opposite directions around the car. For a moment, I was distracted by the muffled shouts of men arguing and hand-to-hand combat above us on the highway. It sounded like Alec was right. This had been no accident.

"Siri?" A voice wheezed from the tree line.

I rushed towards the forest, following the sound of weak coughing. I didn't have to go far. Lying crumpled on the ground against a tree, was Holly. Blood was streaming from her mouth, running down her head, and out of her ears and her nose. She didn't look good.

"Holly! Oh my god. Don't move, let me get someone."

"No." She coughed again, more blood spattering her torn jacket. She reached out and grabbed me. "Don't go. Stay with me. I'm not...I'm not going to make it. I landed on something, I can feel it in my back. Listen...you need to take care of Rowan. Promise me. Okay?"

"I promise, I will. But you aren't going anywhere, either." I called for Rose over my shoulder, and then I placed my hands on Holly's hands, pouring as much love as I could into her. I had healed Miko. I could heal Holly. I had to.

The world began to fade away and I could feel the energy of the earth pulsing through me and into Holly. I could feel her pulse pick up and energy begin to shift as she began to heal. Dimly, I heard Rose run up behind me, felt her body bump mine as she knelt beside me.

"Siri, stop!" Rose grabbed my hands off of Holly.

I glared at Rose. "What are you doing? I'm healing her!"

"No, you aren't." She pointed to Holly, whose eyes were glazed, looking slowly back and forth between us as her breath came in short pants. Blood was streaming out of her mouth. Rose was right. She was getting worse.

"But why? I could feel it, she was healing. Why is she worse?" Then it hit me. "Oh no! She said she was lying on something. Quick, help me lift her!"

Rose moved to the other side and we gently lifted Holly off the ground, moving her to the left. In the dim light, my fae eyes could clearly see the sharp end of a cut sapling, covered in blood.

"She couldn't heal while the tree was still in her. The blood just flowed more strongly," I muttered. I turned back to Rose. "I'm going to try again."

I knelt down next to Holly. She had passed out when we moved her, and I gently stroked the hair out of her face.

"You're going to be okay. I promise," I whispered. "Don't you give up on me."

I cupped her face in both my hands and reach down into the earth again. This time, the healing power flooded through me even more powerfully, but it was like water rushing up against a dam. The energy continued to build and build, filling me until I thought I would burst, but it didn't go anywhere. Holly wasn't taking it in.

My eyes flew open. I shifted my hands from her face down to her neck, feeling for a pulse.

There wasn't one.

"No, no, no!" I ranted. "Not tonight, you aren't going to die on me now!"

I rolled her over with a shove, turning her face to the side, and pulled up her shirt. Quickly, I covered the rough-edged wound in her back. Again, I tried to release the energy I had called up, to force it through the wound, to restart her heart, to bring her back to life. Again, the raw power braked at my fingertips, turning back around and flowing up my own arms, swirling around inside my head and my being threatening to explode.

Rose shook me, screaming, "Siri, stop!"

But still I tried. I called up more energy, more light. I placed my hands on the earth next to Holly, trying to cocoon her in light, thinking maybe if I could heal her aura it would jumpstart her body, but nothing happened.

Finally, the energy burst out from me in a flash of light over the ground, knocking Rose off her feet, and I collapsed. The last thing I heard as my eyes fluttered closed was the harsh sound of the Morrigan's laughter echoing all around me as the wind howled through the trees.

CHAPTER 13

"Siri, get up. Siri!" I came to, Rose shaking my shoulders desperately. "Oh, thank the gods. Siri, something is happening up there. We need to check on the rest of the group."

"But Holly-"

Rose looked at me grimly. "Holly isn't going anywhere. We'll get her home safely, I promise. But we need to see what's going on."

The wind was picking up and a tree branch above us cracked ominously, bringing me back to my senses.

"Alright, let's move!" I grabbed her hand and we ran towards the road. When we got near the top of the hill we veered towards the Scout, hiding behind it while we scanned the scene on the dark freeway.

By my count, there were five Shades from the SUV that had caused our crash. Two women were fighting Alec while he protected Rowan, who looked hurt, and Mialloch, who was propping Rowan up. Two more fighters were cornered by their vehicle, facing the enraged onslaught of Amber and Ewan. Where Amber was lightning fast, Ewan was pure force. Together, they presented an impenetrable front, and I could see what Ewan had meant about the way Lasair was enhanced by the connection of the surge. Watching them flash was hypnotizing, and I had to tear my eyes away from them to find the fifth Dark fae. He was standing on top of the black SUV, holding his hands out and chanting loudly in a language I didn't understand. His dark, long hair flew wildly around him.

"What is he doing?" I whispered to Rose.

"He's casting a dark air spell, calling up a malevolent wind. Do you hear the wind howling through the trees? Shades can't usually connect to powerful elemental magic the way you guys can, they have to tap into dark energy to fuel their power first. He's raising up the angry spirits of the dead, promising them revenge if they help him."

"You can understand him?"

"No. But I can understand them. The ghosts." Her eyes looked wide and frightened. "Siri, we have to stop him. Magic like this, it can get really out of control. Once the spirits are agitated, they will lash out at anyone in their path."

"Okay, I'm on it. It looks like Rowan's hurt. Is there anything you can do to help Alec and Mialloch?"

"I think so," she answered, her face screwing up looking anything but sure. "There's a spell Vala's been teaching me, it creates a sphere of impenetrable light around whatever I am focusing on. It's just a basic warding spell."

"Great. Do that. Shield Mialloch and Rowan so Alec doesn't have to worry about them."

"What about Alec?"

"He can take care of himself," I winked at her, hoping I was right, and took off into the darkness, sneaking around the mayhem to the far side of the SUV. Up close, I could see strands of darkness in the wind that flew around the Shade on the roof of the car. A small dust devil had begun to form with him in its midst, and it was quickly gaining both speed and fury.

I backed up several steps and got a good running start, stepping up onto the running board and vaulting myself up behind the air Shade. He whirled with the wind to face me and I crouched down, aiming a kick at his legs. Instead of making contact, the wind absorbed the attack, buffeting my foot to the side as he laughed.

"You can't harm me. I've called up the spirits of this land, and they answer me with power!" The guy's eyes gleamed with mad fury.

"Wanna bet, Shadow Shaman?" I muttered under my breath. The guy had given me an idea.

I leaped down from the SUV, hunkered down and put my hands to the earth, gathering up energy like I had before with Holly. Wind Dude wasn't watching me anymore, he had turned to face the rest of the Guards and gone back to chanting. He seemed to think I'd fled in fear. He was wrong.

As I pulled the energy from the ground, I called out my own words. I started ranting, explaining to the spirits that this man was not their savior. He would not return the forests to their people. If they helped him, they were helping the same power-hungry men that had decimated their tribes and stolen their women in the first place. I talked about how the Shades wanted to destroy the forests and enslave the people. I talked until I wasn't even sure what I was saying anymore. And the whole time, the energy continued to flow up my arms, into my body, begging for release. Finally, I said a last prayer. I promised them that I would never stop trying to heal the land and return harmony to their people, to all people. It was a promise that I had no idea how to keep, but the air ripped it from me even before I finished speaking the words and I knew I'd made a pact.

I put my hands under the bumper of the SUV and for a moment, everything was silent. The wind stopped.

And then, I let the power out. This time, I maintained consciousness, watching in awe as the shockwave from the release of energy sent the vehicle flipping end over nose. I slumped back on the pavement, unable to stop a slight giggle from popping out as the air Shade flew through the air.

I got up, dusting myself off, and grinned. "Where are your friends now, Shadow Shaman?"

I looked over at Amber and Ewan, and saw that they had used my distraction to knock out the pair they'd been fighting. Ewan was already on the phone, calling in a backup crew to take the captured Shades in for questioning while Amber sat on the back of one of the women and used a belt to secure her hands and feet together.

Ewan stuffed his phone back in his pocket and jogged past me, saying, "They'll be here in ten minutes." He headed past the van to make sure the wind guy stayed down, cuffing him once more on the back of his head for good measure.

I looked over to see how Rose and Alec were faring, and saw that Alec was still in the thick of things, fighting two brutes. Mialloch and Rowan were far off to the side, sitting with Rose. The air seemed to shimmer slightly around them, and I knew she was holding a sphere of protection for all their safety.

Well, I'd said I wanted to practice Lasair more. I shrugged to myself and sprinted over to Alec.

"Wanna spar?"

"Are you kidding?" he laughed. "I thought you'd never ask."

He flashed a brilliant smile at me and I saw the light around him flare, as it had it the club. Gods, I loved that dimple of his.

"Right. Well, here I am."

"Hey, Sam, that's the girl!" One of the thugs seemed to have just caught on to the fact that I was the one they wanted.

"Yeah, that's me. Awesome girl, at your service. You want me to go with you?"

Big guy nodded at me.

"You gotta earn my ticket. Are you in it to win it?"

"You bet, girlie!" he laughed and came at me with a roar. "The Morrigan's gonna reward me handsomely for bringing you in."

Even though Alec was busy fighting his own Shade, I could feel his light, guiding me, empowering me. Showing me moves before I knew I needed to make them. I flowed and flipped and danced and kicked, and before I knew it, our cotillion was done and my thug was lying on the ground out cold.

Alec swept me up in his arms, kissing me as he swung me around. "You did it! I've never seen anyone master the flash so quickly."

"Yeah, well, I've had some really great teachers," I laughed.

He set me down and quickly saw to restraining the two thugs, then stood up again, grabbing my hand. Warmth flowed through me, replenishing any depleted reserves I had from calling up the earth power earlier. He looked at me in concern, sensing the empty spaces that the energy was filling.

"What did you do?"

"Not now, okay? Can we talk about it later?"

"Yeah, alright. As long as you're okay?" His eyes raked over me, taking in every disheveled detail.

"I'm okay." I thought of Holly, and chewed on my lip. I'd learned how to call up the healing power of the earth more strongly than ever before so I could use it as a weapon. Why hadn't I been able to use it to save Holly?

"Come on, there's something we need to do." I pulled Alec with me, striding over to see Rose and Rowan.

"Rose, you can stop now." I knelt down in front of her, watching the air shimmer between us as I looked her in the eyes. "We're safe. The attack is over."

Relief flooded her features and I saw a brief flash of iridescent light wink out as she dropped the shield. She sobbed and threw herself into my arms for a hug.

"Oh, thank gods!"

"Have you told them yet?" I whispered in her ear.

"Told them? No, I...No. I needed to keep them safe. I haven't told them."

"Told who what?" Mialloch asked innocently, watching my face.

I swallowed, and looked at Rowan. "There's something you need to see."

Fear flashed across Rowan's face. He glanced back between Rose and I.

"Where's Holly?" Blood was streaming down the side of his head and he was cradling one arm. "Rose, you said Holly is back at the car. Is she okay?"

I squeezed Rose's hand and answered for her. "She is down by the car, Rowan. Rose told you the truth. Come on."

I stood up and held out my hand, waiting for Rowan to take it. He stood up, ignoring my hand. "I can walk on my own."

"Alright," I agreed quietly, putting my hands in my jeans.

We started down the hill towards the car, the rest of the group following behind us. I looked at Rowan's arm.

"What happened?"

"I think it's dislocated. It's not a big deal, it's happened before. Holly knows how to set it." He shrugged, wincing at the pain the slight movement caused.

"Oh." I wondered who would set it now.

We got to the car and Rowan paused. "Oh wow. I can't believe you guys are all okay. This car is totaled. Where's my sister?"

He looked around, his voice rising.

"Over here." I nodded towards the trees and led the way. The further we walked from the lights of the highway the more my earth-powered eyes lit up. As we drew near the spot where we'd left her, I began to wonder if someone had moved her. Where was her body?

When I finally saw it, I gasped. I'd missed it at first, because she was entirely entwined in flowering vines.

"Siri," Rowan turned to me, exasperated, "what is going on. You're acting really strange, and your eyes are glowing, which is really freakin' weird, and honestly, I'm too tired to deal with any more of this-"

"I'm so sorry, Rowan. Really, I am."

"What do you mean? What are you saying?"

"Oh my Gods, Siri, look!" Rose rushed past me, kneeling at Holly's side, and any chance I'd had at lessening the shock was gone. Rose was already brushing the green tendrils away from Holly's face, and Rowan's own lost all its color.

"You said she was at the car." Rowan murmured as he rushed to her side, pushing Rose out of the way. "You said she was at the car! What the hell is she doing out here, covered in vines and, and..." His voice trailed off and he began ripping the vines off of her in a frenzy.

Finally, he stopped, and just sat there still as ice, holding her hand in his.

I sat down next to him and placed my hand on his leg. He flinched, and I pulled back.

"She was thrown from the car when we rolled. I tried to heal her, I did, but it only made it worse, because she had landed on a broken tree and the healing made the blood pump faster. By the time I figured out that I had to remove the source of the injury it was too late. She was dead. I'm so sorry, Rowan. I really tried, I did."

"She did everything she could," Rose offered, "it was just too serious an injury. All the energy she called up from the earth, that's what made these vines grow – the earth is honoring your sister's light, even now." She pointed to the tendrils he had torn off his sister. They were slowly creeping towards Holly again, new flowers of purple and red blossoming even as they grew.

A strangled groan escaped Rowan's lips, and his hands fisted in his lap.

I placed my hand on his back to comfort him, and said, "Another team is on its way. They'll make sure the Shades answer for this."

For a long time, he didn't answer me. I sat by him, trying to lend support. I didn't know what else there was I could do. How did you comfort someone who had just lost their twin? I hadn't really experienced loss before, and I felt out of my depth. I'd never even been to a funeral. For the hundredth time in a week, I wished my mom was here.

One by one, I heard the others start to head back up the hill behind us.

"This is all your fault."

The words startled me. In the silence, I'd begun to drift away. Now, I felt like I'd been slammed back into the ground.

"What?" I whispered.

"This. It's all your fault." He said it simply, easily. Like I was silly or stupid not to see it.

A tear slid out of my eye as I tried to deny it.

"No. I tried to help her."

"But all of this, don't you see?" He leapt up and started pacing, gesturing wildly as he spoke. "If you hadn't come to Falls Depot, this never would have happened. We wouldn't have decided to choose the Light. We wouldn't have come to Montreal. We wouldn't have been seeing you and your new friends off at the airport. And Holly wouldn't have been in the car. With you."

"I'm not sorry I met you, Rowan."

"You should be." He stopped pacing and glared at me. "You will be. Now leave. I don't want you here with me. I don't want to see your stupid, love-filled face. Tell your team to bring another car, one for just Rose, Holly and I. After tonight, I don't ever want to see you again."

"But, I-"

"No, Siri. Not this time. I'm done letting you hurt me. She was my sister, Siri! My twin! You think you can undo the damage you've caused? Just, go. Get away from me."

I flinched at the venom in his voice. "Fine." Getting up, I was afraid to look at him and see the hate in his eyes. I walked away quickly, breaking into a run past Rose's car, feeling every bit as torn up and wrecked inside as that vehicle.

CHAPTER 14

Five hours later, listening to the drone of the engines on the small private jet we were on, I couldn't get Rowan's words out of my head.

Once the backup Ewan had sent for arrived, goodbyes had been rushed and teary. Amazingly, Mitch had arranged a special transport visa for Rose and Rowan to bring Holly's body back, and they would be heading straight home after a quick stop in Montreal to pick up their gear. Rose had held me, assuring me that everything would be okay, and that she would talk to me when she got home.

Rowan hadn't approached me after our conversation, and I hadn't felt strong enough to try talking to him again. Had it really been my fault? Should I not have tried to heal her? Was there any way I could have avoided all of this? Somehow, I didn't think so. It's not like I'd ever asked to be involved in any of the drama between the Light and the Dark.

Still. Here I was, hours after the death of a friend, on a private plane to Ireland, planning to meet one of the most ancient living fae on the planet. I never could have guessed where I would be if you'd asked me three months ago.

I had discovered the hard way that even the pure, loving energy of the surge wasn't a balm for emotional pain. It was good in a way, I suppose. Nice to know that no matter how comforted I might feel, I could still have regular feelings going on top of it all. Alec had passed out on my shoulder a couple of hours after takeoff, urging me to do the same with concern. I hadn't told him what had happened with Rowan. I hadn't told anyone. Everyone thought I was broken up over Holly's death, and I was, of course I was, but the pain of being blamed for all of it, by someone I had considered a true friend, was more than I could bear.

I couldn't possibly sleep. Instead, I stared out the window of the plane, watching the night sky lighten slowly as we flew towards the dawn, tears leaking down my face. Alec's hand was still in mine, and the warmth of his touch was a bittersweet reminder that love couldn't cure everything.

I sighed, and petted Miko, who was fast asleep on my lap. He was the only one who knew the whole story. He had the privilege of hearing the thoughts that cycled around in my head endlessly. He hadn't said a word though, only nuzzled me gently with his soft head and purred gently. I knew he was trying to calm me down, to let me know without words that everything was going to be okay.

I appreciated the gesture. Too bad my own faith was dwindling fast.

If I couldn't save my friend with all that power I'd called up, how could I ever be expected to save the world? Why did the Morrigan even want me so much? What was so special about me, really? From what Rose and Mialloch had said, it sounded like Airmed was a much more powerful healer than me. I wasn't special.

Carefully, I picked up Miko and moved him onto Alec's lap without waking either of them. I gingerly moved Alec's head aside and got up, grabbing my small pack. Everyone was taking advantage of the long flight to catch up on their sleep before we landed. Everyone except me. I walked quietly through the aisle so as not to wake anyone.

By my count, we'd been flying for four hours, which meant we were over halfway to Dublin by now. I shut myself in the posh onboard toilet and stared at myself in the mirror.

Well, it wasn't called a red-eye flight for nothing.

I grabbed one of the courtesy facial wipes and cleaned off what was left of my makeup, which wasn't much. There were several plush looking creams and lotions secured to the counter, so I smoothed some over my face, hoping it would help repair some of the salt damage.

Next, I checked out my hair. During all the action I'd lost one of the gorgeous barrettes Amber had loaned me, but I knew she wouldn't mind. I pulled the other one out and brushed my hair with my fingers before braiding it to one side and securing it with a rubber band from my pocket. I clipped the barrette back over one ear. Maybe it would distract people from noticing the red rims under my eyes.

Yeah, right, I snorted. Not bloody likely.

I stared down at my pants, noticing short rusty streaks. Tracing the marks, I realized that I must have wiped my hands there earlier without even realizing it. I lifted my hands and inspected them. Sure enough, hints of Holly's blood remained. I turned the water in the sink on, grateful that the posh plane had better running faucets than the economy steerage I was used to. Lathering my hands in generous amounts of soap, I started scrubbing, washing away the dingy flakes of my former life. That life, like the bubbles popping and running down the drain, was gone.

I squared my shoulders and looked at myself, willing myself not to start crying again. Willing myself to keep it together.

"Get a grip, Serious." Somehow, using Rowan's old nickname for me helped.

I stripped off my pants and shirt, putting on my dark spare jeans and one of my standard issue gray tanks. Much better. I felt like myself again. I stuffed the soiled jeans in the garbage. It was like saying goodbye to two friends in one night. But I could get another pair of pants. There would never be another Holly.

"Keep it together, Siri," I gritted out between my teeth, reaching to unlock the door. What I really needed was a punching bag or a good run, not a good night's sleep.

I opened the door and came face to face with Alec leaning against the doorjamb

"Hey," I said.

"Hey. You alright?"

"I will be if you let me out of this bathroom," I grumbled.

He moved away from the door without smiling, looking me over from head to toe.

"You changed," he noted.

"Hello, Captain Obvious," I retorted. Maybe it was just my lack of sleep, but suddenly I was feeling very snarky.

He reached out and placed a hand on my shoulder, "You know it wasn't your fault, right? There's nothing you could have done."

"Who said it was my fault?" I shrugged his hand off, ready to pick a fight.

"No one. I just...I felt what you were feeling all night. The guilt. The self-blame. And I can tell you, you helped us all come out of this okay. Who knows who else might have been hurt if you hadn't joined the fight when you did. Maybe if I had braked more carefully, veered a little less to the right, maybe then Holly wouldn't have been thrown from the car. Maybe if I had told her to wear her seatbelt. I don't know. But sometimes we just can't outrun our destinies. Sometimes, it's just our time."

"Really, is that what you think? Do you think it was your mother's time all those years ago? Your sister's?"

"No, you know I don't." He glowered at me and stepped up so he was toe to toe with me. "But what happened tonight was just as much the Dark's fault as what happened to my family. If she hadn't died, they would have willingly tortured her later if they got their way. Either way, it was not your fault."

I bowed my head, feeling defeated. "Rowan blames me," I whispered.

"How can you say that? No one blames you. You tried to heal her. You did your best. There is no shame in that."

"Rowan does. He told me so. He blames me for moving to their town, for getting them involved in all this, for all of it. Don't you get it? He blames me. And he's not entirely wrong!" I pushed him back, hard, slamming my hands against his chest. "If I hadn't tried to heal her before we took her off that tree, she might never have bled out."

"Of course he's wrong. And you're wrong if you let him make you doubt yourself. There's only one person who has the right to judge you, and that is you. Are you really saying that you think you caused all this? Did you choose the town you moved to? Did you break into your house and abduct your mother? Did you ask someone to infect her with the anti-serum? Did you even ever make a plan to go to Aeden before all that happened?"

"No."

"Of course not. That's how destiny works. It just strings you along sometimes, taking you for a ride. You didn't ask them to come up to Montreal. No one did."

"Holly wanted to come," I shrugged.

"So should we blame her, then? Maybe it was simply her time."

"Dammit!" I turned and punched the wall behind me, which was unfortunate for my hand, since it happened to be made out of some unyielding metal alloy. "I'm not okay with that! We were going to visit Aeden together. She was so excited. It was not her time!"

Alec's arms came around me from behind, holding me close. "Hey, take it easy on the walls. If you want something to punch, I'm right here." He spun me around kissed the tip of my nose before pushing me away and dropping into a standard glima stance. "Bring it, blondie." His dimple flashed as he beckoned me toward him. "If you can."

"Oh, kiss off." I punched angrily him in the shoulder and dropped down low to avoid his answering strike. I spun around to his other side and aimed a kick at his thigh, followed by a jab to his ribs. He blocked the punch, but didn't follow up with an answering attack. Annoyed, I flew at him with a flurry of strikes, and he let each one land, always going through the motions of a parry but never really trying to hit me back.

I knew what he was doing, trying to let me work out my anger and frustration by being my heavy bag. His patience just ticked me off more. I didn't want to be forgiven. I didn't want to be excused. I wanted to take the blame. If it would make things better somehow, if it would help keep anyone else from getting hurt, I needed to accept responsibility for what happened. I knew it didn't really make sense. Part of me felt like everything wrong that had happened in the world was somehow my fault at that moment. If I could just figure it out all, then maybe, just maybe, I could also fix it. Maybe I could stop the bad things from happening. That was all I really wanted.

Little by little, my anger started to dissipate. I wasn't filled with hope, exactly, but I felt better. Emptier. Lighter. Part of the burden had been lifted, and I knew that Alec had taken part of it onto his own shoulders. When I finally lowered my hands and really looked at him, he laughed ruefully and massaged his shoulder.

"You've got a mean left hook, you know that?" He grinned at me and I managed to smile.

"You were supposed to fight back, you know."

"Yeah, well, I'm a lover, not a fighter."

"Yeah, right," I chuckled. "Okay, well, at least now I have someone to practice my healing powers on. Come on, let's go sit down and I'll see what I can do."

We walked back to our seats arm-in-arm, giggling and flirting.

"Dude, couldn't you guys wait until you got a room?" Amber yawned.

"Huh?"

"We could totally hear you guys back there, you know, all that grunting and thumping. Gives a girl naughty thoughts, you know?" She looked over at Mialloch's wide eyes and laughed. "Don't worry, Loch, you're safe from me."

"Um, Amber, I don't think that's what they-" Mialloch started to speak, but Alec cut him off.

"Siri was beating me up, not covering me with kisses, much to my disappointment."

"What?" Amber just looked at him sleepily, rubbing her eyes.

"What Alec means to say," I answered, "is that he was letting me show him the new moves you've been teaching me in glima. That's all."

"Oh," Amber pouted. "How boring. Well, I suppose if we're all awake, we might as well have some food. I'll go gather up some grub from the flight kitchen."

Mialloch opened the window shades near him. The first rays of sunlight were starting to creep into the cabin, dawn decorating the clouds outside in pale violets and furious fuchsias.

"Is it not a beautiful morning? Look at those colors!" Mialloch seemed especially chipper. It couldn't be healthy.

"Are you feeling okay?" Alec eyed him doubtfully, clearly thinking the same thing I was.

"I'm great! You know, this is my first time in a human airplane?"

"You've flown before," I answered dumbly.

"Yes, but it's the first time I have been completely outside and removed from the earth – in no way in contact with Aeden at all. It's an amazing thing. Simply amazing. And the sunrise! Have you seen the sky out there?! It's amazing. Simply-"

"Amazing. Right. Got it," Alec and Mialloch grinned at each other like they were old friends. Which, I suppose, they actually kind of were. Maybe this trip would be good for them.

"Right!" Mialloch clapped and rubbed his hands together. Then he turned his bright eyes on me. "So, Siri, I heard what you guys were talking about before."

"Excuse me?"

"Destiny, healing, you know," he waved his hand dismissively.

"Really? Eavesdrop much?" I retorted peevishly.

Mialloch continued on, ignoring my snark. "I feel like I must tell you, Alec is right."

"He is?"

"I am?"

"Yes. You are," Mialloch smiled at Alec. "My grandmother used to talk to me a lot about how healing works, before she realized that her gift had not been passed on to me. I miss those talks." He stared out the window for a moment, lost in thought. "But I digress. She said that Light has its own consciousness, that the spark within us that humans refer to as soul is indeed animated and full of divine will. In this way, Fate also exists – it is the consciousness that animates all matter on this planet on a quantum level, the Light that emanates from the red sun of Aeden, the core generator of all life on earth. Fate and soul, they work together."

"I don't get it, what are you trying to say?" I asked, frustrated.

"I'm saying that souls, especially the souls of fae who are intertwined with the Light, they often choose their own exit point. There are far fewer accidental deaths than you would think. Fewer real victims, fewer true tragedies. My grandmother, she says that there are many possible exit points in every life, and that at each point our soul chooses whether we want to stay and learn more, or travel back to the Light."

"Okay, that sounds pretty new age-y to me. So?"

"So. Your friend chose her time. I bet she even told you she was dying before you admitted it to yourself."

I glared at him, refusing to acknowledge he was right. As usual, though, my tutor didn't need any confirmation and plowed on.

"Even the greatest healer cannot halt the progression of death during a willful exit. My grandmother couldn't stress that enough. She told me stories...well, they were painful for her to share, I know. One story was similar to yours, where the healing only made the person bleed more, die faster. She said she realized then that sometimes her power couldn't heal, but it could make death come more easily, less painfully. It was a facet of her power that she resented having to use. I think it is part of why she refuses to live in Aeden. She says there are too many memories."

I flopped down in my seat, stunned. "Are you serious?"

"Is he ever not?" Alec muttered.

"Yes," Mialloch answered, glaring at Alec, "I do tend to be serious. I also tend to be right. I try to only speak when I know what I am talking about, unlike some people. Siri, you couldn't have saved your friend, I am sure of it. No matter how much more you practice, some things are past the realm of possibility, and with good reason."

"You think she wanted to die?" I asked disbelievingly.

"No. I think it was her time. It might not ever make sense to us, but you can at least rest easy knowing that she rests with the Light now. She is part of you, of all of us, now."

I closed my eyes, trying to process what he was saying. I had no ready response in my brain or on my tongue. I literally had no words. I heard Alec murmuring quietly to Mialloch, and footsteps retreating. The seat next to me creaked, and a warm hand took mine. When I opened my eyes, I expected to see Alec, but it was Amber's dark eyes that stared kindly into mine.

I should have known that it wasn't Alec's hand holding mine, it was a testament to how frazzled I was that I hadn't even noticed the difference.

"Alec took Mialloch in back to make some coffee. I found some divine looking fruit and cheese. You want?"

"Yeah, thanks." I reached out and broke open a small sourdough roll, spreading some butter and brie on it numbly.

"I heard what Mialloch was saying. You know, I've heard similar stories, passed down through the old legends of the Ancients. I suppose there isn't any way for us to really know, but...well, it is a comfort, isn't it?" She smiled hopefully at me.

"I don't know. I don't know if I can believe all that stuff he said. But there is one thing," I paused. "She knew she was dying. When I found her lying there, she told me she wasn't going to make it. She made me promise I would take care of Rowan."

I leaned my head against the seat and closed my eyes, tears threatening to overtake me again. I willed them back down.

"Oh God. Rowan. He hates me. I promised I would take care of him, and here I am, flying thousands of miles away while he drives his sister's body home. He told me he never wants to see me again." I leaned forward again, looking Amber in the eyes. "How can I take care of him if he hates me?"

"Siri, calm down," Amber soothed me, but she looked troubled. "Whatever he said to you, I'm sure he didn't mean it. He's in pain, and people lash out when they are in pain. But he knows you, right? I mean, you guys connected, I'm sure he knows that you would never do anything to hurt anyone."

"Right, sure," I scoffed.

"Oh, come on. You think I haven't noticed what a softie you are? You might be a natural at martial arts, and you might have developed a tough shell after moving around all those years, but on the inside, you're all sweet and forgiving like that brie you're eating."

"Watch it, Amber, I think I might deck you in a moment."

"Nah, I'm safe. You wouldn't dare hit your guru," she giggled and I snorted.

"That's what you'd like to think," I said and I launched a grape at her face. Unfazed, Amber caught it between her teeth, grinning at me.

"See? I teach, and you feed me. You learn quickly, young faeling."

133

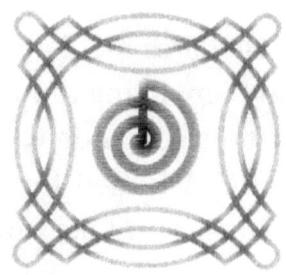

Chapter 15

Amber, Miko and I were eating in companionable silence, interspersed with the occasional blissed out food moan, when the boys finally made their way back with coffee. They were carrying a tray loaded with small shots of espresso, frothy cappuccinos, and some mugs that looked miraculously like hot cocoa with whipped cream on top, complete with tiny slivers of shaved chocolate.

"We couldn't decide..." Alec shrugged.

"So we made everything!" Mialloch grinned like a little boy on Christmas morning.

Alec looked at Mialloch, suppressing a smile. "Yeah, golden boy here doesn't get to cook too often."

"Never!" Mialloch practically giggled. I knew that he was more innocent than most boys I'd ever met, but I'd never really seen this fun, enthusiastic side of his before. It was refreshing. For the first time, I could begin to imagine the boy he had once been, and how he and Alec could have been good friends. It was like meeting him for the first time, and I said as much.

"What do you mean? I'm always like this," Mialloch said, perplexed, and slightly stiff, more like the tutor I had come to know and endure.

Amber snorted. "Oh man, you have no idea, do you?"

"What?" he asked, looking at each of us in turn.

"Mialloch, I hate to break it to you," I began gently, "but you are almost never like this. You almost never smile. And you certainly don't get giddy, like you are now."

"Oh," he paused, placing his cappuccino down on the table. "I'm sorry if I am offending you."

"No!" I reached out and placed my hand on his, and he raised his eyes to me, a flare of interest apparent in them. I hastily grabbed my hand away, but not before Alec noticed the look in Mialloch's eye. "You aren't offending anyone, Mialloch. I like this side of you, it's hard to remember sometimes that you're young, you know, because you take most things so seriously. And I appreciate that, too, I do. But this, this is nice. Thanks for making all these, by the way – is that hot chocolate I see?"

"Yes, it is." Mialloch smiled proudly. "I've never had it made with milk before, it's amazing. All the machines in that kitchen there, the things they can do...I thought only the fae had technology so fine, but I can see now that the humans also have some wonders of their own."

"Truer words were never spoken. Thanks for your hard work, boys." Amber grinned at them over the rim of her mug.

I picked up a cup of cocoa and sipped the divine goodness within. "Mmm, yes, this is the perfect ending to the food fest we just had," I agreed.

"Yeah, I see you guys didn't leave us much," Alec chuckled, reaching over and grabbing a banana and a rind of bread from my plate. "There we were, slaving away, and this is all you left us?"

"Ah, you know me so little, Alec." Amber sauntered over to the sidebar and grabbed another tray. "That tray was for me and Siri. This one is for you guys."

"Oh, thank god!" Mialloch moaned, standing up and stealing the tray from her. "I wasn't sure I could remain a gentleman much longer, so hungry was I."

Alec let out a guffaw. "Yeah, what he said."

We all took a long moment of silence, appreciating the fine beverages and breakfast. The food had made its way to my stomach and I was starting to feel supremely relaxed.

"So. We're what now, a couple hours from Dublin?" I asked.

"Yeah, just about," Alec nodded, leaning back and reaching over to hold my hand. It was his turn now to fall into a food coma.

"What's the story when we get there? Do we just wander around, looking for Airmed? Do we even know where she is living?"

"I don't have any idea where she lives, exactly," Mialloch shrugged.

"That's okay, Siri knows someone who does," Amber winked at me.

"I do?"

"You do."

"But I don't know anyone," I insisted. She looked at me, allowing me to work it out on my own.

"The only person I know who lives in Ireland is...oh! My Aunt Jade! I mean, my grandmother! Oh, well, wow, that's cool, we get to see her? Does she know what's going on?"

"Yeah, she knows. And she hasn't been super cooperative, she doesn't really work with Aeden much, or approve of the fact that her daughter got mixed up in Shade business. She has a reputation for always putting the protection of humans above all fae matters."

"We never saw her much growing up. Things were always kinda tense between her and my mom. But I thought it was just a sister thing."

"Mmm, more likely, a mom disapproving of her daughter's ties to Aeden, thing. But she loves Frederika, and she wants to see you. Plus, she knows Airmed. She's one of the only fae who meets with her regularly – apparently they've had a mean game of cribbage going on between them for the last century."

"Okay, I don't even know what that means," I laughed at her, "but I have to admit I'm psyched to meet up with my grandmother again, now that I know who she really is. So what's the deal? Is she meeting us as the airport?"

"No, that would draw too much attention to us. We are meeting a Light student at Trinity College, and she is going to take us to your grandmother. You know she's a dean at the school, right?"

"No! I knew she was up for some big promotion a couple years ago, but I thought it was just to get tenure. I had no idea. Good for her!"

"A lot of the deans at Trinity are fae, some are Shades and some are Light, they actually manage to work together at the school somehow."

"Like Snape and Dumbledore," I muttered.

"Sort of. The college is safe for both sides, neutral ground. Still, it would be best if we don't stay there too long. We don't want anyone to recognize you, which is why Jade didn't want to meet you in public. She's waiting at her country house for us to get there. So we're meeting a student at the school, and she is supposed to be driving us to your grandmother's."

"Why didn't they just give us the address so we could drive ourselves?" I wondered.

"Rose said your grandmother has some tricky wards around her house, only a few people know how to get through them. I guess this new student of hers knows all the moves, though. Amber said she's taken a special liking to her, even though she's just a freshman. Something about the families being close or something, Rose said. Anyway, that's the plan."

"Okay, cool. I totally wanted to check out Trinity anyway. I haven't had a chance to look at any colleges yet this year."

"Are you sure you want to get your hopes up?" Alec asked me gently.

"Hope is all I have, Alec." I squeezed his hand.

"Not true." He smiled. "You have me."

"Blech. You guys are too damn cute. Stop it before you spoil my breakfast, please." Amber pulled a face and made us all laugh.

"Sorry, didn't mean to go all John Hughes on you," I apologized.

"John Hughes?" Mialloch asked.

"Romantic yet pithy teen movie director, lots of cult classics," I explained.

"Now I'm even more confused," Mialloch shook his head in dismay.

"Never fear!" Amber exclaimed, jumping up and rushing over to a small cabinet and pushing a button set into the wall nearby. A massive flat screen TV revealed itself as a panel slid upwards. She opened the cabinet and begin flipping through a huge folder of DVDs.

"Pretty in Pink or Sixteen Candles?" She quizzed me, holding up two discs.

"Pretty in Pink, obviously," I retorted. Alec groaned and pulled a blanket over his head. "Hey now, none of that," I teased, pulling the blanket off, and him towards me along with it. "You need to explain all relevant scenes to the newbie here, you'll have a better sense of what he doesn't know."

"Try, everything," Alec mumbled under his breath. "Fine, but then you owe me."

"Owe you what?" I asked, narrowing my eyes at him.

"For starters, you can come over here and sit down." He patted his lap and I climbed on, snuggling into his arms.

"Perfect," he murmured into my hair, clasping his arms around me.

Mialloch and Amber sat side by side on the other side of the aisle, Amber already explaining the opening credits in her animated way, waving her arms around, and bouncing around in her seat. I had no doubt that Mialloch was in for a crash course in humanity. Me? For the first time in hours I felt at ease, and as Molly Ringwald pulled her rose-petaled socks on to get ready for school, I leaned my head against Alec's strong shoulder and drifted off to sleep.

CHAPTER 16

I woke as our wheels touched down on the runway. I caught a glimpse of Molly Ringwald and Andrew McCarthy making out onscreen just before the film cut to the credits. At least there, all was well.

I burrowed further into Alec, who had also fallen asleep at some point during the movie, and gave him a kiss on the neck.

"Wake up, sleepy head. We're here."

Alec groaned and started to stretch, jostling me on his lap. When I began to slip off, he put one arm back around me.

"Mmm. I think you'd better move over to your own seat, love. I can't feel my own legs."

"Aw, who needs legs?" I teased as I unwound myself from his body and shifted over to the seat next to him. "So, you're a big Molly Ringwald fan?"

"Oh yeah, the biggest," he said, rolling his eyes. "Actually, I prefer blondes. And I fell asleep right after you, I think."

"Yep, you did," Amber acknowledged. "The snoring was kind of a dead giveaway."

"I don't snore!" Alec protested.

"Whatever, rumble-nose," Amber joked.

"You were a bit distracting for a while, until I sent a whiff of air over and you closed your mouth," said Mialloch.

"You-"

"Honestly," Mialloch continued talking over Alec, "I'm surprised you could fall asleep. That tale was strange, but truly riveting. Tell me, are all human schools like the one in the film?"

"More or less," I laughed, starting to pull on my shoes. "Minus the crazy eighties fashions."

"Ah, yes, Amber's been explaining the various clothing styles of the last thirty years to me. Fascinating."

I giggled and finished lacing up my vans and pulled on my jacket. The onboard speakers crackled on and the pilot welcomed us to Dublin, announcing the weather (cold and misty) and the time (2:41pm). The warm sunlight we'd watched dawning earlier had disappeared behind a blanket of drab gray skies.

The plane taxied into a private hangar. Once we'd parked and the stairs had been set up, we disembarked single file. So far, I couldn't really tell we weren't in Canada anymore. Airplane hangars all looked the same on the inside. We stood around for a moment at the bottom of the steps.

"What now?" I asked.

"We called a cab for you on approach, it should already be waiting outside." The pilot answered from behind me, and I turned to see the attractive pilot pulling her long hair out of its ponytail. I caught a glimpse of pointed ears before she fluffed her hair over her shoulders, hiding the tell-tale sign of fae and human parentage.

"What about going through customs?"

"You were all pre-screened and cleared at take-off. One of the benefits of flying private," she flashed her teeth at me and shook my hand. "I hope you enjoyed your flight, Ms. Alvarsson. Your father has me on standby here in Dublin until you are ready to fly back to the States. Call me when you're ready to leave." She passed me her card and a thick envelope, said her good-byes to the rest of the team, and walked away to the flight offices.

"Well, that seems almost too easy," I said, opening the envelope and flipping through the generous amount of colorful Euro banknotes.

"What do you mean?" Amber asked, nonplussed.

"Ha! I bet none of you have ever flown commercial before, let alone coach, am I right?"

"How does one fly in a coach?" Mialloch looked confused.

"Never mind," I smirked. Memories of my last flight to Ireland made me smile – taking our shoes and belts off to go through security, drawing straws for the aisle seat with my mom, comparing our tiny bags of crackers, people watching at the baggage carousel. All the mundane annoyances seemed trivial now in comparison to having my mom by my side. "Let's go, taxi's waiting."

And it was. A sporty Volkswagen was waiting just outside the hangar, the driver reading a battered paperback behind the wheel. When he saw us he scrambled out of the car and greeted us, opening the trunk so we could all stow our carry-ons. Alec nodded at Mialloch to sit up front and the rest of us climbed in the back seat. Amber explained where we were going and the cabbie nodded.

Amber sat back and pulled out her phone, calling Mitch to let him know we'd arrived. After some back and forth, she hung up.

"Okay, our, um, friend is going to meet us at the Old Library in the Long Room by the William Shakespeare bust."

"By the what?" I asked.

"The Shakespeare bust. The Long Room houses over 200,000 of the library's oldest books, and a ton of marble busts of famous authors and philosophers. Will, of course, is family, so it's as good a place as any to meet."

"What do you mean, family?"

Amber glanced at the human driver up front, who was deep in conversation with Mialloch.

"Family, like, he was born in Aeden," she whispered. "That's the real reason no one can ever find conclusive birth records or evidence he existed. He was born and buried in Elysielle, another city in Aeden. It's sort of an artist's enclave. John Lennon was actually from there, too."

"Wow. Cool! You've been holding out on me. When this is all over, I think that's a place we need to check out."

She laughed. "Totally. They have the best parties. Just you wait. Normally it would have been my first stop as a tour guide, but, well, you know – training comes first."

"Yeah," I sighed. "I know."

I leaned my head against the cool glass window, watching fields and tree-lined highways near the airport quickly give way to the suburbs of north Dublin. As we entered the city, nostalgia overtook me. I had loved the time we'd spent here when I was twelve. The old Georgian buildings had impressed me in ways that most architecture never had. There had been a tangible atmosphere to the place that had made me feel at home, at peace.

I had begged my mother to stay here for another year or two, or even forever, but she'd just shook her head sadly. She'd liked it here, too. After all, she had grown up in Ireland. But she'd been committed to her work. Now that I knew her real job was more about protecting the world and other light fae from the dark, I could imagine how she must have really felt. When I was twelve, and believed she was just a regular security consultant, I hadn't been quite so understanding. Only the fact that we'd moved to Colorado next, and I'd been able to get back into snowboarding, had consoled me.

By the time we arrived at Trinity, Mialloch had become fast friends with the cabbie and gleaned more information from the poor man than an FBI investigator. After we had climbed out of the cab and tipped Mister Corby copiously, I inhaled my first full breath of Dublin air and smiled. Even the air here tasted different.

Amber handed me my pack and I put it over my shoulder, adjusting the strap as I took in our surroundings. The massive front gates of the college loomed in front of us, the dark arched corridor seeming more ominous than I remembered. When I was little, Mom had brought me by often enough, letting me read outside while she had "adult conversations" with Aunt Jade. I had loved watching the older boys play rugby on the grand lawns amidst the courtyards. Five years ago, stepping through the front gates of Trinity had seemed like falling down the rabbit hole to Wonderland.

This time, I wondered if I would like what I found on the other side.

I squared my shoulders and marched forward. "Right, let's go."

We walked through the gates, through the darkness, and back out into the light. For a moment, the sun peeked out through the clouds, and I was blinded. Then the world returned to gray.

I scanned the courtyard that had seemed so vast to me at twelve. It wasn't so big anymore.

"There, just past that building on the right. That's the Old Library."

"Right," Amber nodded. "Let's go find Shakespeare."

"I'll wait here, suss out the locals" Miko told me, and scampered away to a tree.

We approached the building, an impossibly long and narrow structure. The door at the end was locked, so we headed around to the main entrance, halfway down the length of the building.

"Shakespeare better not be back at the other end, or I am gonna be pissed," Amber warned.

"Hey, I told you, you shouldn't have worn those heels."

"Bah. What would you know about footwear, you go everywhere in those trainers. These are my fighting boots, they are both fashionable and dangerous. You should see what I can do with these heels."

"Really, like what?" Mialloch eyed her shimmering pink shoes with interest and Amber rolled her eyes.

"Never mind, tutor. Eye on the prize." She pointed to the door and he dutifully held it open for us as we all passed inside.

At the front desk, a young woman smiled and asked if we were there to see the Book of Kells exhibit. We shook our heads, but she started to ramble on and on about what a treasure it was and how it was one of the best examples of illuminated art in the world. Mialloch's eyes lit up and Alec took pity on him, clapping an arm on his shoulder.

"Yeah, sign us up for the tour."

"Are you kidding?" Amber hissed. "We don't have time for this."

"Aw, come on. Look at the poor guy. He might cry if we don't let him go. Besides, you heard her, the tour doesn't take long, and it finishes up in the Long Room, anyway. We'll meet up with you in a few. Just don't go anywhere without us," Alec winked, and walked away with Mialloch to follow the guide.

"Fine, but I'm not catching you up on any conversation when you guys get there," Amber called out after him, frustrated. One of the librarians shushed her, which she took as an invitation to find out where Shakespeare sat in the Long Room.

The librarian pointed to a set of stairs and Amber thanked her, looping her arm through mine. We set off up the stairs. At the top, I was stunned into feeling like a child again. The room was insanely long, I mean, like, really, really long. I had never made it to this part of the library, having only come into the building to use the bathrooms. Both sides were lined with alcoves housing shelves upon shelves of ancient books. As if that wasn't enough, the two story ceiling showcased a second floor of alcoved books, topped off by beautiful wooden archways.

When I realized that the entire ceiling mimicked the sturdy ridged binding of a well-loved book, I think I actually stopped breathing. Forget the library in My Fair Lady. This place pulled out all the stops.

"Pretty cool place, huh?" Amber smiled, shrugging as if she had seen better, and started off toward the other end of the corridor. I guess she wasn't a big reader.

Me? I had lost all desire to meet this student liaison. All I wanted was to sneak into the roped off areas and fondle a book or two. Really, just one would work for me. Okay, five would be better.

"You coming?" Amber paused and looked over her shoulder at me. "Dude, how much of a geek are you, really?"

"Apparently a pretty big one," I muttered. I started to follow her, but the heady aroma of old books and wood was totally distracting me. I swear, some girls go all gooey over a fancy cologne; me, the sweet clean smell of old books would do it every time.

Finally, we came to find Will's bust hanging out by himself next to stall BB.

"I guess they're not here yet," I shrugged happily. "Now can I stare at the books?"

"Sure, knock yourself out," Amber laughed.

"Actually," a familiar voice said from behind me, "I think you can do better than that. We have a particular collection in this stall that I think you might find especially interesting."

I whirled around and found my childhood friend and confidante standing in the stall holding a severely delicate, aged book.

"Claire!" I hopped over the museum ropes and gave her a huge hug.

"Watch it," she laughed, "very valuable book, getting crushed as we speak."

"Oh gods, sorry!" I let go quickly.

"Don't worry," she laughed, "that one's a total bore." She set it back on the shelf and hugged me again. "It's been too long, Siri! I can't believe how tall you've gotten."

I topped her by several inches now. Claire hadn't grown much since we were fifteen. She still wore her hair in a shaggy bob, but now it had bold highlights of red and blonde running through the dark curls.

"What are you doing here?" I asked, possibly even more stunned than I had been by the Long Room.

"I'm waiting for you," she laughed.

"Um, yeah, ok. But I mean, why are you here, waiting. We're supposed to be meeting a student, um, for a project."

"I know everything, don't worry. Your grandmother is my advisor, and when she found out I knew you she sort of took me under her wing. She's been tutoring me for months. It's a good, thing, too, since once I went through the Choosing my powers totally went haywire and-"

"Wait, I'm sorry. I need to sit down." I headed to a chair near the window and collapsed into it. "Are you telling me you are fae?" I held up my hand, stopping her before she could answer. "No, don't answer that. Of course you are. Your dad works for the same company that my mom set up security for last time we were here. Which means it's a fae company, and he worked at the other place she contracted for in Egypt, so yeah, of course, obviously you must be fae. Dammit, Claire, how long have you known? How could you not have told me?"

"I'm sorry, Siri, when we met I just assumed you knew. Then one day your mom took me aside and asked me not to say anything. I felt weird about it, but I also thought you were kind of lucky, getting to grow up all human and normal. So I agreed I'd keep it to myself. Okay?"

I sighed. Somehow, it always came back to my mom. When she woke up, we were going to have quite the talk about keeping secrets from family. Claire was watching me with concern, while Amber was doing an admirable job of staying quiet, although she was clearly itching to ask some questions of her own.

"Yeah, we're good. I get it, I do." I stood up and hugged her again, then turned to Amber. "Amber, this is Claire, my best friend from Egypt, who apparently is also Light fae, and working with my grandmother. Oh, and she's a big fan of Dave Matthews, don't judge."

Claire punched me in the arm and laughed. "You'll never let that go, will you, just because I like Dancing Nancies? You ought to talk, you were sooo into that T. Swift song all summer."

"Shh. Bite your tongue!" I warned her.

Amber chuckled. "Alright girls, I get it. You're bosom buds. Now what?"

"Now, we go to see Siri's Grandmother," Claire smiled. She put the book she'd been looking at back in its proper place and started to leave.

"Hold up, we have to wait for Alec and Mialloch, they should be here soon enough," Amber explained.

"The rest of your team?" Claire asked.

"Yeah, this is Mialloch's first time in a human library. They're checking out the Book of Kells exhibit."

"Ah, okay. Well, I guess we wait then. So how are you, anyway, Siri? I was so worried when I didn't hear from you for so long, and then your grandmother told me what happened with you and your mom. Have you really been living in Valhalla all this time?"

"I have, can you believe it?" I rocked back on my heels. "I mean, come on, what else could keep me from Facebook? I would have contacted you, but there isn't really any communications tech down in Aeden. Of course, if I'd known you were fae I would have tried contacting you or your parents through the waters. I still can't believe you held out on me for so long."

"Yeah, well, cut me some slack. At least I was planning on coming to your Choosing, you know. Especially since I found out your grandmother's been planning the guest list for a party at her place for over a year."

"Wow, really? I had no idea."

"Yeah, she said she was hoping it would bring Siri's father out of the woodwork finally, but I guess you've got that all taken care of, huh? Is it true? Is Bran Le Fay really your dad?"

"Yep, the Commander himself," Amber piped in, grinning. "You should see his face light up whenever Siri's around."

"He's nice," I said lamely. "I mean, he's been really great. Mostly we talk about my mom and the anti-serum, though, so it's been a bit intense getting to know him. But I think when my mom gets better, that's when he's really going to light up. You should see the way he watches her sleep."

"That's so awesome, Siri. I know you didn't miss having a dad around, but I'm happy that you found him and he's not just some jerk."

"Who's not a jerk?"

Alec's voice startled us all, and I looked over Amber's shoulder to see him smirking at me.

"Ah, we weren't talking about you, Alec, I was telling Claire about my dad."

"Maybe you should have been telling me about him instead," Claire whispered appreciatively in my ear.

"Shh," I whispered back and smiled sweetly at Alec. "If we'd been talking about you, I would have been telling Claire not to mind your weird sense of humor."

"What, me?" Alec asked innocently. "You know I live to make you laugh."

"Ha, no, you live because you make me laugh." I wagged my finger at him in mock threat, and then beckoned for the boys to join us. "Claire, this is Alec and Mialloch. Mialloch is my tutor in Valhalla on all subjects fae, and this is his first time outside of Aeden, so be ready to answer lots of questions. And, this here is Alec, another Light Guard."

"Not just another Light Guard. Team leader, and the light of her life," he quipped, throwing an arm around me and smirking as he shook Claire's hand.

"And not full of himself, at all," I laughed. "Alec, this is Claire, an old friend of mine who apparently has been

153

keeping a lot to herself over the years. She's the student liaison we were supposed to meet."

"Well, obviously I'm not the only one who's been keeping something to herself," Claire teased, looking Alec over speculatively. She raised an eyebrow and glanced at me. "You sure you actually want to keep this one? I don't know, he looks a little..."

"Too perfect? Too hot? Insanely manly?" Alec puffed out his chest.

"Actually, I was going to say skinny. But hey, we can go with deluded if you want."

"Siri, I like your friend," Amber clapped, and a librarian scowled at her as he walked by.

"Me, too. You may keep her," Alec nodded as he stroked his chin.

"You guys are impossible," I laughed, nudging Alec in the ribs.

"Well, I, for one, am honored to meet you, Claire. You are a sight to behold." Mialloch reached out and held Claire's hand, giving her a slight bow. "I look forward to speaking with you more on our trip."

"Um, okay." Claire stared up at Mialloch looking slightly dazed. I widened my eyes at her and she shook her head slightly, as if to wake up from a daydream. She pulled her fingers back from Mialloch's grasp and held them in her other hand. "Sure."

"Well, now that we're all here, shall we go?" Alec drawled, seemingly oblivious to the social awkwardness that was going on. Typical Alec.

"Sure. Yeah. I mean, yes! My car is just outside. It's going to be a little bit of a squeeze, I hope you don't mind."

CHAPTER 17

Alec laughed when he saw the car. "Wow, you weren't kidding, Claire."

Parked neatly in front of us was a tiny blue Ford Fiesta.

Miko chirruped on my shoulder, wondering why Alec thought the car was so funny. "Aren't all cars the same?" he asked me.

"Mmm," I answered him quietly, "some cars are bigger than others. This one's going to be a tight fit, I think."

"Seems pretty big to me," Miko shrugged and went back to eating an acorn one of the local chipmunks had given him.

"Looks like you get to sit up front again, Loch." Alec clapped Mialloch on the shoulder. Alec was close to six feet tall, but Mialloch topped him by several inches.

"I do? Thank you, Alec, I will enjoy having such a good view." I caught him looking at Claire, and he hastily added, "of the road, of course."

"Of course," I grinned.

This time, I volunteered to sit in the middle, squishing my legs up against Alec and elbowing him as I buckled in. After what had happened to Holly, I doubted I would ever ride without a seatbelt again, back seat or no.

"Well, this is cozy," Alec grimaced.

"Sorry guys, I tried to borrow my dad's car. It's way bigger, but he said he still doesn't trust my driving on the left side yet. At least, not with his fancy car. I pointed out that I haven't had a single accident since we got here, but he says I've got my own car to beat up, and to leave his alone."

"Ah, I noticed that people were driving on a different side of the road here than in Canada. Why doesn't everyone follow the same rules?" Mialloch asked.

"Well, every country has its own rules and customs, foods, clothes, even attitudes and religion. But most countries drive on the right. That's how I learned in Egypt. My dad says driving on the left is a holdover from when you had to keep your sword arm exposed and ready to fight while you were walking or riding. Plus, it kept your scabbard from hitting people as you passed, since that was usually worn on the left side of your hip, too."

"So why don't they still drive that way everywhere?" I asked.

"I don't remember, something to do with the industrial revolution and larger carriages, I think. You'd have to ask my dad," Claire shrugged as she navigated the busy Dublin traffic.

"I believe I would very much like to do that," Mialloch said. "Perhaps we will have some time at the end of this trip. I am sure that Siri would like to see your family again as well."

Claire laughed and looked in the rearview mirror, catching my eye. "What do you think, Siri? Think you guys will have time for dinner with the family before you leave?"

"I don't know, ask team leader over here." I pointed to Alec.

"Oh no, I'm not falling in that trap. We have no idea where we're headed, or how long this is all going to take. How about, we'll see if I can even walk after sitting back here."

"Hey now, Ocean doesn't like it when people make fun of her size," Claire warned.

"Ocean? You named your car?" Alec asked.

"Well, yeah, doesn't everyone?" Claire and I both laughed. We both had a thing for naming inanimate objects.

"So, Claire," Mialloch interjected, "tell me about Trinity. What is it like to go to college? What do you study? Do you have classes every day?"

"Well, for starters, we don't have classes every day. Students have the weekend off, thank goodness, since I don't know when else I would get all my studying done. You can study pretty much anything you like, so long as your grades are good enough to get into the program you want."

"What are you studying?" I asked.

"Right now I'm undeclared, but I think I'm going to focus on archaeology and anthropology. I'm really interested in helping people piece together more of their history, fae and human. There's a lot of knowledge that has gotten lost through the ages."

"But why anthro?"

"Well, I'm also interested in what makes people tick. I'd like to see different aspects of society be able to get along more harmoniously. I have to admit, what happened to your mom is a big factor in my decision."

"What do you mean?"

"The Dark and the Light used to work together. We were all one people. I'm curious about the stories each side tells about its history, and where the truth really lies. I imagine the truth is somewhere in the middle."

"Keep imagining," Alec bit out. "Shades are a menace. There is no middle ground with them."

I held his hand and gave him a look meant to both silence and reassure him.

"I'm sure you know more about it than me, having worked as a Guard." Claire responded slowly. "But that's how they are now. I wonder how the divide really happened, how they got that way. I imagine that at one time both sides may have been at fault, and the leftover anger has driven the wedge even deeper between us. I think it's sad."

Alec snorted and turned to look out the window, crossing his arms over his chest.

"You'll have to excuse my friend," Mialloch said sarcastically. "He doesn't have much patience for anyone's beliefs but his own."

"How can you say that?" I protested. "You know what happened to his family."

"I do know. And it's clouded his judgment, from what I can see. He's been on a mission to punish the dark ever since we were kids."

"Oh please," Alec yawned. "I never heard you complaining when I was fending off bullies for you. No, you think you are too good to get your hands dirty, or know someone who does."

"I may have thought that way, once. Or maybe I was just scared."

"Yeah right. Scared of what?"

"Not scared of anything, in particular." Mialloch studied his fingernails. "Just scared. After all your stories, I didn't want you to join the Guard. It seemed too dangerous. But you wouldn't listen, and I couldn't watch you kill yourself just for some, some idea of revenge."

"Gah!" Alec threw his hands up in disgust, straining against the seatbelt as he leaned forward. "Revenge? How about standing up for what you believe in, how about protecting people who can't protect themselves? That's why I joined the Guard."

"I know," Mialloch sighed. "I see that more clearly now."

Alec laid his head back against the seat and echoed Mialloch's sigh.

"There, see?" Amber said brightly. "I think this is exactly the sort of thing Claire is talking about. Am I right, Claire?"

Claire looked at her thoughtfully, choosing her words with care. "Yes, exactly. I think if we can understand social dynamics and cultural divides better, a lot of conflict would be avoided. Being at Trinity has been a real eye opener in that regard."

"How so?" Mialloch asked curiously.

"Trinity is unique in that it is the only English-language university that is an open sanctuary for both the Light and the Dark. There is another university in Peru, a monastery in Tibet, and a small college in Kyoto, but those are pretty much it for places where young fae who have already chosen sides can openly study together and feel safe. Trinity's neutrality actually has a lot to do with the founding of Dublin, which was a major focal point of the early wars between the light and dark. The Light founded what is known as "Viking Dublin." Archaeologist believe it was founded by ordinary Vikings, but many of the northmen were actual Guardians, like your mom's family. The Alvarssons were some of the most renowned Viking Guardians."

"My mom told me about that. She said that our family took vows to protect humans and the earth from the Dark."

"Yes, they did. And they have. They traveled to the same places that the Dark were trying to conquer, and tried to balance the fight so that humans wouldn't be annihilated or enslaved. For the most part, they've prevailed, although for the last few centuries the Dark have succeeded in gaining large areas of control through economic and political means instead. When your side always fights fairly, it can make it more difficult to maintain an edge on the competition."

"I am still curious about these neutral grounds you claim exist. How does that work?" asked Mialloch.

"It's pretty simple, really. I go to school. If I come in close contact with a Shade, I smile politely and move along. We don't interact much, unless we're forced to work on a project together, but a lot of the professors are fae, too, so that rarely happens. Like I said, there have always been a lot of fae in Dublin, so they've had to find ways to coexist peacefully, at least some of the time."

"Do the professors have some kind of master list they can refer to so they know who is who?" I joked.

"Actually, yeah, they do. They don't give it to us, though. The Shades are pretty much kept too busy outside of class to bother with the rest of us students, anyway. They have a group named "The Nightshade Society." Most people think it is a regular cheesy secret society, but it's really just a cover for all their Dark mind-warping programs run by Shade upperclassmen."

"You know, Rowan's dad was talking about sending him here to school next year. Their whole family is Dark, and Sullivan said they've all gone to Trinity. My mom never mentioned it to me though, even though I have dual citizenship. Did she go here?"

"I imagine she was probably still hoping you could stay in your little human bubble forever, no offense," Amber offered.

"Yeah, you're probably right. You, know Rowan wanted me to come with him."

Thinking about the conversation we'd had made me sad, reminding me of a time when Rowan had wanted me to stay with him. Now, I imagined he wanted me as far from him as possible. I could feel some serious moping coming on again.

"Well, you're here now," Amber smiled and squeezed my hand.

"With much better company, too," Alec said softly, kissing me on the cheek.

"Thanks, guys." I smiled at them both, grateful for the comfort offered. Still, I was getting really tired of being cooped up so much. I hadn't had a good run in days. The gorgeous Irish countryside was calling to me, and I hoped my Grandmother's home was still as fun to explore as I remembered.

"Hey, Claire, how come we needed you to get through to my Grandmother's house, anyway? Not that I'm not glad to see you, or anything, but I don't remember having to do anything special when we came with my mom."

"Were the gates to the estate closed when you came?"

"Well, yeah, but my mom got out to open them, and she didn't use a key or anything."

"Ha, that's what you think. Jade's always had wards up, and now they are even stronger. Your grandmother doesn't let just anybody into her estate. Since the attack on your mom, she's tripled the defenses, and she's been very, very careful coming and going at school. The people who are looking for you are not very nice, you know."

"I know," I grimaced. "So are we putting her in more danger by being here?"

Claire burst out laughing.

"What, what's so funny?"

"I'm sorry, it's just, you," she apologized when she finally stopped laughing, wiping a couple tears from her eyes. "Your grandmother can handle herself, trust me. Anyone would have to be crazy to come after her directly. Besides, no one knows you are here. No one would ever think to be watching me, I'm a nobody."

From the little she'd said, I couldn't help think that wasn't quite true. It sounded to me like Claire had gained herself all the right attention. Someday, she's probably be quite powerful. But she was right. There was no likely way anyone could know we were connected, or that we were traveling together now.

We crossed a bridge over the River Liffey into North Dublin. The wide stone-lined river was calm and smooth today, reflecting the afternoon clouds clearly. Claire turned west, taking us into Dublin's playground, the famous Phoenix Park. Wide manicured lawns and mature forests spanned both sides of the long avenue, bringing back memories of long jogs and tai chi on the grass with my mom.

Picnics. Frisbee. We had spent most of our weekends here at the park, and I had loved it. Now that I knew I was an earth fae, it made sense that I had always had this connection to the forest. Wherever I went, if there were woods I felt at home.

I leaned my cheek against Alec's own stubble, pointing out some of my favorite spots. The more I saw, the more I remembered, the happier I should have felt. But instead, I started to feel like I was sinking, bloated with a saturated feeling of sadness and loss. This place was important. This place was -

My home. My home was burning. All around me, the flames of the invaders were overtaking the trees. The sacred grove had already been burned, the beautiful carved monument to our ancestors had been the first to catch fire, after they had filled in the healing well during the night with stones and dirt, so that the fire could not be put out.

I should have stayed anyway and tried. As an earth fae, I could have maybe smothered the embers. But I was with child, and I had to warn the others that the Shades had found us. The animals were right, dark fae had crept out of the darkest shadows and everything they touched died.

I stopped to catch my breath, crouching to the ground for a moment and rested my hand on the earth. Looking around to make sure no one was near, I sent out the faintest of tremors, a warning to animals near and far to gather their families and run for their lives. The trees, I could do nothing about. Dear gods, the trees. I wanted to weep for them, but there was no time. If the Shades had any earth fae with them, I might have just alerted them to my position.

I had to run.

I had to run.

"Siri, where are you girl? What are you doing? Why can't I find you? Sullivan Carey is looking for you." Far away, I could hear Mikael calling to me. "He knows what you did to his daughter. We are coming for you. You can run, but we will find you."

I had to run.

I had to run! I leapt up and began streaking through the forest, leaping over fallen trees and small streams, faster, and faster, running for the Great Hall.

"You can't run from us, Siri!"

Ahead, I saw the gleam of river through the trees, glinting in the moonlight.

"We will find you, Siri! Where are you! Siri!"

"Siri!"

I blinked and focused my eyes on Alec's face.

"Hello, space cadet. Where'd you go? One minute you were talking about Frisbees, the next you were totally spacing out on the woods. What did you see?"

"How do you know I saw anything?" I asked grumpily.

"Come on, Siri," Alec whispered patiently. "You know I can feel what you are feeling. And just now, wherever you went, there was a whole lot of anger, sadness and fear."

"No. Not fear," I corrected him as I stared off into the woods. "Urgency. I had to warn them."

"Warn who?" Claire asked over her shoulder.

"Warn the-" I paused. "Huh, I'm not sure. The rest of my family, my friends, I think. It was weird. I'm usually me, an observer. But this was...different. I didn't feel like me. I was taller. My thoughts didn't feel like me. I think I was someone else, and I was pregnant."

"Pregnant?" Alec squeaked nervously.

"Yeah. But I told you, it wasn't really me," I said absently. "Anyways, I was watching the forest burn, there was fire everywhere. The Shades burned it, and I was trying to save the animals and warn everyone that danger was coming. I felt like I was here, but it was different. The trees were bigger, older. Was it the future?"

"I don't know." Claire bit her lip. "That's what you usually see, right, because of your Skuld Norna blood? So it should have been the future. Do you really think you were someone else?"

"Yes, I am sure of it."

"We'll have to ask Jade about it when we get there. I've heard about the other visions you've had. I don't think it's a good idea to ignore any of them, even if some of them seem different. Did anything else happen?"

"Yeah." I shivered, and Alec rubbed a hand up and down my side. "Mikael was there."

"The Morrigan?" Claire asked fearfully.

"Yes. He was there, too, at the end. He said they don't know where I am, but that they are looking and they'll find me. He said I can run, but I can't hide."

"I don't get it," Mialloch interrupted. "Why her? Why does the Morrigan want Siri so badly?"

"We still don't know," Alec answered grimly.

"My dad and Vala both think the Druid prophecy is about me, and if it is then Mikael needs me to destroy the Light once and for all, so the Shades can take over the world or whatever. But I don't know why they would need me, or how I could help them destroy anything."

"It doesn't matter," Alec growled, hugging me tightly. "They can't have you."

"Agreed," Claire added, and Amber nodded.

"Well, at least everyone is all in agreement," Mialloch said seriously. "Siri stays with the Light, of course."

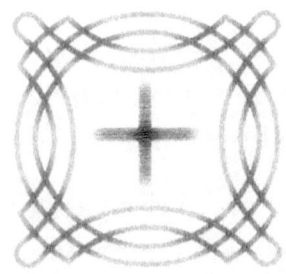

CHAPTER 18

Suburbs with names like Castleknock had given way to pastures and villages. Spricklestown. The Ward Cross. Four Knocks. We passed through town after town, and still we kept driving. We even drove through the town of Kells. Claire pointed out megaliths and other fae landmarks from the front seat and fielded inquiries from Mialloch.

Not much had changed since the last time I had been here about two years ago. I recognized even more landmarks when we started nearing my grandmother's home. Claire had kept to smaller roads, rather than the highways that my mother had usually taken. I knew she was doing it because she thought we would be nervous on a highway this soon after the accident. And she was right. Even though she had reassured me that we were safe here and I knew that Mikael didn't know where we were, I still felt like I had to keep checking over my shoulder. I'd spent half the trip watching out the back window to make sure no one was following us. I knew Amber and Alec were both watching the side view mirrors, too.

Mialloch seemed to be the only one unfazed by our dangerous situation. But then, you never really knew what was going on in Mialloch's mind.

Finally, we pulled up to the gate of my grandmother's estate, the glacial waters of Lough Ramor glimmering in the distance under the setting sun.

Claire hopped out, stretching while we waited for her to open the gates. She poked her head back in the car and looked at me.

"You coming? You should know how to do this, just in case."

"In case what?"

"I dunno, just in case. She is family, after all. Eventually these gates will belong to your mom, and then to you. Come on," she prodded, and ducked back out of the car.

"Okay, guess I'm up," I shrugged.

Alec opened the car door, standing up and sighing in relief.

"Oh, the torture has ended!" He hopped up and down, warming up his legs and jogging in place. "Please tell me I do not ever have to get back in that clown machine, please."

Claire laughed and wagged a finger at him. "Now, now, I told you, no trash talk about Ocean! You are welcome to walk up to the house on foot, it's not quite one kilometer."

"Sweet, open this thing up and I'll race you," Alec winked at her and turned to me. "How about you, you coming?"

"Sounds great, but I think I'll meet you there, hot shot."

"Suit yourself," he grinned. He stood back with his hands in his pockets. "Well, go on, go do your stuff, ladies."

I walked over to Claire. "Okay, what now?"

"The wards around Jade's home use old magic and rely on two things. Blood and Intention. You have to be with a Light fae to get in, that's the blood."

She pulled a pin out of her pocket and pricked her finger, rubbing the dot of blood on the iron gate.

"Ew, seriously? That's so gross!"

"The wards rely on magic that was put in motion thousands of years ago, back when this was an important place of power. In those days, blood power was used a lot more, until people realized that it had the ability to be warped and twisted, and used for ill gains. For this purpose, though, it is the best protection a girl could have."

Still, I thought, pretty creepy.

"So, is that it?"

"Not anymore, now we have to pass the earth wards Jade has put in place. We have to state our purpose here. The wards read sincerity and intention, if the magic senses a discrepancy or wavering of intention, it won't let us in." She placed her hands on the ground and said, "I am here to see Jade Alvarsson, and with me I bring three other Light fae and Jade's grandchild, a faeling. They seek advice for the Light."

"What if someone in the group had bad intentions?" I asked.

"It doesn't matter. The wards work through me and broadcast out to read everyone in the group. If there are more people than who I mention, or if their intentions are false, the ward will not let us through."

"Oh," I said, feeling a little small. "So this is what my mom did whenever we visited?"

The lock gave way and the gate swung open. Claire rose, dusting off her hands.

"Back then she just had to work the blood magic."

"Okay, but then, how did it work before there was a gate?" I wondered.

"Probably like the wards we have in the tunnel," Alec mused from behind me.

"How do those work?" Claire asked.

"Anyone who is dark or human can't get through them, they feel an overwhelming urge to turn around, and they just see a wall in front of them," Alec answered.

"Yes, the wards here are similar. In fact, there are parts of the property that are not fenced in. In those areas to cross the boundary you must place the blood on the earth, say the words, and then you can pass. If you try and you haven't followed the sequence all the energy from your body will be drained and you will collapse to the ground, like you've fainted. It's impossible to get through, and most people don't try more than once, anyway. They usually just assume they aren't well and go home to rest."

"Does that happen a lot?"

"Every few years, according to your grandmother. She says there are a few stubborn poachers who really want access to what they claim are prime hunting grounds for coney and pheasant."

"Coney?" Alec asked.

"Rabbit," Claire and I answered at the same time.

"Cool. Okay, last chance, Siri, you coming?" He gestured to the lane ahead.

"No," I chuckled, "but I do want to go out later, you still going to be up for that?"

"Honey, I'm up for whatever you can throw at me. First one there gets to drive the car next time!" He taunted and took off running down the driveway. When the drive curved, he continued straight, diving into the forest and disappearing among the leaves.

"Okay, well, guess we'd better get going!" Claire and I jogged back to the car, laughing. We buckled up quickly and Claire took off, carefully driving as fast as the winding gravel driveway would allow. "He's totally going to get lost in the woods, anyway. There's no straight path to the house." She said confidently.

A few minutes later we pulled up to the house. Alec was sitting on the front steps, leaning back lazily.

"What? No way!" Claire slammed the car door as she got out and marched over to him. The rest of us watched, trying not to laugh. "How did you beat us here?"

"I ran through the woods." He shrugged.

"But how did you know the way?"

"I didn't. The plants showed me."

What do you mean the – arg! You're an earth fae?! That is so unfair." Claire whirled on me. "You totally did not tell me that. He is not driving my car. No. Way."

"A bet's a bet," Alec tsked.

Claire stomped a foot and squealed.

"We'll see about that," she huffed, pushing her hair out of her eyes. "Cheater."

The sound of a large door creaking grabbed all our attention, and we stared up the steps at the vivacious woman who had just appeared.

"Aunt Jade!" I exclaimed and ran up the steps, hugging her tightly.

"Technically, I suppose you should start calling me Grandmother now," she laughed in my ear.

"Too weird," I mumbled into her bright red shawl. "How about just Jade?"

"Sounds good to me," she answered. "Now, let me get a look at you, Siri. My, but you've grown fine and tall, haven't you? You are the spitting image of your mom, with Bran's coloring."

"You know my dad?"

"We met, a long time ago. I just never knew that we were family," she chuckled. "Until now."

"He never mentioned it."

"He might not even remember, it was a very brief meeting and I don't think he was much older than you are now. But enough about ancient history. Why don't you introduce me to your friends, darling?"

She straightened her cream sweater set and shawl. My grandmother might have been over a hundred years old but she didn't look a day over fifty in her dark-washed jeans and buff suede boots. Her dark hair sported a shock of white at one temple and she had a couple laugh lines next to her eyes, the only real tells that she was even older than my mother.

"Oh, right. Well, you know Claire," I started.

"Yes," my grandmother smiled warmly at Claire, "when I learned she knew you, I made sure to spend extra time getting to know her."

"This is Mialloch Airron, Airmed's grandson, and this here is Mikowa."

"The life-bond?" My grandmother asked me intently.

"Yes."

"Mmm. Your father told me. Very interesting. A pleasure, Mikowa," she nodded at Miko where he perched on my shoulder.

"And here, this is Amber Slaight and Alec Ward. They both work for Bran in the Guard."

My grandmother smiled at them each warmly and welcomed us into the house.

Entering the great hall, Alec stared. Amber whistled lowly and whispered in my ear, "You never told me you came from money, honey."

The house was large, but inside it seemed even bigger. A double winding staircase arched into the foyer, wrapping its pale marble arms around the hall. Gold scrollwork wound up them, glimmering under the bright crystal chandelier that dangled above us. Ancient Norse tapestries and antique Tibetan rugs lined the walls and floors.

"I never really thought about it," I said truthfully. "I always sort of figured it was all from my aunt's marriage, since my mom and I lived so differently. Anyways, it's just, I don't know, stuff, you know?"

"Our family has had a long time to accumulate things, it is true," my grandmother said offhand. "We live quite simply, compared to the money we have at our disposal. Our main focus has always been maintaining the safety of our people, and of our charges."

"Clearly," Alec said sarcastically. My grandmother gave him an appraising look and sniffed.

"Why don't I have Marie here show you all to your rooms, and you can freshen up?" she gestured to the tiny, elderly woman who had materialized at the top of the staircase. Marie had been my grandmother's housekeeper for as long as I could remember. She had bathed me, fed me, played with me, always with a gleam in her eye and ready with a quick story about little people, Picts and the old gods.

"I'll get tea ready," Jade continued, "and we can all meet back here in the library in twenty minutes. Siri, you can stay in your mother's room, and Claire will sleep in the adjoining room. Amber can sleep across the hall, in the pink room. Marie, please put the young men in the east wing."

"Um, grandma, I was kind of hoping I could take a run tonight. Are the paths still lit along the Lough?"

"Yes, dear. Why don't you get ready and you can go out after we've caught up a bit at tea. Dinner will be served late, so you will have plenty of time. See you in a flash."

She kissed my cheek and walked away towards the kitchen.

CHAPTER 19

Claire, Amber and I all walked back downstairs together, giggling as Claire recounted a story about finding a naked boy sleeping in a closet after the last party in her Dublin flat.

Laughing with the girls, I felt lighter than air. It had been heavenly to take a shower. It'd been over twenty four hours since my last shower, and washing off the lingering grime of travel and death had made me feel one hundred percent better. My damp hair was back in braids, my feet were buoyant in their running shoes and I felt ready to take on the world again.

We entered the library through its large arched doors. Alec and Mialloch were already there, and my grandmother was setting up the silver tray on the low tea table between the settees. Alec was lounging insouciantly by the stained glass windows, watching my grandmother from behind a lock of wet hair. Clearly, he had showered as well. His skin was practically glowing and a plain gray t-shirt clung to his damp skin in all the right places. He'd put on some gray sweats and trainers, so I guessed we were still on for our run later. Mialloch was standing on the other side of the room, clearly absorbed in the titles on the shelves. A small stack of books in his arms was growing by the minute as he continued to pull every third or fourth book off the shelf.

"Ah, girls, have a seat, please." Jade gestured to the seats around her. "Mialloch, I'm glad to see you have found some books that interest you, please feel free to take any of those to your room later if you enjoy late night reading. Now, though, if you wouldn't mind joining us," she said, eying him with amusement and gesturing to the seating area. "Alec, you, too. Please, won't you join us?"

Everyone settled into the overstuffed chairs and dainty sofas around the tea tray. Before us lay a mighty spread: neat little sandwiches cut into quarters, warm cinnamon scones with freshly hand-churned butter, and my favorite, butterscotch shortbread cookies shaped like miniature oak leaves. Suddenly, I felt ravenous. I'd eaten on the plane, but apparently still not enough to make up for the amount of energy I had channeled earlier. I grabbed half a sandwich filled with smoked salmon, two scones and a cookie, arranging them on my plate with expectation. I waited patiently while my grandmother poured and handed me a steaming cup of Irish Breakfast tea cut with milk. The heady, malty aroma wafted up to me, bringing back more memories. Jade never drank anything else, she claimed all other blends tasted like water.

She passed teacups around the table, gracefully pouring cup after cup until everyone had been served. Even Miko received a small platter of milk and a sweet oak leaf. Once everyone had a plate and a cup in front of them, Jade moved next to me and wrapped an arm around me and thanked everyone for coming.

"I cannot tell you all how much it means to me that you have chosen to accompany my granddaughter on this trip to see Airmed. Siri is the dearest thing to my heart, rivaled only by my love for her mother. I have no one else left in the world that I care for so deeply. That she is surrounded by such great friends and fine warriors, that is no small thing to me. So please, eat, drink," she urged.

We all dug into our platters, everyone quietly slaking their thirst and nourishing their bellies. Finally, the soft clinking of china subsided, and the pace of chewing slowed. I was the first to set my plates down.

"So, now what?" I asked. "I understand that you know where Airmed is living?"

"Yes, I do. It is a very secret place, hidden from the view of humans for the last six hundred years, not to mention most fae."

"Why?" asked Amber.

"Because Grandmother wearied of visitors," Mialloch supplied.

"Yes, it is true," Jade confirmed. "Airmed was continually sought out because of her abilities as a healer. But she has also been hated and envied for her skill, and for her occasional failures, for all things must come to pass eventually, even the Ancients. Life is a circle, not an unending line which we travel. We must die, to be reborn. But not all understand this. Airmed lives in secret to protect herself from the jealous whispers of those who would have her power. Most people don't even know that she is still alive. She guards the most holy of wells. For centuries, the Christians tasked themselves with blotting out the old signs of pagan worship. Holy wells, which used to dot every countryside in number throughout the world, have been filled in and eradicated in so many lands, none more so than these isles. Airmed took it upon herself to protect her favorite."

"Fionnaeda Clootie," Mialloch said.

"I'm sorry, what now?" Amber asked.

"The well – in Ireland and Scotland, a clootie is a well with particularly powerful healing powers, able to remove physical and emotional ailments from the seeker," Claire explained.

"Exactly so," Jade smiled at Claire. "Young Mialloch's grandmother lives near the Fionnaeda Clootie. Its name and location have long been struck from the books of history, but Airmed and I get together now and again for tea. She likes my scones, you see, and I like her company. Actually, she was my own mother's best friend. When mother passed, I kept up the habit of visiting occasionally. Now, I am especially glad I did, if it will help poor Freddie."

"Is it far?"

"It's a couple hours away, you can leave after breakfast tomorrow. There's no rush, you see, for Airmed does not take kindly to visitors after dark. She says it disrupts-"

"Her nightly beauty routine," Mialloch laughed. "I thought that was just something she said in Aeden to get out of having dinner with the family."

"No. She's quite serious about maintaining her health. Already, she has long outlived other Ancients her age. And she's not even close to finished yet. No, Airmed will outlive us all. Would that she would share more of her beauty secrets. She won't even tell me what she puts in her herbal tea, let alone what she does after the sun goes down."

"Okay, well that is all fascinating, but are we sure she is going to be willing to help us?" Alec interrupted.

"Dear boy, we can be sure of nothing. But I think between getting to meet Siri, my granddaughter, and the joy of seeing her own dear grandson, she may very well be agreeable."

My grandmother let that sink in for a moment, and then continued.

"Of course, I also have something which I believe will ensure her cooperation. Airmed, it is true, can be difficult sometimes. But," she said, rising and walking to a small writing desk by the window, "she has always admired this amulet my great-grandmother received from Tyr."

In the light, she held up an intricate silver necklace dripping with tiny, dangling arrows and a faceted blue crystal in the middle. The light lit up the pale stone, sending tiny rainbows out through its many facets to sparkle over my grandmother. She smiled and walked back over to me.

"It is said to hold the power of justice and light within. The blue topaz encourages clear communication, trust and honesty. The arrows represent black, white, and all the shades of gray in between. I had always hoped to pass it on to you, Siri, and I do so now. If you find that Airmed is not willing to help, perhaps offering her this will change her mind."

She walked over and clasped the necklace around my neck, moving my braids out of the way gently. I expected the necklace to feel cold, but it warmed against my skin, humming slightly.

"It feels alive," I said in wonder, touching the stone.

"It is," my grandmother answered simply. "The silver, the stones, they are all of the earth. They were mined and crafted carefully, with intention, awakened by Tyr himself using his own Earth abilities. From the beginning, the stones agreed to work for justice and truth, and they have never stopped. They recognize your earth energy, it makes them happy."

"Why would my grandmother want it, then, if she is a water fae?"

"Why does any woman want jewelry?" my grandmother laughed. "It's a beautiful piece and she has always loved it. Perhaps she feels it would help her navigate society again, by showing her what another's intentions really are. Who could say? I would rather Siri keep it, of course, but if it can help our cause, do not hesitate to use it."

"Okay, thank you, Jade," I said. But I couldn't quite imagine giving this necklace up. Already, it felt as if it were a part of me. Its low hum had shifted to a barely discernible pulse that kept beat with mine and I felt more clear-headed and confident than I had in weeks.

I watched as my grandmother wrote out directions to Fionnaeda Clootie and handed them to Alec.

"You can take my Land Rover. It's old, but it will get you there in one piece."

"Sweet," Alec said, "Thanks."

"Wait, isn't Claire coming with us?" I asked.

"No dear, Claire has class tomorrow and she has quite a bit of work to do for me, too."

Claire groaned. "Oh, come on!"

"Sorry, dear. But your parents made me promise I would be a proper advisor. Nose to the grindstone and all that," she winked at Claire. "Besides, she needs to drive me back into town."

"Bright side, Claire, at least now you don't have to let me drive your car," Alec laughed.

"When you put it that way," she grinned.

"I'm so glad we settled that." My grandmother laughed, "Now, I believe Siri wanted to go for a run, and I have a few things to tend to before dinner. Siri, if you'll remember, the paths to the right of the boathouse are lit and follow the lake for some way until they turn to ramble through the woods. Enjoy yourself, everyone, please feel free to explore the library and the grounds. They are quite extensive."

Jade left the room and Mialloch returned to browsing the bookshelf.

"So, who's up for a run with me?" I asked.

"Not me," Amber yawned and Miko chattered in agreement, gathering up some more food in his arms and settling next to his saucer of milk. "But I would like to see the gardens and the lake."

"Oh, I can show you around. There is a tiny secret garden behind the carriage house that has the most amazing labyrinth," Claire offered.

"Sounds like a plan," Amber agreed.

"Hold on, I will join you. I am curious about this labyrinth." Mialloch neatly arranged his piles of books by an armchair and walked over to the girls.

Alec hooted. "Maybe you can find yourself while you're there, Loch."

Mialloch glared at Alec and rolled his eyes. "Yes, well maybe you can run into some class while you are out there, too."

"Oh, really, Loch? Class? That's what it always comes down to with you, isn't it?" Alec's lip curled and he started towards him.

I stood up in his way and started to push him towards the exit. "Ok, yeah, well, this is fun and all but I need some outdoor time. Like, now, Alec," I shoved him into the hall.

"Out. Now." I frowned at him and pointed to the door.

CHAPTER 20

Outside, I took off down the steps and jogged around the house to the rear lawn. The sun was setting behind the house, casting us into shadow while the lough glistened in hues of indigo. The lights were just beginning to flicker along the lakes edge, awakening with the night, and I shot off towards the boathouse, following the path that meandered between the rocks, moor-grass and rose hedgerows. In the summer, the path would be rampant with rose blooms and honeybees, but now the plants were pale and slumbering in their winter raiment.

I could hear the slight crunching of gravel underfoot behind me, so I knew Alec still followed me. We ran in silence along the lake to the southeast, the sun's last bit of warmth fading on my back. If I wanted to stay warm, I'd have to pick up the pace.

We ran in silence, along the lake, then entering woods, where the lamps twinkled through the trees. When I was little, I had thought they looked like fairies. How ironic was it that they remained lamps, while I, instead, had become what I'd imagined.

I was glad I didn't glitter in the dark. That would have put a severe cramp on my nightlife.

We came to a small fork in the path and I turned onto the smaller trail, coming to a circular clearing in the woods. Great ash trees stood all around us as the night sky loomed above. I stopped running and stood in the middle.

"This was my favorite place as a child. I used to just come here and sit for hours at night, staring up at the stars. During the day my mom would come and we would train here." The ground was still springy beneath my feet despite the cold, the fallen leaves and forest loam creating a soft cushion below.

Alec wrapped his arms around my waist from behind and dipped his face towards my ear.

"I was watching you run. I love watching you run, it's like watching the wind dance, and tonight, the sun was on your hair and it looked like firelight."

My breath caught, and I noticed he wasn't even breathing hard from our run. Incongruously, I wondered, did the boy never tire?

I spun in his arms and wrapped my arms around him, reveling in the feel of his body against mine. God, he was better than chocolate.

I placed my hand against his cheek and felt the surge flow through me, rippling against my skin trying to escape the confines of this small fae body. The feelings that simple touch brought seemed too large to be contained by something so mundane, so mortal. Yet I wanted more. I knew there was more. So I rose up and kissed Alec, brushing my lips against his, gently teasing, until he pulled me closer to crush his lips against mine. The waves continued to build, creating a pressure in my body that begged for release and made my knees go weak.

I moaned, and Alec stopped. Now, finally, he was breathing heavy. But I didn't understand why he'd stopped. My mind could not compute, and I stood feeling dazed, satisfied and frustrated, all at once.

"I thought we came here to work out, not make out?" Alec teased.

"Well, you know, plans change," I said, wrapping my arms back around his neck and brushing my fingers through the shaggy hair at the base of his neck.

"Not these plans," he said, kissing me lightly on the nose before gently moving my arms back to my sides and stepping away. "I don't want to take advantage of your grandmother's hospitality."

"I'm pretty sure that it's my hospitality," I quipped, stepping forward.

"Either way. Loch reminded me that as the elder in your family, I will need your grandmother's blessing some day and that maybe I should try not to antagonize her."

"You're listening to Loch now? Wait, what do you mean, her blessing?"

"Well, you know," he blushed, not finishing.

"I'm not sure I do, maybe you should spell it out for me," I said, crossing my arms and giving him a blank look.

"Marriage, Siri, I'm talking about marriage." Alec ran a hand along the back of his neck. "Not now, obviously, you're way too young, you still have school and everything, but eventually, you know-"

"No, I didn't know," I said quietly. "I wasn't sure you really wanted...well, I didn't know."

He came forward and held me. "Well, now you know."

"Any other big plans I should know about?" I squeaked.

"I've actually been thinking maybe I could go to school with you. I've spent the last ten years fighting and training. When I am with you, I am reminded of my human side, and the things I have missed. I want us to move forward through life as equals. I want to do what you do, experience what you experience. I want to know everything about you."

"Can you do that? Go to school, I mean? What about being a Light Guard?"

"I don't know. I will have to talk to Mitch, see if I can convince him it would be useful as part of my training to fit in above below. Or maybe I can sell myself as your live-in bodyguard. We could share an apartment."

I snorted. "Yeah, I am sure Bran will be totally ecstatic with that idea. Not. But I'm all for trying to talk him into it."

"I'm sure Amber would love to go to work on Mitch, too, get him to talk to your dad."

We stood quietly for a moment, just staring into each other's eyes. The violet ring around his pupil was glimmering in the twilight, and I imagined he could see every twig in the forest. What could he see in me?

"You're wondering what I'm feeling?" he whispered. The telempathy of the surge had shown my feelings to him, and his to me.

"Yes."

"I'm looking at the love of my life, the woman I never want to be without. Where you run, I will follow. Where you sit, I will wait."

"Are you sure?"

"I'm done fighting it, Siri. I surrender. I can feel your faith in me, and it humbles me. I'm not going to second-guess the wisdom of it, or worry what other people might think. All that matters to me anymore is what you think. Everyone else can go to Hel."

"I think I love you, too. And I would love to go to school with you. I haven't really ever thought about marriage, but I think if it's with you, I'm in."

"Well, you know, I haven't actually asked you yet," he smirked at me, the dimple in his cheek flashing.

"You jerk," I laughed, smacking him in the arm. "Alright, well then, good luck with that. You can spend the next several years trying to convince me. And, of course, you have to catch me!" I taunted him, dashing off into the woods.

His rich laugh echoed all around me through the woods and I picked up my pace. Every so often I would cut through the woods rather than follow the immaculate trail around a corner, cutting my distance and employing my parkour skills as I vaulted over rocks and kicked off trees.

Still, Alec was always right behind, not breaking a sweat. It would probably take me a lifetime of training to be able to outrun him.

And I would never want to.

CHAPTER 21

Two hours later we were all seated at the long table in the formal dining room. I knew my grandmother rarely used this room, usually choosing to eat en famille with Marie in the kitchen, but the size of our dinner party demanded it. I'd taken another shower, quicker this time, and let down my hair. It had dried into thick waves, thanks to my braids. As long as it didn't rain and I didn't run a brush through it, I figured it just might behave itself through the evening.

I sat at my grandmother's left, with Alec and Marie on my side, and Mialloch, Amber and Claire across from us. As always, a place had been set and left empty at the foot of the table for the little people. Everyone looked relaxed and happy, a testament to the hospitality of Jade's home. It was interesting that my mother had managed to duplicate the same quality of comfort and ease in every house we'd lived in, despite the short duration of our stays. I supposed that

I had my grandmother's example to thank for that, and I could only hope that someday I would have the same ability, wherever I wound up.

"Is someone else joining us?" Mialloch asked, looking at the empty plate.

"Och, no," tsked Marie. "That there is for the fair folk."

"Fair folk?"

"Aye, the little people."

I giggled, earning me a reprimand from Marie.

"I'm sorry," I said, "but I don't understand. What little people? Jade?" I looked at my grandmother, not sure how much I should say. I mean, Marie had to know we were all fae, right?

"Don't be daft, Siri," Marie snorted. "You cannae have forgotten all the old stories since last I saw ye. The wee people, the fair folk. Most call them fairies, but of course they are not the same as ye and me. But that doesn't mean they don't exist. The little people are the elementals, and they enjoy a good cuppa as much as ye or I. If ye learn to work with them, and don't go disrespecting them, they might even teach ye a thing or two."

"Vala mentioned elementals once, too. What are they?"

"Elementals are them that make the wind blow, and the green earth grow. They are the energy and the spirit of the fire, the air, the water, the earth. Not all that looks dead is. Everything has a soul, a living energy within it. Even the rocks. And not everything that looks as if it is empty, is. The elementals do not have bodies like ye or me, but they are the breath of life on the wind. They can shift the atoms around them to work as they want, without dipping their hand into matter."

"Huh," I said. "I'm going to have to think about that for a while. So explain to me why we leave out a plate for them?"

"It's good manners, that's all," Marie huffed. "Honestly Jade, didn't yer daughter teach this lass anything?"

Jade chuckled and shook her head. "Not what you or I would have taught her, no. But she taught her well in her own way. Siri, like Marie said, the elementals don't eat the way we do, but they do sample and enjoy the energy all around them. They live off the life-force of food and light, rather than through the physical process of digestion. If you don't leave out a bit for them to eat, they may very well eat the energy right off your plate, and then you are truly eating dead food. This way, they know what they are welcome to, and everybody wins. And, of course, like Marie mentioned, it pays to be friendly with the elementals. They can help you tap into your power more easily."

"Wow. Okay, I had no idea. I thought it was just a superstition or something."

At that, Marie got up to serve the warm cheesy potato soup, muttering to herself all the while.

"So, Siri, Claire tells me you were thinking of coming to Trinity. I think that would be a lovely idea."

I chewed on my bread, thinking. "Well, I do like the idea of it. But I also kind of liked the area around Bennington, and it'd be nice to go somewhere with good mountains for snowboarding. I don't know, I haven't given it that much thought. I guess everything is sort of in limbo right now with my mom. I've already missed a big part of my senior year."

My grandmother waved her hand dismissively. "Pish tosh. There are plenty of schools you can go to without finishing your year, I can see to that. I will get a list of places together for you. A phone call from me and you could start at any of them within a week."

I blinked in surprise. "That would be great, Jade, I would really like that. You know," I continued bravely, "Alec is considering going to school, too, but of course he only attended the academy in Aeden. Do you think you could help him, too?"

"I don't see why not. I am sure that wherever you go your father will want you to have companions for safety. Perhaps, Alec, you could go with Siri," she said nonchalantly.

Alec coughed and I blushed. "Yes, ma'am, I am sure you are right. I shall discuss it with Bran."

"Excellent," she replied, returning to finishing her soup.

"Actually," said Claire, "all this talk about Trinity and schools reminds me. When we were driving through North Dublin, Siri had a strange vision."

"Really, strange in what way?" Jade asked.

"Well, we were driving through Phoenix Park, you know how much I loved playing there when I was little," I said. "But all of a sudden I was running through the woods and everything was burning. I was me, but I wasn't, you know.

My clothes were different. I was different. I was running, and worrying about a sacred well the invaders had destroyed, and how I was going to save my friends and family in time."

"In Phoenix Park?" Marie asked.

"I think so. But the woods seemed older."

A look passed between Jade and Marie.

"Caill Tomair," Marie whispered.

"What?"

"Thor's Wood," Jade answered. "As you probably know, Dublin was originally settled by people known as Vikings. Some of the settlers were actually your relatives, Siri. The sacred grove and much of the forest were burned to the ground during a Dark raid in 999AD. The well allowed them to communicate with the council back in Aeden, so of course the Shades would have destroyed it. But I'm curious. How is it that you were able to see into the past? Your father led me to believe that you had inherited the sight from our side of the family, tapping into possible future events?"

"Yes, everything I've seen was in the future. I don't know what this vision was. Like I said, it was as if I was in someone else's body."

"Well, maybe you were," offered Amber, chewing thoughtfully on some bread. "Last year I started hanging out in this little new age shop in Montreal, they have some really amazing jewelry, you know? Anyways, I heard this guy talking about his past lives, and then the lady who owns the shop said he could be experiencing genetic memory, too. She said that strong ancestral memories are passed

196

down in the DNA, encoded for future generations to tap into. So maybe you were doing that? What do you think, Jade?"

"Hmm, that's an interesting idea. I have heard similar theories popping up in mainstream genetics lately. It certainly seems to fit." Jade pondered her wine. "Whatever the case, it would seem your powers are still expanding."

"Well, whatever it was, it was not fun, I'll tell you that much. When I was in Aeden I thought I was getting a handle on my visions, but now they seem to be just as bad as before."

"Have you been meditating?"

"Gah, yes! You sound just like Mom. She wanted me to meditate all day, too," I sighed in frustration.

"Not all day, dear," my grandmother laughed, "just enough to 'get a handle' on your emotions. Visions can be triggered by emotions and strong memories. Just stay calm, and you'll learn how to influence what you see more clearly."

"Can't I just turn them off?"

"Now why would ye be wanting to do something like that," scolded Marie. "Yer visions are a blessing. Ye should be proud to have them. Not everyone has access to powers like yer family does."

"Sorry," I grumbled, put out at being scolded like a child.

"Marie," chided Jade as the other woman got up and began clearing the bowls, "I don't think Siri meant to offend you." Marie harrumphed and left the room with the stack of dishes. "Sweetheart, Marie is descended from fae, like us, but her family line is so diluted with human blood that there hasn't been anyone in her family with a long life span or elemental abilities in several generations. It's a sensitive subject."

Marie came back into the room and placed the main course on the table, a massive whole grilled pike from Lough Ramor accompanied by caramelized carrots and greens.

"This looks amazing, Marie," I beamed at her. The rest of the table quickly joined in, murmuring their agreement. Marie smiled, accepting the compliment, and started dishing out plates for everyone.

We all set ourselves to the task of eating, with occasional murmurs about how good everything was. Mialloch, in particular, was impressed by the food, especially by the deep color of the greens.

After dinner, Mialloch excused himself to his room to read. Amber had told Claire that she would teach her some simple glima moves, so they headed to the large sunroom with its warm stone terrace. I promised I would meet them in a minute, after I grabbed a hair tie from my room. I could see the humidity was already starting to have its wicked way with my hair, which was fast starting to frizz up. No doubt it made a lovely halo above my angelic head.

I bounded up the stairs and wasted no time putting my hair up into a messy bun on top of my head. There. Much better. I nodded at myself in the mirror, taking a moment to look at the necklace around my neck. I hadn't taken it off since my grandmother gave it to me; it felt like a part of me now.

"Tyr-wise and Tyr-brave," I whispered, fingering the tiny arrows. I really hoped I could be both. Could a necklace really help me do that? The necklace seemed to warm for a moment, almost as if in response. I brushed it off as my imagination and headed back downstairs.

By the door to the library, I heard Alec talking and started to go in, figuring he would want to help Claire train, too.

I stopped when I heard his words.

"I want to be honest with you from the start, Jade."

"I appreciate that, Alec. What is it you need to talk about?"

"I'm not just the team leader here, or a Guard that will protect Siri when she is at school. I don't want you to think that I haven't always been clear with you."

"Of course not, why would you think I ever would?" My grandmother sounded like she was humoring him, hiding her own amusement.

"I plan to marry your granddaughter and I-"

"Well, I would hope so!" I swear, she practically cackled.

"I – wait, what do you mean?"

"You think Bran didn't fill me in on all the details before you got here? Please. The boy has more sense than that. Why do you think you and Mialloch are staying in a separate wing? I've heard all about the surge, young man.

My own marriage was arranged, as was proper in those days, but I'm pretty sure the surge had a hand in how young Siri was conceived, and I can tell you right now that there better not be any funny business going on between-"

"No! No. Of course not," he stated emphatically. "Siri hasn't even had her Choosing yet."

"Wonderful. Well, thank you for being so honest with me, my boy, I appreciate it. I think you will make a fine addition to the family."

"You do?" He sounded stunned.

"Of course I do. Bran told me all about what a great warrior you are, leading your own teams already and at such a young age. And I can see that Siri cares for you, which in the end is really all that matters to me."

"As I care for her, I assure you. Thank you, Jade, I was worried you might want Siri to marry someone more like Mialloch."

"Bah. Rank can be gained. Or not, if you are content. All I ask is that you make my Siri happy. Do that, and I will be happy. Otherwise..." I heard the glasses on the sidebar begin to clink against each other, and a slight tremor shook the floor beneath my feet, rocking the house for a full ten seconds.

Alec coughed, sounding shaken. "Point taken. Don't worry, I will do everything in my power to see that Siri laughs every day for the rest of our lives," he pledged.

"Good. Then we are agreed. Of course, you will still have to convince her mother when she wakes up. My daughter has been coddling that child for her entire life, I don't know if she is going to be ready to see her settling down just yet. But, I have a feeling she will like you."

"Actually, we've already met. I've taken a few of her martial arts training courses for the Guard. She's an amazing woman."

"Indeed she is. Well, if you don't mind, I think I will call Siri in now, what do you say? Siri? Are you ready to join us yet?"

Ugh, caught!

I could feel the tips of my ears burning with embarrassment as I trudged into the room.

"Hey, guys. I was just walking by. Did you need me for something?"

"Come now, child, tell the truth. I could feel your vibration in the earth waves when I rattled the house. You should know better than to listen at doors." She clucked. "I know we taught you better than that. Now, run along you two, I think you are supposed to be helping Amber teach Claire some defense moves, are you not?"

"Absolutely," I grinned, hauling Alec off the settee and hurrying out of the room, successfully avoiding any rehash of the conversation. "Goodnight, Grandma!"

CHAPTER 22

The next morning, I awoke with the dawn. It was strange to see the light creep into the room after living in Aeden for the last few months. I had become used to sleeping in the total darkness of the shuttered windows of my room. Now, the early morning light was both comforting and invigorating, a much more natural awakening than finding Amber or Auroreis creeping through my room. I stretched in bed, looking at the clear skies. It seemed like it was going to be a rare sunny day over Lough Ramor.

I hopped up and threw on my running clothes, lacing up my sneakers. This was the perfect morning for a run to the lookout over the lake, where the sun would be rising soon. Miko stirred, sitting up and regarding me intently.

"Where are you off to?"

"I thought I'd take a run up to the bluff before everyone else wakes up. Want to come?"

"Sure, why not."

I held out my hand and he scampered up my arm, perching on my shoulder.

I crept quietly down the hall, careful not to wake anyone, and slipped out the front door.

I walked briskly over to paths through the trees to the north of the house. Miko hopped off my shoulder and zipped up a tree. "Okay kid, you lead, I will follow."

We set off at a gentle run, Miko leaping from limb to limb above me while I padded softly through the trees. Soon, the terrain started to climb, and trees became taller and stronger. We kept on, until finally we reached a barren bluff overlooking the lough. The sun was just starting to crest over the hills across the water to the east, and I dropped into the warrior's pose, beckoning the sun with my outstretched hand as if I called it forward.

Miko chuckled and sat on a ledge nearby as I moved into a complex tai chi form.

"Don't you ever stop moving?" he asked. "How can you hear the sun rise if you are busy concentrating on your dancing?"

"First of all, it's not a dance, it's the dragon form, which is great practice for defensive combat." I answered him slowly, my words keeping pace with my movements. "And secondly, what do you mean 'hear the sun rise'? Don't you mean watch the sun?"

"No, I mean hear the sun rise. Maybe you can't hear it because your ears are untrained. I don't know. But you must know that the sun has its own song it sings as it approaches. Everyone knows that. Why do you think the birds begin to sing before it rises?"

"Um, the light wakes them up?"

"No, it is the song that wakes them. The rush of the light toward the planet has its own song, and as it crests over the horizon it is at its strongest, ringing off the land, coming over the hills and through the trees likes a horn, waking the plants with their own chorus of greeting."

"Wow, Miko, that sounds beautiful. I wish I could hear it."

"Well, maybe if you stop moving, kid. Why don't you come sit here with me? Do some of that meditating your family is always on you about."

I walked over and sat down on the cold rock beside him, drawing my knees up in front of me as we watched the sun hover over the hills.

"That's right. Just gaze at the sun, quiet down. Reach into your earth power – that might help you access your senses. You can hear the animals, so I think there's a good chance you'll be able to hear this."

I pulled my hood up over my head to ward off the chill and block some of the direct light from the sun, allowing only its outer rays to filter through my lashes. I thought about the red sun of Aeden, and then I let that thought go like a balloon on the breeze, quieting my mind. I imagined roots growing down from my spine and feet down deep into the hillside, spanning ever outward, intertwining with the roots of the trees. As the sun rose, I felt the roots begin to hum and throb with life, awakening to the light. I felt life begin to flow through them, through me. Overhead, birds sang as they flew towards their breakfasts and morning sips from the lough.

And then I heard something. At first, I thought the wind was singing through the trees, the way it does sometimes, whistling among knotted branches. But then I realized there was no wind, and the song was rising. It was like the sound of water glasses being played, but more harmonious, more ethereal.

"Is that-"

"Shh, just listen," Miko shushed me.

As the sun rose, so did the song, as if an angelic chorus had joined in, toning in harmony. Finally, the sun crested the hill completely, and I actually *saw* the waves of sound burst over the horizon like a tsunami of light, washing over the hillside in a triumphant flash of sound and light. Birds took flight in concert, and the trees rippled as if stirred by the wind.

And then all was silent. All was still.

I sat in silence, too, all cares in the world erased by the beauty of what I had just experienced.

Eventually, the rumbling of my stomach brought me back to my senses.

"That was amazing."

"See? I knew you could hear it. Now you know why the birds sing, and where the wind is born."

"Wow. Okay. Like, really, wow. I've never heard of anything like this. Thank you for helping me hear it, Miko."

"Anytime, kid."

"Do you think I could teach other people to hear it?"

"I don't know. Maybe. Or maybe not. You have better ears than most, you can hear us talk. Not many can anymore. But, maybe."

"I wish everyone could hear it. Maybe then we'd all be a little more careful about what we do on the earth. I mean, that was like...like the sun is watching us. Singing to us. The whole planet is alive, Miko."

"You're telling me," he chittered in amusement. "About time you woke up."

"Alright, alright. Come on, let's head back. By the time I get cleaned up Marie should have breakfast on the table. You up for more running?"

"When am I not? You're not the only one who's been training in Valhalla, you know."

"Seriously? You didn't tell me."

"Yeah, well," he groomed his ear. "I've been working with a couple squirrels and a hawk to practice combat diffusion techniques. Running, too."

"Diffusion techniques?"

"You know, jumps to the face, eye clawing, neck biting, things like that. I know I probably can't take out a Shade on my own, but I want to be able to help you whenever I can."

"Miko, you already have."

"I know, I know. But that time at your house might have just been lucky. I want to be prepared. You seem to attract all the wrong kind of attention, no offense."

I chuckled. "None taken."

I stood up and dusted myself off.

"Alright then, let's see what you can do. I'm going to run my fastest, back to the house, and you see how often you can tag me. Ready?"

"Oh, you're on!" He took the trees and I sprinted away through the forest.

Almost immediately, he leapt and landed on my back.

"That's one," he said gleefully, jumping back off my shoulder into a tree as I passed by.

After that, our run became a raucous game of tag. I threw in as many evasive tactics as I could think of, utilizing my freerunning skills to create a less predictable course. Instead of taking the quickest, shortest route, the way I usually did, I started looking for places to spin, to twist, to hide. We dashed through the woods, blurs of gray and black. Time and again he jumped towards me. Sometimes he landed, sometimes he crashed to the soft ground only to clamber up another tree. I vaulted over trees and boulders, twisting to the side in midair to land where I shouldn't.

Where the path went straight, I tic-tac'd off a tree to detour through patches of dried ferns.

As unpredictable as I tried to be, he must have determined a rhythm to my moves, because by the time we approached the edge of the woods he was landing every jump on my shoulders.

Smiling, I slowed to a walk, cooling down as I crossed the wide lawn.

"Well, Miko, I think you've won. Was I that obvious?"

"No. But you forget, I can hear your thoughts. Once I stopped trying to outwit you and began really listening, it was more like a dance. Easy pickings."

"Oh, you cheater!" I laughed.

"I am not!" Miko took on a tone of mock offense.

"You totally are. But you are also hella awesome. I think you can tell your friends in Valhalla that they trained you well."

"Thank you, Siri." I swear, I could hear him blushing through his fur. "I promise, I will use my skills to honor our life-bond."

CHAPTER 23

After a shower and a full Irish breakfast, everyone was ready to hit the road. Miko was perched on Alec's shoulder, sniffing his hair while Alec pretended not to notice. The squirrel was seriously messing with his "I don't care" attitude. I bit the inside of my cheek and looked away, focusing instead on the happy blush that crept up my grandmother's cheeks when Mialloch bowed over her hand, kissing the smooth skin as he thanked her for her hospitality.

"It was my pleasure, young man. I am happy to see that Aeden still produces fine-mannered gentlemen." She eyed Alec with a sparkle in her eye. "Although, of course, many of us still have a bit of Viking raider in us, blood or no."

"You should meet my fiancé, Ewan," Amber giggled. "He is a fine northern specimen, even if his family hasn't lived above below in a couple hundred years."

"I always thought he was Scottish," I said.

"Some Scots, some Viking, and lots of fae in all the right places," Amber raised an eyebrow and wiggled her hips.

My grandmother gasped and I stifled another laugh. My grandmother, great as she was, had her limits. I decided to save her any embarrassment and rushed over, enveloping her in a hug.

"Thank you, Jade. I wish we could stay longer. Will you come see us in Aeden soon?"

"I will, I promise. I should wrap some things up at the University, but I managed to arrange to have the winter semester off for a sabbatical so I can come and stay for a couple of months. I'm not planning to come for another week, at least, but I will be with you for your Choosing."

"That's amazing! I can't believe you didn't tell me before!" I squeezed her tight. "I can't wait to see you again. I love you so much."

"I love you, too, sweetheart. Now, off with you. Claire is going to drive me into Dublin to my apartment, so we'll be right behind you."

Everybody said their goodbyes and we piled into our cars. This time, the drive through the grounds was more sedate, Alec being careful as could be with my grandmother's Land Rover.

I leaned over and whispered in his ear.

"Don't worry, I won't tell her if you break the speed limit when we're out of sight."

"I would never," Alec said in mock outrage.

I pecked him on the cheek and sat back, appreciating the beauty of the wrought iron gates ahead of us. Alec stopped and I jumped out to open the way, waving both cars through. The gravel crunched as they rolled by, parking to wait a few meters away.

I was just shutting the gateway when the attack came.

A blue arc of electricity flew out of the woods and hit the metal scrollwork above me, creating a shockwave that pulsed through both my hands, throwing me backwards. I smashed into the rear hatch of Claire's car and slid to the ground in a daze.

Instantly, I heard car doors opening behind me, shouts and feet on gravel.

"Siri, are you okay?" Clair held my face in my hands. "Say something!"

"Yeah. Yeah," I shook my head, trying to clear the fog.

I hopped up onto my feet and crouched low behind the car to see what was going on. I counted at least twelve men and women circling our smaller group. Alec and Amber were already fighting the nearest Shades.

"This is bad. Get back through the gates, Claire."

"No, not without you."

"No, Claire, you can't fight these people, you're not trained. Get back where it's safe."

"Not without you!" She sobbed, her eyes wide. "You're hurt! You were, you...dammit, Siri, you were just hit by lightning."

"I'm okay," I insisted, realizing at the same time that I really was. "I mean it. Please, I can't help the others if I am worrying about you. Please, just go, now."

I stared at her, willing her to give in. After a few moments, she sighed. "Fine, you win. But I swear, Siri, you better not die on me."

She turned and fled to the safety of the gates, pausing as she scraped her hand against the raw iron to gain access through the wards. I watched her close them behind her just in time, letting go moments before more lightning arced over the cars to hit the arches.

I zeroed in on a woman clothed in black, a large hood drawn over her head. I could see that her hair was dyed an impossible shade of orange, the tips peaking out wildly from the darkness around face. From the depth of the shadows, I saw her smile at me slightly.

"Come, Siri! No one needs to get to hurt. We just want to talk."

"Talk? Sure, let's talk." I reached down, yanking the hubcap off Claire's tire with both hands. "Sorry, Claire," I muttered, standing up. I cracked my neck, judged the distance and sprinted forward, running over Alec's car and flying at the woman. I saw her hand begin to rise up, strange flickers building over her outstretched palms before I brought my arm out from behind me and flung the plastic wheelcover at her like a giant throwing star.

I'd never been one to play Frisbee, but apparently it wasn't the size of the star that mattered.

The heavy disc caught her in the forehead, ripping back her hood. Her eyes widened in shock for a moment, a surprising mixture of unnatural blood-red and glowing orange, and then they closed as she went down unconscious at my feet.

I didn't waste time gloating. Three more Shades were right behind the woman. One man sneered at me at lunged.

"You're going to pay for that," he said.

"Really? Are you sure about that?" I taunted. "Don't you need to bring me in alive?"

"Alive, yes. Unharmed? Well now, all sorts of things can happen in the middle of a fight. And, of course, we will have plenty of time in the plane to get to know each other."

"Good luck with that," I snorted. I aimed a roundhouse kick at his head, which he dodged. It didn't matter. Even as he was coming out of his defensive move, I was moving in with a fast flurry of punches to his ribs and heart.

While he began to flounder, I could see the other two Shades creeping up to flank me from either side. I was outnumbered, but not unprepared. As he reached out to grapple with me, I feinted left and slipped around to his other side. Using my elbow, I threw all my weight into him, shoving him at the massive fae approaching. They both went down in a tangle of limbs, gifting me with several precious moments.

I spun and jabbed the woman who thought she was sneaking up on me hard in the throat. When in doubt, throw some Krav Maga at them, Mom always said.

I turned back to deal with the two men, but there wasn't any need. A small but ferocious whirlwind of dust, small stones and dead leaves blocked them from my sight momentarily. I braced myself, expecting an attack from another Shadow Shaman, but the whirlwind enveloped the Shades, not me.

Wails and screams pierced the air, and then everything went silent. The wind stopped and the leaves fluttered to the ground, drifting over their knocked out forms. I looked around for the source of the wind and saw Mialloch, leaning against the car breathing heavily.

"You okay?" I asked.

"Yes, I just need a moment to recover. You see, you aren't the only one who has learned new things on this trip," he smiled tightly at me.

"Thanks, Loch" I said, and then vaulted over the car to check on Amber and Alec. I needn't have worried. They had made short work of the fae they were fighting.

"Siri," Miko practically screamed in my mind, "there are more coming!" At first, I peered blindly into the woods, and then I saw them, thirty or more Shades were converging on us. There was no way we could take them all.

Suddenly, behind me, I heard Jade calling my name.

"Siri! Alec! I need you, now! Everyone, fall back."

We ran over to her.

"What is it, what do you want us to do?" I asked.

"Alec, you are Earth fae, correct?"

"Yes, ma'am."

"Perfect. With three of us, we'll have plenty of juice. Link hands with me, now."

We did as she asked while she kicked off her shoes and bowed her head.

A low rumble shook the ground, a disruption to everyone's balance but not enough to knock any Shades off their feet. They paused, and then laughed, continuing forward.

"No offense, ma'am, but I think we might have better luck if you let us fight," Alec offered.

"Hold your tongue, boy. Watch and learn," Jade retorted, lifting her head momentarily to glare at him, her eyes gleaming brilliantly. Then she bowed her head again and began to emit a low, keening sound, holding a constant tone.

For a moment, nothing happened. The Shades all grinned at each other and continued forward, some brandishing knives, others, simply pounding their fists in anticipation, I suppose, of what they would want to do to our faces.

And then, the first one went down.

And then another. And another. One by one, the men and women were being yanked off their feet by an unseen force.

When I finally saw it, I gasped. Because it wasn't an unseen force at all. My grandmother had called up the plants in a way that I had never imagined possible. Roots and vines were tearing our enemies to the ground, pulling all the Shades into the forest wrapped in heavy blankets of green.

"Are they dead?" I whispered.

"No. Not yet," my grandmother answered grimly.

I gasped, surprised at the venom and determination in her voice.

"They must be dealt with by the authorities, Jade," Alec warned her. "Otherwise we are no better than they are."

"I know, I know." She ripped her hands from ours. "But dammit, they came after my granddaughter, at my own gates. No one attacks me and gets away with it. Nobody!"

I'd never seen my grandmother so angry.

"Jade," I put my hand on her shoulder. "Alec is right. Please. We have to stay true to who we are."

"Fine," she sighed. She smiled weakly at me, gesturing to Alec. "Like I said before, Siri, you have a good man here. Better than me, it would seem. You really are made for each other."

She looked at us both with determination. "Now, you must hurry. Don't worry, Claire and I will gather the local council to deal with these louts. They will rue the day they ever thought to attack anyone under my care. Go quickly, in case they are sending more. You must get to Airmed without being followed."

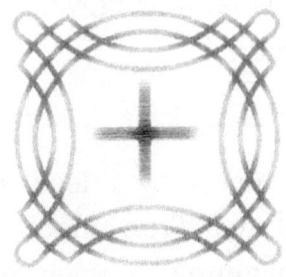

CHAPTER 24

The sun, as I had predicted at dawn, gave rise to a beautiful midday sky.

Each road we took was more picturesque than the one before it. Sheep dotted sleeping winter meadows, barren trees stood on walled hills, white cottages sent peat-scented smoke out their chimneys.

The beauty mocked me.

It was hard to believe that the sun that shone above us was the same one that had witnessed our battle by the gates. The same sun that had nourished my soul at dawn.

Of course, the sun hadn't changed. It still sang, somewhere, for someone else's dawn and it would sing for me again tomorrow. I had the ears now to hear its song and it made me wonder all the more at the divide between the light and dark.

How could the Dark have degenerated so much? How could they have turned away from that song? How could any of us?

I could hear Vala in the back of my head, coaxing me to stay strong, to stay on track.

I thought back to the last time I'd seen her.

"Fear is the one true enemy, it leads to all conflict in the world," she had told me. "True empathy, true light, comes from within by imagining yourself in another's shoes, feeling their pain as your own, their joy as your own. When we face our fears head on, then we can be truly empowered and follow our soul's purpose here on earth. Our hearts open up, our minds become unclouded and we can see our way more clearly."

I was still trying to see my way clearly. And I couldn't quite place myself in the shoes of these dark fae. I just didn't get it, the compulsion to turn away from the Light. I had been afraid again and again, angry more times than I could count, but there was nothing appealing to me about the Dark side. What did she mean?

"Are you sure about that?" Miko asked me telepathically. "I know you are hurt, but I know you also understand the pain Rowan is feeling right now, and you know how even Alec's memories of his family's deaths still affect him. Just take those feelings one step further, and imagine what it would be like if someone had a fear or a pain, and decided that the only way to never feel that way again was to be the one in charge, the one making all the decisions. I've heard how these Shades think. They believe that as long as they are in control, they are safe. Some of them even feel like they are doing humans a favor, like everyone else is too weak to make the decision for themselves."

"But that's ridiculous," I whispered. "No one has the right to do that."

"Of course, not," Miko answered. "That is the illusion of control. We animals know better than to pretend we have any control over life, death, and the natural order of things. But both fae and humans like to believe they can control the chaos of life. The illusion of control gives them a feeling of safety – until the illusion shatters."

"I still don't get it," I thought. "Don't they see the pain they cause? The damage they do to people's lives? To the planet?"

"Oh, come on, you've met these people," Miko persisted as he crawled over my shoulder and under my chin, nestling around my neck, rubbing his ears behind mine own. "Can't you sense the pain they are in? The emptiness and bitterness they have from believing that they are disconnected from the Light? Of course they are still connected. But by denying the connection, they lose its comfort. It is a very painful existence. Life becomes about survival. About fighting to prove they are valid, valuable beings. Special. They don't remember that they already are."

"God, that's sad," I said out loud.

"What is?" Alec looked at me.

"Oh, um, just something Miko said about Shades. I'm still trying to work it all out, but I think I am getting closer to understanding how the Dark works."

"It's spreads like an infection," Alec scowled. "Too bad there isn't an antidote for that."

"Hmm, maybe there is. I wonder..." An idea was starting to form in my mind, something I couldn't quite put into words. Somehow, I knew there really was an antidote. If Alec and Miko were right, and the Dark was just a distorted expression of the Light, then that meant that all we had to do was figure a way to light the Shades up again.

Oh yeah. Easy peasy.

"What are you thinking?" Miko asked.

"I don't know. It's like this idea is in there," I thought, but I can't quite get to it. I'm too distracted, I guess. Maybe it'll come to me later. I don't know," I sighed.

"You okay?" Alec reached over and rubbed my hand.

"Yeah, I'm fine. How much farther do we have to go?"

"Hey, don't ask me, you're the navigator."

"Right," I drawled. "But my grandmother didn't mark any distances on this sheet of paper, just the directions. I thought maybe she told you when you guys were talking last night."

For maybe the first time ever, Alec blushed. "No, we didn't get to talk about it."

"Hmm, right. Well, looking at what she wrote, we've gone through most of the roads on here, just a few more turns left. Of course, that could mean anything, distance wise."

"Great. Well, we've been driving for a couple hours already, it can't be too much longer."

"Hey," Amber said, leaning over the front seat and pointing ahead. "Didn't she say the clootie's near the Slieve Bloom Mountains?"

"Yes," said Mialloch, "she said the water in the clootie is fed by the water from the tallest hill, Arderin."

"Well, that must be them, it was on that sign," she pointed again to a sign as we passed it, and then to the softly rolling range ahead of us to the southeast.

"Ancients below, it's about time," Alec yawned. "I don't think I've ever spent so much time sitting down in one week."

Amused, I quirked an eyebrow at him.

"What? First I was on a completely useless mission to Palm Springs, then I had to fly back to Canada, drive to get you, drive back, drive again, fly on the plane again, then more driving, and more driving. I'm an earth fae. That doesn't mean I like to sit around like a rock."

"You're not kidding," Mialloch snickered. "I don't think I ever met anyone else that was as restless as you, Ward. Do you know, one of our teachers used to actually tie him to the chair to get him to sit still?"

"That's terrible!" I exclaimed.

Alec shrugged, smiling in the mirror at Mialloch. "Actually, I think Mrs. Kaxun helped me become a better Guard. If it wasn't for her, I might not have ever learned how to tolerate hours of surveillance on mission. After a week of being tied to that chair, I managed to master my impulses. But, I can't say I ever learned to like it."

"Well, I still think it's awful." I shook my head. "Is that a normal thing for teachers to do in Aeden?"

"Definitely not," Mialloch retorted. "In fact, when my mother found out she went straight to the school and had a talk with Mrs. Kaxun."

"I didn't know that," Alec said thoughtfully.

"Why do you think she stopped? You might think you had tamed your impulses, but trust me, I still had to sit behind you. I don't think I've ever watched someone fidget so much. It was most distracting."

"Well, lucky for you, you didn't have to put up with it for long," Alec chuckled.

"No. You made sure of that when you decided to pursue a different skills track," Mialloch said with a hollow tone. "We never shared a class again." He crossed his arms over his chest and looked out the window.

Alec frowned, looking in the mirror at his old friend. "I'm not the one who—"

"Alec, turn here," I cut him off, realizing we'd almost missed our road.

He focused on making the turn, and an awkward silence descended. After a minute, Amber spoke up.

"Okay guys, I don't want to interrupt the emo bromance you've got going on, but we really need to talk about what we're going to do when we get to Airmed's. Mialloch, she's your grandmother. Do you have any tips for how to approach her?"

"Are we even going to be able to get in?" I wondered. "I mean, if Jade has so many wards on her place, what about Airmed?"

"We'll get in," Alec said confidently. "Jade says the wards on Airmed's all focus on scrambling your emotions. If you don't have a real need to see her, and you don't already know exactly why you are going there, then as you approach you will become confused and turn back. It's similar to the wards on Vala's and the entry-wood in Canada. We should have no problem."

"That doesn't sound like much of a ward to me," I muttered.

"You don't know my grandmother. She will have keyed the wards very specifically to the entrant's intentions. She is nothing if not precise, even when she is one of her moods," Mialloch said.

"Sounds like someone else we know," Alec grumbled.

I hushed him and looked back at Mialloch. "Okay, so about these moods of your grandmother's. This isn't the first time it's been mentioned that she can be difficult. What do we do if she won't help us?"

"She will," Mialloch vowed.

"Don't worry, Siri," Alec said, grasping my hand firmly. "Everything is going to work out."

"I'm not worried," I said, pulling my hand away. "I just think we should have a game plan. Be prepared."

"I have a plan," Alec said, glancing at Amber.

"What do you mean?" Mialloch asked.

"I mean, that I am the team leader and I have a plan. I believe that your grandmother will help us. She has always been agreeable to me. But if she does not...Amber knows what to do."

I cocked my head, examining him. "Are you going to share your plan with the rest of us?"

"No. I am not."

"Amber?"

"Sorry, Siri, I have my orders," she smiled tightly at me, the gesture not reaching her eyes.

"Fine," I huffed. "Whatever."

A furrow appeared in Mialloch's brow. "Alec, if you are planning on harming my grandmother in any way, I must warn you—"

"Stuff it, Loch. Nothing is going to happen to your grandmother. And what would you do about it, anyway?" he taunted.

Mialloch's gaze turned cold and he just stared at Alec's eyes in the mirror.

After that, there wasn't any more discussion. We drove on, and eventually came to a hidden road turning off into a wood. The road was barely maintained, strewn with rocks and sand and small fallen branches. I was glad my grandmother had loaned us her Land Rover.

"Who needs wards? I bet most people avoid this road just because it's a hazard," I grumbled, bracing my hand against the roof of the car as we bounced over another rock.

Another hundred yards and we passed through the barrier, the fine hairs along my body rising as they connected with the energy, transmitting the warmth and heat of the ward through my body. We turned a sharp corner, and the road smoothed out into an even, hard packed gravel drive winding through the wood.

Along the way, I started to notice ancient, ragged strips of cloth, gold chains and quaint little effigies made from sticks hanging from the occasional tree. The further in we went, the more of them I saw.

"What is all this?" Amber asked.

"Offerings," I answered in a hushed voice. "All the clooties in Ireland have them. You leave a bit of yourself when you ask for a healing. It's meant to be an energetic exchange, according to my mom, though I had a teacher who said it was just a stand-in for pagan sacrifice. With the cloth, the idea is that as it disintegrates with the wind and the rain, it is returned to the earth, feeding the well, and your prayers will be answered."

"Creepy," said Alec.

"I dunno," said Claire. "I think it's kind of pretty."

"Well, either way, it means we must be close," Mialloch said, excitement creeping into his voice.

We turned another corner and had to slam on the breaks to avoid colliding with a massive boulder blocking the road. Two worn footpaths led around either side of the rock.

We all looked at each other, thinking the same thing.

"Not exactly the welcome wagon," Alec said heavily.

"Nope." I wondered if anything could ever just be easy when it came to the fae. "End of the line, people. Now, we walk."

CHAPTER 25

We all hopped out of the car, even Miko. After the exertion of the fight at Jade's gates and then sitting cooped up in the Land Rover for so long, it felt awesome to stretch my legs and arms. As I passed the giant boulder I brushed my hand against its surface and felt a strong tingling sensation. The surface of the rock was worn smooth, as if thousands of hands had rubbed it in the very same spot. Maybe they had.

We headed into the woods at a brisk pace. Alec and Amber started teasing each other, and soon we were all jogging lightly, laughing and running between the trees along the narrow path. Even Loch was joining in on the fun, playing chase with the rest of us. I felt giddy, free. The wood was vibrant here, and many of the trees were covered with buds and fresh leaves, as if spring had come early here.

Alec plucked a white trillium flower and stuck it behind my ear and dodged away, smiling. I grinned and gave chase, stumbling when I almost fell over a wide silver bowl on the ground in a small clearing.

"Whoops!" I giggled.

"I gotcha," Alec breathed into my ear, catching me before I could knock it over.

I stared up into his eyes, utterly enchanted.

"That's quite enough," a stern voice said loudly, and someone clapped twice, the way you do when you are trying to get someone's attention. Still, I couldn't look away from Alec. Those eyes. The purple ring within the viridian circles expanded, shining brightly into my own.

"Oh, for goodness sake," the voice complained. Suddenly, I was completely wet, doused with ice cold water.

"What the hell?" I shrieked and turned, expecting to see Amber.

Instead, I saw a woman in her forties with long, pale hair holding the now-empty silver basin. Her dark kohl-rimmed eyes stood out in stark contrast with her fair skin, although her cheeks had a natural rosy healthfulness to them.

"Airmed!" Alec exclaimed. "You haven't aged a day."

"Ah, but you have, my boy," she said warmly, rushing forward to embrace him in a hug. "And very finely, at that."

"It is so good to see you again," Alec murmured, adoration filling his voice.

Behind us, Mialloch and Amber burst into the clearing hooting, "ha, found you!" Airmed released Alec and looked over the newcomers.

"Loch, my sweet, darling boy. It's been too long," she enfolded him in a hug and Mialloch hugged her back, blushing. "Are you boys going to introduce me to your friends?"

"Certainly, Grandmother. This is Amber Slaight, a Light Guard, and this is Siri Alvarsson."

"Jade's granddaughter? Do you play cribbage?" she looked at me speculatively.

"Um, no, sorry, I don't. I actually came here to—"

I started to explain why we had come, but she had already turned away, apparently uninterested in me now.

"Come children, the sun grows high in the sky. It is time for the midday meal. Some conversations are best had indoors."

She clapped her hands again and a small cottage shimmered into view behind her, wood smoke and all.

Mialloch and Alec grinned at each other while I just asked, "How?" and stood there looking like an idiot.

"Water fae," Amber whispered to me. "They are great at affecting emotions, and some can cast illusions. Basically, she just manipulated you into not seeing what's right in front of your eyes."

"That's a disturbing thought."

"Could be worse, trust me. I've seen Water Shades use their abilities to bring your worst nightmares to life. Now that, that's disturbing."

A tingle of unease spread across my back, but I ignored it and followed Airmed and the boys. As I passed the small artesian pool in the clearing, I saw that a single lotus flower bloomed at its center. Could lotuses even bloom in winter? I knelt down and dipped my fingers into the clootie and found it strangely warm, almost body temperature. A slight sulphurous odor rose from its surface in a fine mist. The lotus bobbed in the middle of the small pond, its hue shifting from periwinkle, to violet, to mauve, and back to blue in the light. Its beauty drew me in and when I looked round I realized everyone had already entered the cottage.

Quickly, I hopped up and dried my hands on my jeans. "Miko," I called out with my mind, "are you here?"

"Yes, up here," he chittered from the roof of the cottage. "Her illusions don't affect me."

"Good. Come with me, and let me know if you hear or see anything strange. I don't entirely trust Mialloch's grandmother."

"Okay, look out below!"

He hopped down off the roof and landed in my hair.

"Ow! Watch it!" I complained out loud.

Miko apologized, and the door to the cottage opened.

"Is everything okay out here? A friend of yours?" She eyed Miko curiously.

"Just a pet," I said quickly. Miko squealed at me, but I telegraphed reassurance to him, letting him know I meant no offense. For reasons I couldn't quite explain, I didn't want her know we had someone on our side who couldn't be fooled.

"Well, come, come. Don't just stand there on the doorstep." She ushered me in.

Inside, the air was warm and fragrant. A long channel of hot water steamed in a wide trough along one stone wall. Airmed caught me looking and explained.

"The water is diverted here from the clootie, running in a closed circuit. It provides all the heat and hot water I could need."

"It reminds me of the stonework I saw at a Roman bath when I was younger."

"How very astute of you. Yes, this cabin was built for me by a dear Roman friend. Such a sweet man, he was."

"Roman? Like a Roman invader in Ireland, Roman? But that would mean you are at least two thou—"

"Shh, a lady never tells her age." she winked. "And, besides, the Romans never invaded Ireland. They just...visited."

Mialloch laughed. "Yes, and you made sure they were well entertained, did you not, Grandmother?"

"Of course," she retorted. "I am a very good hostess. But in my old age, I do seem to find my own company to be the most pleasant of all. Except, of course, for the rare occasion that I have such charming guests such as you all." Her smile beamed, but the light did not reach her eyes. "But please, sit, and we will eat."

We all sat around the heavy round oak table and watched as she began to set platters in front of us – fresh, herbed farm cheeses, a large artisanal bread, and a heaping bowl of berries. A steaming pot of sweet herbal tea completed the offerings, which she encouraged us all to sample.

"I am sorry I do not have more to offer you, but I wasn't expecting anyone today."

"Ah, I am sorry if we are intruding, Airmed," Alec smiled at her apologetically before he ripped a hunk of bread off the loaf and smeared it with a peppery cheese.

"Nonsense, Alec," she patted his hand. "I am so happy to see you boys. Perhaps now you will visit me more often. I suppose Jade told you where I was?"

"Yes, she did."

"I see. I am surprised she gave up my secret, even to family." She narrowed her eyes at me, "Tell me, why have you come? I get the sense that this is more than just a social call. Unless Loch has come to announce something important? An impending engagement, perhaps?"

I almost choked on my tea.

"No, Grandmother," Mialloch sighed. "I remain unmatched."

"Ah, my dear boy, don't worry. You have all the time in the world to find love. Just don't let your father pair you up with some simpering council ninny to feed his ego. No. You deserve a fine, accomplished young woman."

"Thank you, Grandmother," he said, turning beet red. "I shall be sure to pass that on to my father."

"Better yet, I will tell him myself. You are still my favorite grandson, you know."

"Your only grandson," he muttered.

"What was that?"

"Nothing, grandmother," he sighed.

She harrumphed, and Alec jumped into the conversation.

"Actually, Airmed, we have come to you on urgent business. The Shades have developed an anti-serum for the Light, and they have used it on some of our people already."

"Really?" Airmed sounded intrigued. "What sort of anti-serum? Do you know how it is produced? What does it do, exactly?"

"Our scientists do not know how they are making it. Every Light fae they have used it on has fallen into a sort of suspended animation. They aren't sick, but they are unconscious and they continue to age at their natural rate."

"A pity you could not have brought me a sample."

"Actually, I did." Alec reached into his pocket to remove a wooden box. He opened it, and handed a small vial of red liquid to Airmed. "Not the anti-serum, itself, but some of the affected blood."

"I didn't know you had that," I said, surprised.

"Bran gave it to me to give to Alec," Amber explained. "Sorry, Siri, it was 'need to know' only."

"Need to know?" I glared at Alec, who ignored me.

"Airmed, can you tell what it is?" he asked.

She opened the vial and sniffed. She carefully tipped one brilliant crimson drop into a glass of water and closed her eyes as she held her hand palm down over the glass.

"No. It's not natural. It's something...dark. Unnatural. Created by a merging of the elements in all the wrong ways." She frowned, and poured the water into the bucket of ashes by the hearth. I jumped at the startling crash of glass as she threw the now empty cup into the fire. "It is not a true virus yet, it can't spread on its own. How can they hope to use this against the Light with any great effect? What are you not telling me? Start at the beginning."

"Well, I guess it all started with Siri's mom. Mikael Morrigan is after Siri for some reason, we aren't entirely sure why, but he wound up taking her mom as leverage and used the anti-serum on her."

"But the doctors can't figure out a cure," I interrupted, pleading. "And I tried to use my own healing powers, but I'm not strong enough—"

"You have healing powers?" Airmed stood up and started pacing. "That doesn't come through your mother's line. Who is your father?"

"Bran LeFay." I answered.

She grunted and started talking quietly to herself while she kept pacing.

Each time one of us tried to say something she would shush us. Eventually, we all just continued eating, quietly watching her wear a hole in the floor.

Finally, she stopped.

"You are descended from Tyr," she said, glaring at me accusingly.

"Yes?" I said, confused about where this was going.

"The god of bravery and wisdom, but also he who had the power to decide any battle. And Bran, he carries the blood of both Skuld Norna and Morgaine Le Fay, through Yvain and Kalila. So again, the power to affect future outcomes, and of course the ability to heal and work with living energy."

"If you say so," I shrugged, popping another gooseberry in my mouth.

"Silence, child!" she lashed out at me. "Don't you see? No one has manifested a viable healing power in centuries, other than me, and most people believe I am dead. Even if they could find me, I could not do what you can do. With your bloodlines, you fulfill an ancient prophecy – you have the power to remove light from the world, or to expand the reach of the light and bind it here forever!"

"You're joking, right?" I practically choked on the fruit in my mouth. Incredulous, I leaned back in my chair, seriously doubting her sanity. "I've heard you could regenerate limbs and piece people back together. I couldn't even stop my friend from bleeding out."

She waved my protests away with her hand.

"Your power is still developing. How old are you? Nineteen? Twenty?"

"I'll be eighteen in a few weeks."

"You haven't had your Choosing yet, and you are already exhibiting powers?"

"The visions started several months ago. So?"

Airmed threw up her hands and resumed pacing. "You have no idea of your inborn power. Your self-doubt may very well be your downfall. Once you have your choosing, who knows what you might be able to do." She stopped in front of me and slammed her hands down on the table, making the dishes rattle and jump. "The Dark needs someone like you to jumpstart their anti-serum. A powerful enough healer could potentially awaken their poison and mutate it into an airborne virus. Every man, woman and child would be affected within weeks, fae and humans alike. A virus like this, something that shuts down the Light in the body would be a disaster. It would put all light fae to sleep, like your mother, and lull humans into mindless compliance – they'd become slaves."

Alec inhaled sharply. "We have already encountered a few strange humans on our search for the cure at the Shade research facilities, some lab assistance and night guards. They were extremely simple-minded and accommodating and did whatever we told them. They weren't even afraid."

"I suppose that information was 'need to know', too?" I glared at him.

"Anyways, you can't be sure it's the anti-serum," I argued. "Maybe they have a water fae on staff who makes everyone feel good."

"We don't know. But it makes sense."

"I'm sorry, but how are we supposed to trust this woman?" I stood up. "A healer, who shuts herself away from the world? Why are you really here? Why would you make it so hard for your own people to get healing from you? Don't you care that there are people suffering?"

Airmed stiffened and Mialloch stood up to rush to her defense.

"No, Loch. Sit." She nodded for him to sit back down.

"You're right. I have retreated from my duties as a healer."

"You've shut off this well, made it secret. Who are you to own a clootie? What gives you the right?" I wasn't sure why I was so angry, but the words poured out of me. "I saw all the clothes and offerings in the trees. How do we know they aren't clothes left by the Dark?" Behind me, Mialloch hissed, but I persisted.

"Who do you heal?"

"No one. No one comes here. Only your grandmother, and the rare visit from my son. That is all. Through the waters I can hear the prayers of people at the other holy wells, and I leave the offerings myself, in their stead. It's an old habit, and I find it comforting." She exhaled and returned to her chair, looking deep into her cup of tea before she took a drink.

Amber reached up and tugged gently on my sleeve, urging me to sit, too. I scowled at her but she pulled on my jacket again, so I sighed and gave in. As soon as I was seated, Airmed continued.

"I made a decision a long time ago that my powers would never be used by the Dark. Back then, life among the umans was much more violent and lawless. It was easier for the Shades to cause devastation without drawing undue attention from the humans. I had trained so many other healers, and passed on all my knowledge of herbs and the way light works in the body. Hadn't I done enough? I decided I had. How many people would I have to endure dying before me? Every time I healed someone, the energy flowed through me, rejuvenating my own cells as well. I did not want to live forever." She raised sad eyes to mine, imploring me to understand. "I do not want to outlive more of my own children. I want to be the one being remembered, not the other way around."

I reached out and took her hand. "I do understand. I can only begin to imagine what your life has been like. But tell me something. Did you really pass on all your knowledge? Is there not perhaps one remedy that you didn't trust anyone else to use?"

"I don't know what you mean," she said, and rested her hand on her belt.

I looked at Miko, shooting him a silent question, and he nodded back, confirming my hunch.

"Really? How about whatever you have in the pouch on your belt? You know, the one you are hiding from me, right now?"

She shook her head.

"Grandmother?" Mialloch said gently, "Please, won't you tell us?"

Again, she refused to speak.

I leaned forward and rested my chin on my folded hands.

"Well, let me tell you what I think. My friend Rose found an old incantation of yours, except it's different from the one most people know. It has a few extra lines that go like this:

> *Water to water*
>
> *Flower to flower*
>
> *Combine the two*
>
> *At light's last hour.*

Which sounds to me like it could be referring to exactly what you described – a viral epidemic that steals everyone's light, and destroys Aeden as we know it. And you know what? Mialloch here says you make a powerful healing essence from that funky lotus that is blooming right now, right outside that door, in your well." I pointed with my thumb over my shoulder. "So tell me. Is it true? Do you have something that can reverse the anti-serum? Or should we just leave, and let you stay here, outliving the rest of the world?"

Airmed closed her eyes and sighed.

"No. You are right. I do have such an essence that works particularly to harness the power of the Light to repair cells. It is how I was able to regenerate King Nuada's arm so many years ago. After my father and I built this clootie, the true Well of Slaine, the simple lotus I placed within it was transformed into the Nelumbo Lux. But I only have a small amount of the elixir, because there is only one flower each year to harvest. What I have is barely enough to cure a handful of people. If that anti-serum goes viral, my Nelumbo Lux will not be enough."

"How can this be the Well of Slaine, I thought that was at Heapstown Cairn? My mother and I visited it when we were here last time."

"Bah. A story we made up to protect the true clootie. This is the Well of Slaine. The water has restorative properties, but truly it is the Nelumbo Lux itself that holds such great potential."

"Then you understand why we had to come." Alec placed a gentle hand on her shoulder and asked, "Will you give us the elixir, Airmed, or must we return to our people empty handed?"

She removed the pouch from her belt and held it, considering.

"If I give this to you, you must be very, very careful that it does not fall into the wrong hands. Who knows what the Shades would do with it, how they would use it to create something twisted and dark. You must promise me, all of you."

"Of course," Alec vowed. "We will protect it with our lives."

We all agreed.

"I hope it will not come to that," she smiled sadly at us.

"No, I'm pretty fond of living," Amber gave me a twisted grin.

"Aren't we all, dear girl?" Airmed laughed mirthlessly. "Aren't we all?"

CHAPTER 26

A phone rang just as we were finishing eating. The strains of The Eagles' Witchy Woman sounded strange in the rustic cabin.

"That's Vala's number, excuse me," Alec said, pulling his phone out. "Hello?"

He listened, glancing at me.

"She's right here. I'm putting her on." He held the phone out to me. "It's Rose. She sounds really upset, says she needs to talk to you."

I grabbed the phone and walked outside the cottage. "Rose? What's up? Is everything okay?"

"Oh my god, Siri, I'm so glad I finally reached you! Your phone's been going straight to voicemail."

I pulled out my phone and looked at it. Dead.

"Sorry," I laughed. "I kept it charged the whole time I was in Valhalla with no reception. Now I finally get somewhere with cell towers, and I forget to charge it. Classic!"

"Yeah, well, I had to drive to Vala's to get Alec's number. She wouldn't give it to me over the phone. Listen, we have a problem."

"Don't we always? What's happened, have the Shades done something?" I gripped the phone tightly in my hand.

"No."

Relieved, I knelt by the pool of water and trailed my hand through its silvery surface.

"It's Rowan."

"What? What's happened?" I removed my hand from the water and shook it off, standing back up.

"He's so...he's so angry, Siri. You should have heard him, ranting the whole way home in the car. He's so mad at you, at Alec, at all of us. I thought a couple times that he might actually stop and throw me out of the car."

"Oh, come on, he wouldn't—"

"Seriously, Siri. Anytime I tried to defend you, or anyone with the Light, he would lose it. I finally figured if I just let him talk, he'd calm down eventually. But he didn't. He'd go quiet for a few minutes every once in a while, but then, then he'd just start up again. I swear, I've never seen anyone so angry."

I frowned into the phone. "I know. He told me he blames me, back by the highway. He told me he'll never forgive me." Even as I said the words, I tried to shut out the pain of the memory, to focus on Rose's voice.

"Yeah, he told me, several times," Rose was saying. "And I totally get how he was angry at first. I mean, they were twins. He must be in agony. But I'm worried, Siri. Some of the things he's said in the last few days...I talked to Cooper. He says Rowan's going to choose the Dark. He wants Cooper to do the same."

"I knew how angry Rowan was, but I really only thought about how it was affecting our relationship – I never imagined he would take it this far. I mean, how could anyone choose the Dark after what we've seen?" I sighed in frustration. "What about Cooper? What is he going to do?"

"Cooper wants to do whatever Holly would have wanted. So far, I think I have him convinced that means choosing the Light. But I really need you here, Siri. I think you have the best chance of talking Rowan out of making a really bad decision."

"But, he hates me." My stomach flipped a few times just thinking about the way he'd looked at me after the accident.

"I know. But he loves you, too. You can't hate anyone that much unless you love them. He won't listen to me, or to Coop. You're our last shot."

"Okay. When's his Choosing?"

"Tomorrow."

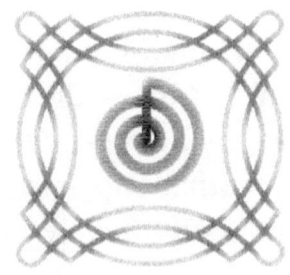

CHAPTER 27

Splashing water over my face from the clootie after I hung up with Rose, I felt my heart slow. My way was clear. I doubted Rowan would listen to me, but I had to try.

I walked back inside and handed the phone back to Alec.

"So?" Amber asked, sipping her tea. "How's Rose?"

"Not good. I need to go home."

"What do you mean?" Mialloch looked up at me. "Back to Aeden?"

"No, not Aeden. Falls Depot. Rowan's Choosing is tomorrow. He's going Dark."

Airmed gasped sharply. "A friend of yours? A faeling going Dark? Was he captured?"

"No," Alec said, watching me intently as he spoke slowly. "A darkling. Siri, you know this was bound to happen. Darklings never Choose the light."

"Don't talk to me like that. I'm not a child. And you're wrong. Cooper is going to Choose the light, and Holly," my voice broke, "she was, too. Cooper's the one that warned Rose. This is all about what happened back in Montreal. Rowan is grieving, and unfortunately, he's still in the anger phase. Rose can't talk him out of it, but maybe I can."

"Why you?" Mialloch asked, intrigued.

"Because he loves her," Alec answered, still watching me.

"Or he did, anyways. It's a long shot, but I have to try. At the very least, maybe my being there will help him retain a bit of the light, even after he becomes Dark."

"Siri, that can't happen. You know what they do to new Shades. You know how they train them," Alec told me gently.

"Still, the girl needs to try," Airmed spoke up.

"I do?" I asked, surprise.

"Of course. You are a healer. This is what you do. There is always a way. You have to believe that. If there is one thing I have learned in the last two thousand years, it is that things usually have a way of working out for the best. And when they don't, the fact that you tried your best is valuable consolation."

Alec pushed his chair away from the table and stood up. "We'd better get going then. Shades have their Choosings at night, which gives us just enough time. I'll call the pilot right now and make sure the plane is ready for us." He walked to Airmed and embraced her. "Thank you, Airmed. You have always been like a second mother to me."

"I love you, too, dear boy." She patted him on the back. "Now that you know where I live, I hope you will visit again."

"You can count on it." He kissed her on the cheek, straightened and walked out the door.

Amber thanked Airmed and followed Alec outside with Miko cradled in her arm while he ate berries out of her other hand. Mialloch stood and hugged his grandmother. "I will be back as soon as I can. There is much more I would like to learn about this world above below."

"I would like that very much, Loch. You are always welcome here, and you can stay as long as you like...just so long as you do not bother me after dinner."

"Right, your beauty routine," he chuckled. "I know."

"If a girl is going to live as long as I have, she might as well look her best." She winked at me over Mialloch's shoulder, squeezing him tightly before letting go. "Now, go on with you. I want to have a word alone with Siri before she goes."

She waited until he had left, and then she went over to an herb-filled cabinet. She gathered several dried flowers from a bowl and placed them into a small mortar and pestle, grinding them slowly while she said something in a language I did not recognize. She poured the ground material into a small pouch with long cords attached to it and walked over to me.

"This will help protect you from what you are going to face. Until your Choosing, you are still vulnerable." She moved behind me and lifted my hair, tying the cords around my neck. "Now you have two charms to keep you safe. You can tell your grandmother that she has passed her necklace on to a wise woman, after all." Airmed's pouch fell between my breasts and I tucked it into my bra. At least the confining contraption was good for something.

"What's in it?" I asked as she walked back around me.

"White rose petals, elder flower and mugwort blossoms. It will help you keep your Light up, even when faced with extreme darkness. Hopefully, you will not need it. But, better safe than sorry."

"Thank you, Airmed." I reach out and clasped her hands. "You have done so much for me. I can't thank you enough."

"Nonsense, child. I just hope I have done enough."

"You've done the best you could, and that is all we can do, right?"

"Exactly so," she smiled at me. "You are a strong faeling, and soon, you will be stronger. No matter what happens, remember to believe in yourself. You carry the brightest light within you, nothing can dim it except yourself. Choose light, and let love guide you, and you will never be steered wrong."

"I will, thank you. Maybe sometime I can come back here, too."

"I would like that very much. Besides, I imagine that before long you will be going everywhere Alec goes, will you not?"

I blushed, but decided there was no point in denying it. "Yes, that's the plan."

"Then you will come visit me together. It's been a long time since I have had an apprentice. Perhaps you would enjoy learning more of the healing arts."

"I would be honored," I gushed, and meant it. "My friend Rose, she is training to be a Druid, she's totally into plants. Maybe she could meet you sometime, too."

"Well, now, let's not get ahead of ourselves," Airmed smiled nervously. "I am not sure I am ready to accustom myself to such a social life."

"Aw, come on, isn't there a plant for that?"

Airmed laughed. "Indeed, young one, there is. You are a fast learner, Siri Alvarsson. I look forward to teaching you, and your friend Rose. Now, take a last sip of your tea, may it fill your heart, body and mind with the blessings and the radiance of Aeden, aho-em."

I did as instructed, downing my tea in one gulp. "Thanks. Well, I'm sorry to eat and run, but..." I shrugged, and she shooed me outside.

"Go on. Go and save your friend. Gods speed you on your travels."

I walked outside, rejoining the group, and Airmed waved goodbye from the doorway one last time before she went back inside.

Before we left, I ripped two small pieces of cloth from my shirt, dipped them in the water and tied them on a bush near the clootie, saying a short prayer for Rowan and my mother.

"Okay," I said, wiping my hands off on my pants, "let's go."

We hiked in silence back to the car. The ride back to Dublin wasn't much better. Alec found a good radio station, at least, with lots of traditional Celtic music. I couldn't understand a word they were singing, but the soft pipes and stringed instruments were soothing. I leaned my head against the window and closed my eyes, thinking about what Airmed had said about love and light. Somehow, I couldn't really see how those two things could ever really save the day against an army of Shades.

My mind wandered and I started to doze off.

The earth rumbled under my feet. Small rocks shook loose from the roof of the tunnel. I ran faster.

"You can't hide, Siri! I will have you. You will help us. You must," Mikael shouted behind me, too close.

Somehow, I knew if I stopped, he would have me.

"Not a chance, scumbag!" I yelled, kicking up my speed. My legs burned with the effort.

Could muscles even burn in a vision? What was this?

"I'm not helping you annihilate humanity, or the fae," I shouted.

"No one wants to annihilate humanity," Mikael cajoled unconvincingly. "We just want to lead them. That's all. And you could lead them with us."

Right then, I knew Airmed had been right about the anti-serum all along. Behind me, I heard more shouts, and one voice stopped me cold.

"Siri!" Rowan yelled.

"Siri," Alec shook me. "We're here. Wake up."

"I wasn't sleeping," I said, rubbing my eyes. My door was open, and Alec was on one knee next to me.

"Could've fooled me," he grinned.

"No, really," I wasn't. "I had a vision. Mikael, and Rowan, underground. Mikael was chasing me."

"And Rowan was with him?" Alec's hand tightened on my thigh.

"I don't know who Rowan was with. He yelled my name, and then I woke up… The things Mikael was saying… He wasn't hitchhiking into my vision, like usual. He was part of it. The things he said, Alec, Airmed is right. Mikael said he wants to 'lead' humanity. You know what he really means."

"Control."

"Yes."

"Well, then, we'd better hurry up and get the Lux essence back to Valhalla." He stood up and held out his hand. "Come on, gorgeous. Time to jet."

I grabbed his hand, letting him pull me out of the car even as I rolled my eyes at his goofy pun. For a moment, my legs felt wobbly beneath me, an aftereffect of the vision. I hooked my bags over my shoulder and beckoned Miko to climb up my arm. Alec and I started toward the plane where Amber and Mialloch were already climbing the stairs to board.

"So, while you were sleeping, I talked to Mitch," Alec said. "He doesn't want us to take Loch with us, says it's too dangerous, that we've already had enough close calls. Apparently his father is really angry about everything that's gone down so far, wants his son home ASAP."

"Okay, so, what, you and me head to the Depot and Amber can chauffeur Loch home?"

"No, apparently that's not safe enough, either. Mitch says dear old dad wants a double security detail."

"But—" I started to protest, but Alec cut me off.

"Don't worry. I told him that's not an option. Ewan is on another mission, so he can't meet us, but Mitch said he would call someone to meet us and help escort Loch home."

"Geez, they're acting like he's a kid."

"No, not a kid, just a very important person's son, who doesn't know jack about fighting." He stood back, gesturing for me to go up the stairs to the plane first.

"I wouldn't say that. You know, he used his air power pretty well at my grandmother's," I said, passing him.

"Yeah, well, he still needs a lot more practice. And he knows zip about hand-to-hand combat. He can practice on

252

his own time, safely ensconced back in his apartments in Valhalla."

We boarded the plane and walked to the main cabin, where we found Amber and Mialloch chatting companionably with my grandmother and Claire.

"Jade!" I exclaimed. "What are you guys doing here?"

"We're coming with you," she answered, a twinkle in her eye.

I rushed forward and hugged her, happy to see her face again. "But, I thought you couldn't come for another week?"

"Claire convinced me it's time I learned to delegate. I have a very capable assistant who is rather ecstatic to take over, to tell the truth. When Mitch called and asked me if I could help bring home Airmed's cure, I realized I didn't want to miss the chance to see my daughter open her eyes."

"And you?" I asked Claire, "won't you be missing class?"

"It's okay," Claire grinned at Jade. "I have a note from my advisor excusing me from school for a few weeks, just long enough to attend your Choosing."

"That's awesome! We are going to have so much fun."

"I'm counting on it. But first, I understand you're having some trouble with your ex?"

Just then, the pilot came in, instructing us that it was time for takeoff. Claire and I sat down together and buckled in.

"Okay, so spill. What's going on with Rowan? Jade said you and Alec are going to try and stop his Choosing ceremony. Why would you do that? Last time we talked you said he and his sister were going to Choose the Light?"

"They were. But since Holly died, he's been furious. He blames the Light for her death, me most of all. Apparently he's going Dark after all."

"And you think you can stop him?" she eyed me doubtfully. "No offense, Siri, I know you two were close, but didn't you break his heart?"

"Hey, he dumped me. But, yeah, you're right. He knew I was feeling something for Alec. It was sort of a pre-emptive dumping."

"Which so does not count as being dumped, I can tell you from experience."

"Well, anyway, whoever dumped who, it doesn't matter. I have to try. If I don't, I'll never know if I could have done something to change it."

"Is Amber going with you?"

"No, she's taking Jade and Loch back. Alec is coming with me."

"Well then, so am I." She leaned back and crossed her arms over her chest, daring me to argue.

"No. It could be dangerous."

"And you think having your new boyfriend there, while you try to reason with your old boyfriend, is going to make it less dangerous. What are you on? You told me before, Alec and Rowan hated each other on sight."

I glared at her. "You're not coming."

"Like hell. You're going to need someone to keep Alec out of the way so you guys can actually talk without extra testosterone flying around. I'm coming, and that's that."

Miko piped up, "You know, she's got a point. Your guy has a hard time keeping it together when he's around the Dark. If this is a ceremony, don't you think there are going to be more Shades? We need all the people we can get, I think."

I sighed. "Great. Now it's two against one. You guys suck." I looked at Claire. "Alright, fine. You can come. But please tell me you've been able to get your new fire abilities under control."

"Yeah, I have a few tricks up my sleeve. After I saw that guy throw lightning this morning, I did some practicing of my own. I don't have the best aim yet, and I'm not great at throwing it over a distance, but if I'm really close I should be able to let off a mean jolt."

"Wait, you mean lightning is a fire power?"

"Duh."

"I kind of figured it had to do with air. Wow. That's crazy! Can you show me?"

Claire looked scared. "Here? On the plane?"

"Well, yeah. Just give me a little jolt. I wanna test how this Taser ability of yours works."

"I don't think that's the best idea," Claire shook her head, looking worried.

"What's not the best idea?" Alec leaned over our seats with Amber.

"Siri wants me to tase her with my lightning ability."

Alec barked out a laugh and Amber covered her mouth.

"Tell her it's a crazy idea," Claire pleaded. "I never even made lightning before today. What if I hurt her, or worse, take out the plane?"

"I think it's an awesome idea. My boots are rubber, they'll stop any charge. I'll hold her, and you just give her a little taste," Alec smacked his lips together.

"Okay, but I still think this is crazy."

"Don't worry," Amber told Claire. "You're so nervous, I doubt you'll be able to get up much of a charge anyway. You got this."

I stood and Alec scooped me up in his arms. "Aren't you going to get shocked, too?" I whispered up at him.

"Totally worth the price of admission," he said, kissing the top of my head.

I looked at Claire.

"Do it."

CHAPTER 28

I woke up still in Alec's arms, except now he was seated and my legs rested on the seat next to us.

"So, the good news is, you didn't piss yourself," he said in a low, bedroom voice.

"The bad news?" I asked, amused.

"You've been out for eight hours. Although, I don't know if I would call it bad news, exactly. I mean, you got to sleep through pretty much the whole flight."

"Eight hours?! I thought Tasers just knocked out muscle control for a couple minutes."

"Yeah, well, Claire isn't a Taser. Jade says that fire lightning actually knocks out the Light circuitry in fae, so that we have to sleep it off. In a way, it's not so different from how the anti-serum works on us."

"Wow. That's crazy."

"Yeah, Jade was pretty angry at us when she saw what happened. She said it could knock you out for days. Apparently she had no idea Claire had been playing around with a new power today. Claire was pretty worried you wouldn't wake up in time to see Rowan, she's feeling really guilty. You'd better go talk to her."

"Mmm, in a minute," I said, running my hand through his hair and tracing his ear. "You know, this is our first trip overseas together, and we've barely had any time to ourselves."

"That's true. It's been Jade this and Airmed that, and Rowan, Rowan, Rowan," he mocked me, an Irish lilt to his voice.

I pulled him close and silenced him with a kiss, allowing everything I felt for him to bubble through to the surface. I could feel his own emotions, his relief that I was awake, how happy he felt just to hold me in his arms. And there was worry. Lots and lots of worry.

I pulled back.

"Something's bothering you."

"That obvious, huh?" he laughed, rubbing his hand along the back of his neck.

"What is it?"

He looked out the window.

"I don't want you to get hurt."

"How many times do we need to go over this, Alec? I'm a big girl. I may not have as much experience in battle as you, but I'm not exactly untrained. I can take care of myself."

"That's not what I mean."

"Then what do you mean?" I placed my hand on his cheek and forced him to look at me.

"You didn't see yourself the night Holly died. The way you were beating yourself up about the things Rowan said to you... I don't want him to hurt you again. I don't think I could stand it."

"Claire was right," I mused.

"What do you mean?"

"Claire said you and Rowan would be a problem. That's why we got on the whole lightning kick in the first place. She said she had to come with us, and I said no way, and she said, hey, I have lightning powers, and I said, hey, let me see. Yeah, I know, it was a brilliant plan. Anyhow, she says she has to come because someone's got to keep an eye on you while I talk to Rowan."

Alec snorted. "I'm not a child, Siri."

"No, but sometimes around Rowan you act like one." I smiled gently at him. "Look, I appreciate you looking out for me. You'll just have to appreciate Claire looking out for you. I'm not expecting things with Rowan to go easily. But I need to know you aren't going to make things worse."

"I can promise I will try my best," Alec grinned, the dimple re-emerging in his cheek.

"That's all a girl can ask."

"Alright, well, how about you go tell Claire the good news, and maybe I can get some feeling back in my legs before we land."

Realization hit me that we must've been sitting like this for the whole flight and I scrambled off his lap. "Oh my God! You must be in agony!"

Alec laughed. "Not really, no. Agony stopped hours ago, when everything went numb."

"Jerk," I swatted at him and skipped over to Claire and Mialloch who were deep in conversation.

"Congratulations, Claire, your power is a hit!" I joked. She sprang up and hugged me.

"Oh thank gods! I was so worried you'd wake up tomorrow. Jade really laid into me after you passed out."

"Nope, everything is good. You saved me having to entertain myself for eight hours. What about you?" I eyed the narrow distance between her and Mialloch. "You two seem pretty cozy."

Mialloch smiled up at me. "Yes, we have been quite comfortable."

I swear, sometimes I couldn't tell if Mialloch was really as uptight and clueless as he seemed, or if it was all an act. Claire coughed into her hand.

"We just ate, actually. Amber spent a few hours showing us glima moves, and a couple Krav Maga tricks she said you taught her. She is so cool."

"You guys aren't so bad, either." Amber walked up to the group, placing a hand on Mialloch's shoulder. "This one here actually has a fair amount of grace once he loosens up. I think some Qi Kung practice would really be great for him."

"Really?" Mialloch asked, intrigued. "Could you teach me?"

"Actually," she said, "I think Siri is your gal for that. Maybe, when we get back to Aeden, Siri can start teaching all of us. I've only studied it a bit."

"Yeah, I would love that. My mom and I used to do some almost every day."

"Perfect. Well, I actually came over because the captain told me it's time for us to land. Siri, maybe you should go sit with your grandmother, she was pretty worried about you, you know."

"I know," I grumbled. "Geez, can't a girl have a little fun?"

Claire giggled and Amber looked at us sternly. "No. Definitely not. No more fun for you two. Off you go, I'll sit with Alec and firm up our plans. Mitch said he'd have cars waiting for us at the airport, so we'll be splitting up right away."

I ambled over to Jade, who spent the first half of the landing ignoring me, and the second half of it berating me for my recklessness. She said she didn't understand why Alec hadn't talked me out of it, but at least he'd had the good sense to make sure the rest of them were protected from any splash effects. Finally, she had ended up hugging me, crying happy tears that I was okay and that she wouldn't know what to do if she lost both her baby girls.

Honestly, I wasn't sure how much of this kindness I could take.

"Hey now," I protested, "What happened to my crazy, fun loving aunt? Just because you're suddenly a grandmother doesn't mean you get to become all sappy now. Buck up, Grandma, life is good."

She sniffled and wiped her eyes. "I think I liked it better when you called me Jade."

I laughed.

Jade was back. Maybe everything really would be okay.

We cuddled companionably and watched out the window as the plane approached the evening lights of Montreal. We'd left Dublin a little after five o'clock, but it was barely nine here in Montreal. When I was younger, I'd always felt like I was time traveling each time we flew back west. It had felt magical, arriving in a distant land just hours after takeoff. Like we had cheated time.

This time around, all I felt was anxiety. Every moment we spent circling the airport, waiting for permission to land, felt like an eternity. I needed to get off this plane. I needed to get to Rowan. Even though Rose had said we had until tomorrow, I felt like time was running out.

Finally, the landing gear came out and the plane made a sharp turn, angling itself toward the runway before straightening out. The plane dipped lower and lower, and then our wheels kissed the tarmac and the plane taxied to the hangar.

By the time we arrived I was already standing by the door with my bags over my shoulder and Miko in one arm.

Behind me, the rest of the crew got their things together with a bit more decorum. The pilot emerged from the cockpit, followed by her partner.

She smiled at me wryly. "You know, you are supposed to stay in your seat until I give the all clear."

"Yeah, well. Shoulda, woulda, coulda. Sorry. I'm a bit anxious to get my feet on the ground, no offense. The flight was great and all. Both flights, in fact."

Claire clapped a hand on my shoulder and I jumped. "Don't mind her. She rambles when she's nervous."

"Really," drawled the pilot, "I hadn't noticed." She opened the door and nodded at me. "Safe travels, Ms. Alvarsson, Ms. Brucie."

"Thank you, Miss-?"

"Mrs. Fenig. It's been a pleasure."

We shook hands, and I exited the plane. The yellow Scout was there, in good shape despite having been at the center of a minor fae battle just two days before, parked next to the dark car of a private cab service.

We walked over to the vehicles, unsure what to do next. Alec walked by, taking our packs and throwing them in the back of the Scout. "Ok, say your goodbyes. The car service is going to take Amber and the others to the cabin."

"Is that safe?" I asked doubtfully.

"Totally. We use this service all the time. They're on our side, half their family lives in Aeden."

"Okay, well then I guess we'll see you guys later," I said, turning to the others. Alec placed the small pouch containing the Lux essence in Jade's hands.

"It's in your hands now. Guard this with your life. See that it makes it back to Bran."

"To my daughter. Yes, I will get it there." She tucked the pouch into her bra, saying "There's only ever been one man brave enough to venture in here."

"Saucy as ever, Jade," I laughed, giving her a big kiss on the cheek and then saying something I'd always imagined only Valkyries or War Boys said. "I'll see you in Valhalla."

"In Valhalla," she agreed, kissing me back.

CHAPTER 29

Four hours later, we finally pulled into Rose's driveway in Falls Depot. The clock on the dashboard read 12:54 am.

"Park next to Cooper's Jeep," I said, pointing at the rusty Wrangler. "She said she'd wait up for us, but not to wake her parents. She doesn't want to worry them."

"Gee, why would they," Claire said, rubbing a hand over her face in an attempt to wake up. "Nothing to worry about here. Just a darkling hanging out with their impressionable young daughter, and another one waiting in the wings to have a freak out."

"Hush, you," I scolded her. "There she is."

Rose waved to us from the side door of her kitchen, putting a finger in front of her lips warning us to keep the noise down. We all got out of the car, closing the doors on the Scout carefully.

We walked inside and followed her down the hall to her room to see Cooper holding a bag of peas over his cheek and Rose's eyes rimmed with runny, black makeup.

"You've been crying. And you've been pounded. What happened?"

"It's over," Rose hiccupped, looking like she was fighting back more tears. "It's too late. Rowan's already Chosen."

"What do you mean he's already Chosen? You said it would happen today!" My voice rose and Claire shushed me.

"It did," Cooper said sadly. "At midnight. Shades Choose at midnight."

"Of course they do," I said, collapsing into a chair and stroking Miko absently in my lap.

"I'm so sorry," Rose said, rushing over to comfort me. "I should have known. I didn't think—"

"None of us did," Alec stopped her. "It's not your fault. It all happened so fast."

"I tried to talk him out of it." Cooper lowered the bag from his cheek to reveal a deep yellow bruise. "He called me a traitor. He said I never loved Holly, if I would join the people who killed her. I tried to reason with him, to point out that it was the Shades attacking that caused the accident in the first place, but he wouldn't listen. When I touched him, he punched me and threw me out of his house. That was over an hour ago, before all the Council members started arriving at his place."

"Are you sure it's over? How long do these things take?" I asked.

"You can't be serious," Claire said.

"That's exactly what I am. How long, Cooper?"

"I don't know, I suppose it might still be going on. But you can't go in there with all those people. The house is full of Shade bigwigs and their bodyguards."

"Well, then, let's go," I stood, looking at Alec.

Rose shook her head. "I can't. As a Druid, there is only so far I can go. We are supposed to remain impartial, however we may actually feel. Vala doesn't want me involved tonight. But I think you should go."

"Okay, thank you for everything you've done, Rose. Really, you've already gone far and beyond the call."

"Hardly," she said. Looking past her for a minute, I saw something in the corner that made my eyes pop.

"Is that my—?"

"Yeah, I saw it in the pile of stuff on your porch," she said eagerly. "Your landlord gave most of your stuff to charity, I think. But I was able to sneak off with your gear."

I rushed over and fingered the gray and purple jacket hanging over my old Anu snowboard. "You put the bindings back on," I whispered.

"Yeah, well, they were just sitting there in the pile. I didn't see any gloves though."

"That's okay, I probably needed a new pair, anyway." Fitting my goggles over my head, I turned and grinned at my friends. "Hey, Alec?"

"Yeah?"

"Is there really no snow in Aeden?"

"No snow. But we do have some killer sand dunes," he said, grinning back.

"Well, then, let's stop wasting time." I hefted the board and jacket on one hip and invited to Miko run up my other arm and sit on my shoulder. "Let's go get our friend back."

I walked back outside and put the board in the trunk with the rest of our bags. The new boarding jacket was way warmer and cleaner than the sexy black one I'd borrowed from Amber back in Montreal, so I ripped off the tags and swapped coats, stowing the black one with the rest of the gear.

Coming around the front, I saw Cooper with his hand on the door. "Coop. You don't have to come. I don't want to cause any more problems between you and Rowan."

"Don't sweat it, Serious. I want to do this. Besides, if anyone sees us, they know me. I'm still a darkling, my own Choosing isn't for another month and no one knows I am going Light aside from Rowan. I can distract any adults so you can get in."

"Okay." It was risky, and I didn't like it. But I wasn't going to argue, either. Cooper was right. He could help. I nodded, and he hopped in the front with Alec.

Rose's house was just a few minutes from the Carey's. Cooper motioned for Alec to park over a couple houses away where we watched car after car pulling out of Rowan's driveway.

"It's over," Cooper moaned.

"It's not over until I say it's over." I jumped out of the car and started walking down the sidewalk. I could hear everyone else getting out, and Alec jogged to catch up with me.

"You have a plan?" he asked.

"Nope."

"Sounds good to me."

We stopped in the shadow of a large tree and peered through the hedges. Rowan was standing on the front steps with his parents and my old nemesis, Emelie Helzer. His mother had an arm around him while she beamed and waved to the last car driving away. Once the car had left the driveway she stood up on her toes and gave him a kiss on his cheek, tousling his hair before she went back inside. The blue had been washed out of Rowan's hair and he wore a plain dark suit.

He looked like a mannequin at Macy's. He hadn't moved since I saw him. Not to wave, not to smile. He stood still, like a statue. Like a stone that nothing could touch. His father turned and smiled at Rowan proudly, clapping him hard on shoulder.

"I'm proud of you, son," Sullivan Carey said. I could just barely hear him at this distance. "A shame your sister couldn't be here to see this."

Rowan flinched, the only reaction I'd seen from him yet.

"Thank you, father," was all he said. His voice sounded wooden, hollow.

"You coming inside?"

"Not yet."

"I understand. Just don't do anything your mother wouldn't approve of," Sully winked at them both, making me want to hurl.

"Yes, father."

"And don't stay out too late. You're going to want to get a good night's sleep before Mikael's men come to escort you to camp. And your father's going to want you home, too, Emelie. I believe he said something about your first job starting tomorrow."

"Camp?" I whispered to Cooper.

Cooper shook his head, looking as confused as I was.

"Mindwashing," Miko clicked angrily. "They take the newly Chosen and they mindwash them, train them to be twisted and evil. I've heard stories from the animals that live near these places. They say no one comes out the same." Miko twitched his tail anxiously.

"What is it?" Alec asked, looking from Miko to me, not understanding what Miko said.

"Tomorrow morning, they take him to be brainwashed, trained to be a good and proper Shade," I spat out, watching Mr. Carey walk inside, leaving Emelie and Rowan alone on the porch.

Emelie sidled up to Rowan and wrapped her arms around his neck, whispering something into his ear.

He shook his head, removing her hand from his neck and stepping away from her.

"I think I need to take a walk. Clear my head."

"I could help you with that," she said suggestively, trailing her fingers down his chest, "how about we just let our fingers do the walking?"

"No. I think I need to be alone. You should go home, Em," he shrugged in a friendly way, but the smile didn't reach his eyes.

"Okay, I get it. I felt the same way when I had my Choosing, like I was going to burst out of my skin," she said smugly. "The powers...they're bubbling up inside you already, aren't they?"

He nodded stiffly and she tossed her long blonde hair coquettishly, leaning up and pecking him on the cheek. "Call me when you get back from camp, Rowan. I think you'll find we're a better fit than you know."

She turned and flounced back to her car, the bounce of her tiny skirt showing more leg than I ever would have deemed decent in public.

"Floozy," I hissed.

"What?" said Claire.

"Nothing," I ground out.

"I don't think Siri likes Rowan's new girlfriend," Alec noted sarcastically.

"She's pure evil, trust me," I said. "No offense, Coop."

"None taken. Emilie's...well, let's just say she's always had issues."

We waited in the bushes as her car passed, watching her primp her hair in the mirror while she spoke into her phone looking like the cat who ate the canary.

I looked back toward the house. Rowan was already heading toward us down the driveway, and I pushed everyone further into the shadows.

"Wait," I hissed. "We'll follow him to a safer area, away from the house."

He emerged onto the road and started walking away from us. We followed at a distance.

When he rounded a corner onto an empty street, we did, too. And when I say empty, I mean empty.

Rowan was suddenly nowhere in sight.

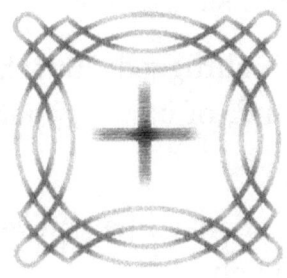

Chapter 30

"Where'd he go?" Claire whispered.

"I don't know." I scanned the road in both directions, wondering how we could have lost him.

"Oh, I'm sorry, were you looking for me?" Rowan shimmered into view, his eyes reflecting the light strangely, almost as if they were glowing on their own. He'd cloaked himself, the same way Airmed had disguised her cottage. "I could hear your emotions buzzing like static on a bad radio station. It's annoying."

"Siri," Alec warned, trying to step in front of me.

"No, Alec, it's okay. I got this." I stepped around him. The fact that Rowan's new powers were already manifesting made me a little nervous. What else had changed in the short time since I'd last seen him?

"Yeah, Alec," Rowan sneered. "She's got this. Geez. Over-protective much?"

"Should I be?" Alec asked calmly.

"Probably," Rowan shrugged. "But then again, you have me outnumbered. And, of course, you're a bit late to the party."

"Yeah, so we saw. Looks like you've fallen in with the wrong crowd," I said lightly.

"Wrong crowd? Oh, I suppose you mean Emelie? But then, you two've never gotten along. So much jealousy and so little of me to go around." He pursed his lips, feigning an apology. "Sorry, doll, if you've come here to say you're sorry and you want me back, it's too late. I've moved on."

"Maybe for us, but it's not too late for you, Rowan," I said calmly. "Whatever and whoever you've chosen. It doesn't matter. I don't think it's possible to ever lose your light, not completely. I can't believe that. The light's still in you, Rowan. You've just turned away from it."

"I don't think so. Do you see this pin?" Rowan said, cocking his head and pointing to a small silver rune pinned to his chest. "This is perthro. It means I'm an empty cup, that I've poured out all my Light and I can be filled with the truth now. Every Shade gets one when they Choose, it's the symbol of our initiation, a declaration that Shades make their own fate. But it's nice to know you still care. Really, I'm touched," he said, touching his chest ironically.

"Look, if you would just listen to me, talk to me, I know we can work this out. I still care about you, Rowan, we all do."

"Yeah, even if you do have a mean right hook," Cooper added, earning a sneer from Rowan.

"What do you want from me, Siri?" Rowan threw his arms wide. "You want me to sacrifice myself to the Light, too. You think your side is all cheery and good? You are so wrong, you have no idea. My father and Mikael, they told me. They told me how the Light lies, how it corrupts. How it kills."

"No, Rowan, that's not true. It's the Dark that kills. Ask Alec what they did to his family, to his baby sister. We're not looking for a fight. We're just trying to protect our people. Protect all people."

"Really?" Rowan laughed. "Who died and made you gods? Because you know, that's what people used to think we were – gods. And maybe we are. Maybe we should be."

"No, that's Mikael talking. That's not you."

"You don't know me. You knew some idiot who let you run off to Aeden with another guy, some dreamer who thought if he turned Light he could get you back. Forget you, Siri. Everything that's happened, Holly dying, everything, it's all your fault. You and that idiot dreamer. I don't want to know either of you anymore."

"Rowan, I—"

"Maybe you should just leave it, kid, the vibes I'm getting off him, they aren't good," Miko burst into my head.

"What's he going to do?" I asked silently. Miko didn't answer, a low growl humming through his body as he stood at attention on my shoulder. An uneasy chill crept up my spine, but I pushed it down. Light and love, I thought, pushing a small stream of healing energy out toward Rowan, drawing up energy from the earth. Light and love.

His faced relaxed as my energy reached him. He closed his eyes and looked blissful, leaning back his head as the tension left him for a moment.

He straightened, and opened his eyes. Now, they were definitely glowing. The rich vibrant blue looked out of place in the evening light.

"Thank you, Serious." He smiled at me and took a step forward. "You've made everything so much clearer."

"Rowan?" I gushed, "It's okay, you can Choose again, you'll be safe with us. I promise." I was so happy I'd reached him.

He laughed, and looked down at his hands. "Yes, I am sure I would be. Safe, and weak and disgusting. Just. Like. You." His words didn't register until he lifted his hands and threw out a massive ball of blue energy that grew as it approached. Two feet across, five feet across, ten feet across. Rowan shimmered out of view and just as I had time to think that it was going to take us all out, Miko leapt off my shoulder and met the light head on.

"No!" I screamed. Miko fell limply to the ground and the light dimmed significantly, but it kept coming. When it hit me, I collapsed in an onslaught of emotions. Sadness, anger, shame, fury, blame, and glee burst through me so powerfully that my knees buckled and I stopped breathing. The last thought I had as my head hit the ground was that my heart had broken into a thousand frozen pieces.

I stumbled hard onto my knees, hard pieces of rubble pelting my back. I wanted to cry out with the pain of it, but I didn't dare make a sound. In the darkness, I scooted to one side of the tunnel, hoping to hide in plain sight. A sharp stone jackknifed the crown of my head and I gasped.

I thought frantically. Where was Alec? Where were my friends? The way out was blocked. The barrier was failing. There was only one thing left to do. I would have to lead the Shades into Aeden.

I started to stand and my head swam, nausea bubbling up from inside. I reached out to steady myself against the cavern wall and misjudged the distance, tilting and hitting the wall hard with my shoulder. More pain rocketed up my arm and I moaned...

"She's coming around."

I could hear another girl moaning in the darkness, but I couldn't see a thing.

"Come on, Siri, open your eyes, dammit. Wake up!" Alec's voice pleaded with me, his hands holding my face. The surge powered through me, making me gasp. I opened my eyes, silver eyes staring up into rings of purple incandescence, the rest of his face shadowed by his hair. I was on the hard ground and it was cold.

"Is she awake? We have to go, man." Cooper's voice broke through the ice. "Who knows if he's coming back with reinforcements."

"Maybe he's just leaving us out here to die of hypothermia," Alec muttered. "Or maybe he's watching us right now and we just can't see him. The coward."

"Whatever. I'm sorry, but I'm not sticking around to find out. Do you want help carrying her back to the car or not?"

"It's okay," I said. "I can walk."

I tried to get up, but my body betrayed me. I could barely even move my arm.

"Forget this." Alec stood and swept me up into his arms. "Cooper, Claire, you guys take point to the car. I'll follow with Siri."

"We should take the long way around the block, just in case he's headed back here with his parents," Cooper warned.

"Fine, whatever. Let's just go. She's not exactly made of air, you know."

"Hey, I can hear you," I slurred.

He ignored me and set off at a brisk pace, following Cooper away from where we had been. Where had we been? What had happened? The details were foggy. I knew we'd been talking to Rowan, but I couldn't remember why, or what had made me wake up on the ground. I struggled to remember, but the effort was too great. Being carried by Alec was making my brain feel like a basketball dribbling about in my head. The constant pounding was more than I could take, but I sensed the group's urgency and didn't dare say anything. I wasn't sure I could speak without throwing up, anyway. I closed my eyes again and gritted my teeth, pushing my head into Alec's shoulder. Instead of clearing my brain, the darkness pulled me back down within its shroud, where the pain grew distant and nothing mattered.

The next time I opened my eyes I was back in the Scout, the bright neon glare of the Depot's all-night gas station slicing through the windows.

"Argh. Turn off the lights," I moaned, shielding my eyes. I was lying across the backseat, my back against the door. Claire turned around in her seat up front while I watched Alec walk into the convenience store by himself.

"Nice to see you awake again," Claire smiled. I could see the worry around her eyes, despite her light tone. "Alec is paying for our gas and getting us some snacks for the road."

"Where are we going? Where's Cooper?"

"We're going back to Aeden, Siri. We just dropped off Cooper at his house."

"Where's Rowan? Isn't he coming with us?"

Claire's smile faltered. "I...you don't remember?"

I frowned, sitting up. My head throbbed gently in protest, but I ignored it.

"I remember talking to Rowan, and he was mad at us. At me. But I got through to him. I remember he smiled and he was going to come with us. Why isn't he with us?" Nothing made sense to me, and trying to suss it out was making my brain hurt again.

"That's the last thing you remember?" Claire bit her lip, clearly not wanting to say anything else.

"Well, yeah. Come on, Claire, I know all your tells. You're holding out on me. Spill it."

"Rowan wasn't ever going to come back with us."

"Yes, he was. I remember." I could see his smile, his easy grin. For a second, I saw his grin twist into a sneer, like a transparency superimposed over my memory, and I shook my head to clear the image.

"He was messing with you. He used his water powers to weaponize his emotions, he flooded you with them. Actually, all of us. I was so surprised, I didn't even get a chance to try out my new power. But you were his target, and you were hit the worst. If Miko hadn't gotten in the way—"

Alec opened the door, interrupting Claire's train of thought, while I was left seeing a flash of blue light hurtling towards me through space, and Miko, leaping straight into it.

The pieces were coming back to me, and each fragment stung like the shards of rock in my vision.

"Alec," I sat up, the effort making my voice shake.

"Hey babe, nice to see you're up." He turned and smiled calmly at me, holding out a small brown bag. "I got you some things."

He spoke softly, like you would to a convalescent.

I snatched the bag out of his hand, tossing it on the seat next to me.

"Where is Miko?"

Alec swallowed. "Maybe you should rest, Siri. We can talk about this later."

"No. Where is he?"

"I have him," Claire said before Alec could speak again, shooting him a look.

"Why didn't you just say that?" I asked, glaring at Alec. "He got knocked out, too, huh?"

"Not exactly," Alec said. I looked at him, not understanding.

"Rowan's magic. Miko took the most of it. That ball was meant for you, Siri. It was meant to take you out. Permanently." Claire looked at me, willing me to understand.

"Where is Miko? Give him to me," I ordered, suddenly finding it hard to breath.

Claire reached for my bag on the seat next to her and handed it to me. Inside, Miko lay limply. He looked so tiny. I picked him up in my hands, cradling him carefully.

"He's cold. I need to heal him, Alec, give me your hand, I need the earth energy."

"No, Siri." He shook his head sadly.

"But he's—"

"He's dead."

"No, he's not, he's—"

"Yes, he is. He's been dead for over an hour. He saved your life, Siri. Maybe all our lives."

"He knew what Rowan was going to do. He tried to warn me." I couldn't cry. I wouldn't.

"He was a brave friend," Claire offered, reaching for me over the seat. I shrank back, cradling Miko's lifeless form against my chest. He was so tiny. He'd never seemed so small before.

A car pulled into the station behind us, and Alec looked through the window with narrowed eyes.

"We can't stay here, we don't know who Rowan may have alerted. I really am sorry about Miko, but he did what he needed to do to protect you. Now, we need to get as much distance as possible between us and Falls Depot." He turned the key and rolled toward the road. "We'll give him a hero's burial when we get to Valhalla. If we drive all night, we can be there by late morning."

I nodded my head, then had a thought.

"No. I know where we need to go. It won't take long. Turn right here, and take the next left onto route 100."

Alec looked at me doubtfully in the mirror, hesitating.

"Just do it, Alec," I ground out. "We're taking him home."

CHAPTER 31

When I saw the sign saying we were almost at Mount Snow I tapped Alec on the shoulder and had him pull over. I doubted I'd ever find the exact spot where I had first encountered Miko, even if it wasn't dark, but I knew we were really close. I crossed the road and walked to the edge of the woods, taking a deep breath.

I wasn't ready to say goodbye.

Behind me, I heard Alec rummaging through the back of the truck before he and Claire joined me. He held up a small emergency shovel.

"Where do you want me to dig?"

I looked around at the frost-covered forest.

"The ground's going to be too hard to dig this time of year. If we don't bury him deeply enough, some animal will just come along and dig him up. There's an old stone wall over there – come on, I have an idea."

I led our small group deeper into the woods, stopping on the far side of an ancient stone wall, the kind you find zig-zagging through the woods all over the place in New England, thanks to a whole lot of sheep-crazy farmers back in the 1800's.

"This'll do. We'll build a cairn over him. If the rocks are big enough, the animals will leave him alone."

I knelt down and cleared a deep hollow in the leaves. I reached up and pulled my scarf from around my neck, wrapping Miko in the warm grey knit. Tears sprang to my eyes, and I kissed the tiny bundle I had made.

"Goodbye, little guy. I am really going to miss you. You did so much more for me than I ever did for you. I wish I could have known you longer."

I placed him in the hollow, nestling him among the leaves. Claire placed a handful of acorns next to the bundle, and Alec started to bring over some large rocks, laying them carefully around Miko to form a small burial tomb. We laid a capstone over the top that required all of us to lift it, and then we set about covering the entire structure with more rocks even as the cold stones turned our fingers numb. When the pile reached our waists and stretched out at least as wide I motioned for everyone to stop.

"It's magnificent," Alec said, rubbing the small of my back. "The best burial any squirrel ever had."

"Thank you, Alec." I hugged him. "You, too, Claire. Miko would have loved those acorns. He was all about the food."

"We really should go," Alec reminded me.

I heard an owl hooting nearby, and I had an idea.

"Hold on. I just want to do one more thing before we go."

I knelt beside the cairn, placing my hands upon the icy granite stones and reached down into the earth with my energy. I sent out a call to the owl, willing it to come closer. I could hear by its thoughts that it was the night sentinel of these woods, and it would spread the call among the animals. I asked her to let them know that a hero had died today, one of their own, and that we had come to honor him.

The owl landed silently in a nearby tree and cocked its head, waiting to hear what I had to say.

"Tonight," my voice rang out, "our dear friend Mikowa gave his life to save four fae from the Dark. It was not the first time. He saved me when men attacked my home, and he helped me understand who I really was. He shared my meals, he journeyed with me to Aeden, the land below, and he lived among the branches of the World Tree, the Tree of Life, under the never-setting Red Sun. He traveled across the ocean with me and showed me how to hear the song of the Sun as it rises. He was the bravest warrior I have ever known, and the truest friend. He comforted me when I had no one else. I loved him with all my heart. On the longest nights and the darkest days, remember to sing of Mikowa the Brave as the sun rises, and remember that we all have the power to be true heroes. For heroism lies in our hearts. In our power to love. It does not matter how big you are, only how brave, how true. When in doubt, remember, Miko, always. Aho-Em!"

The owl bowed its head and flew away, calling out its new song, the song of Mikowa. In the distance, I heard other night birds respond to the owl's song, and a fisher cat howled in the distance, lamenting the fall of its distant cousin. I had vowed not cry, but my face was wet with tears.

I sent one final tug of energy down into the ground and called up one of my favorite wild plants, the small, spicy evergreen vines of wintergreen. Dark shiny leaves forced themselves out the depths of the ground, twining up over the cairn, weaving between and above the stones. The longer the vines grew, the more leaves appeared, small white teardrops of flowers bursting forth. Soon, the tomb was completely enveloped, both in homage and protection for Miko's final place of rest.

It was done.

I stood, and Alec embraced me from behind, his warm coriander scent overpowering the minty tones of the wintergreen. "It's beautiful. Just like your eulogy."

"He told me once that just going to Aeden was enough for him, more than he'd even dreamed of seeing in his life. I hope he is in a better place." I chuckled, wiping the tears from my face. "Somewhere with really, really awesome food."

"No doubt, he is giving the other squirrels in the great world tree a run for their money."

"How can you do that?" I asked peevishly. "How can you believe in the legends of the old gods, when you live in the legends? I mean, the great world tree? Your apartment is next door to it. It came here in a spaceship. Not from heaven. The world was created by your people. Not some god."

"Yes," Alec answered patiently. He dragged a hand through his hair, thinking. "But those legends are not just about our tree, or about our eldest Ancients. The Ancients themselves, they carried those stories with them from our old world. Our tree of life is but a seedling of the great world tree. Our Ancients are but the babies of the old gods. The folktales we grew up on? They are the stories of the stories of the stories of our people. All legends begin with a seed of truth. Do not turn away from the magic of our world, of all worlds, simply because you weren't there when the story began."

"Claire? You've been studying this. What do you think?" I asked, wanting to believe, but feeling perversely opposed to the idea. "Do we really have souls? Do we live on after all this?"

"I don't know. I haven't see both worlds like you and Alec. But yes. Inside, part of me...just knows. The stories carry the song of truth from Spirit, from other worlds beyond ours, from the source of all time, all space, all life. Miko isn't dead. He's just not here anymore."

"God, I hope you're right." I sighed. "Let's go. Wherever he is, we've done all we can for him. Right now, more than anything, I think I'd like to see my mom."

"She's probably eating Jello right now, asking for a proper breakfast," Claire said, smiling at me as we walked back to the car. This time she got in the back, saying it was her turn to sleep for a while. I grabbed the keys from Alec.

"Come on, get some rest. I promise I won't wreck Ewan's precious heap. You need to sleep, too."

"Fine. Just follow the GPS and wake me when we get to the border. It's about four hours away, we can switch then."

"Yeah, yeah, okay." I slid into the driver's seat and connected my phone to the stereo, scrolling through the menu. I selected a Moby album and put the Scout in gear. Alec leaned his seat back and closed his eyes. I ran my fingers through his hair.

"Sweet dreams, Alec."

"Just drive, already," he muttered, grinning even though he kept his eyes closed. "Before this craptastic music of yours puts you to sleep, too."

"Hey, this is classic Moby," I protested.

"Classic lullaby, more like it." He snorted and rolled over on his side, tucking his hand up under his cheek and looking at me.

"Whatevs," I shrugged. "You wouldn't know good music if you had front row seats at the show," I said, and eased my foot off the brake, continuing north on Route 100 toward Canada.

Alec smiled, and his eyes closed for good this time. I knew he didn't really care about the music, that he'd been teasing me to take my mind off of things. I loved him for it.

I didn't need it, but I appreciated the gesture.

He had no way of knowing that nothing would distract me now. Because I knew something. When I'd reached into the earth and connected with its power, I'd relived the

288

moment that Rowan's sphere splashed past Miko and into me. The memory had passed through me in slow motion, second by second, like the earth was trying to show me something important.

We didn't need to fight the Dark.

We needed to heal them.

Because at the center of Rowan's anger was a hard kernel of fear so dark, so intense, so dense, that no light could penetrate it. He could never forgive me, because that fear held him back and tainted each decision he made, every thought he had.

The secret that no one knew, not even Rowan, was that the kernel of fear was like the hull of a seed. It held everything within it that Rowan needed to get past his anger.

The earth knew how seeds worked. And now, I did, too. Somehow, I just needed to expose that kernel to enough warmth that the love inside, the light inside, could burst out, just like the wintergreen from the barren, frozen ground.

I had no idea, of course, how to do that.

I couldn't share my thoughts with Claire and Alec, not after what had just happened. They would never believe me. They hadn't really wanted me to talk to Rowan in the first place, they hadn't thought I had a chance. They thought the darkness inside him was too strong to fight.

If I told them what the earth had shown me, what I had felt, they would chalk it up to wishful thinking. But I knew better. I knew the answer was inside that seed. The best part? It was already planted. I just had to find a way to make it grow.

So I did the only thing I could do. I kept driving.

Toward Aeden. Toward my mom. And, hopefully, toward some answers.

CHAPTER 32

I didn't wake Alec at the border. The customs officials grinned at me over their pre-dawn coffees when they glanced in the car, quietly checking passports while Claire dozed peacefully in the back and Alec snored loudly enough to raise the dead. A minute later we were on our way again.

The drive was peaceful. It gave me time to think. By the time we reached the cabin near the tunnels that led to Aeden, I was feeling a lot better. My mind was relaxed. At some point during the long drive, I'd realized that Vala and Airmed were right. I needed to trust more. I would find a way to honor Miko and Holly, to make their deaths mean something. I would not just give up on Rowan, or any of the dark. If the Shades could make an anti-serum, why couldn't we? I had a thousand ideas and no leads, but hope had given me a new source of energy and excitement. I couldn't wait to get back to Valhalla. I hadn't had any visions to prove it, but I knew that the prophecy was true. Somewhere inside of me, like that kernel of fear inside Rowan, I held the power to change everything. I just needed to figure how to unlock the code.

I parked among the hemlocks behind the cabin and watched the early morning sun sparkling through the pines. I'd missed its dawn song, but in my mind I could still hear it. It was a moment with Miko that I would treasure forever.

"Hey sleepy heads, time to get up." I roused the troops when I got out of the car. I stretched and decided to check out the cabin. Inside was pretty spare, just a woodstove, two cots piled with woolen blankets, a small pantry and a manual composting toilet behind a curtain. After five-plus hours in the car, the last was like a gift from the gods. The seat was freezing, but at least I didn't have to go in the woods.

Checking the pantry, I found a large store of dried jerky, nuts and fruits in glass jars. I munched on some nuts and apricots and grabbed some jerky for the others.

Claire stumbled into the cabin, her breath making little puffs of smoke in the cold air.

"Oh wow, is that food?" She pointed to the jerky and I nodded, biting the inside of my cheek when she groaned. Claire had never been a morning person, but she always woke up starving.

"There's more in the cabinet, too. Lots of fruits and nuts, take your pick."

"I don't suppose there's a bathroom here, too?"

"No running water," she made a face when I said that, "but there's a camp toilet in there. Just sprinkle some of the sawdust inside and turn the hand crank on the side after you go."

"Weird, ok."

"There are directions on the wall if it doesn't make sense."

"Yeah, yeah, I got it." She waved me away and went behind the curtain. I decided to give her some privacy and left the cabin, walking straight into Alec.

"Jerky?" I said, holding up a stick of spicy dark meat.

"Mmm," he said, biting it out of my hand.

"Savage."

"Thanks, Speed Racer. What happened to waking me up at the border? And just how fast were you going to get here in under six hours?"

"That's for me and Sacagawea to know, and you to never find out," I quipped back. "Besides, you were snoring too loudly to hear me at the border. The customs guys got a real kick out of it."

"Who the hell is Sacagawea?"

"Um, famous Native American guide, led Lewis and Clarke across the country?"

"Right, okay, but what does she have to do with your driving?"

"Um, hello, Scout? Guide? Sacagawea? I can't drive a car without a name, duh."

Alec smacked his forehead.

"Ewan is going to kill you. Naming his car. Geez."

Claire spoke up from behind me in my defense. "Sacagawea is a great name. Yay, girl power!"

We high-fived and Alec stalked off into the cabin, muttering about girls and their lack of respect for classic machines.

"So, now what?" Claire asked happily, munching away on a handful of cashews. "Do we walk? Does someone meet us here? How does this whole 'journey to the center of the earth' thing work, anyway?"

"We walk underground for a while, then we ride these awesome machines, kind of like snowmobiles but they fly. We should be in Valhalla in a few hours."

"Hours?" Claire whined. "I feel like we've been traveling for days already."

"Well, we kind of have," I shrugged. "We could cut the time if we run the tunnel."

"Blech. You and your running. Thanks but no thanks."

"It's only a mile or two," I cajoled.

"Not a chance. See these wedge heels? I don't do running, unless I am in mortal peril."

"Okay, fine. Have it your way. But you know, if you were in mortal peril, you might actually be able to outrun it if you started jogging regularly."

"That's okay. I'll take my chances," she said, popping another nut in her mouth. "And please, tell me it's true that

Aeden is really warm all the time? I am so over this winter already. I can't tell you how much I miss Egypt sometimes."

"It's definitely pretty warm where we are going. In Valhalla, at least, the temperature is pretty constant, along with the sunshine."

"Oh, I can't wait. Sounds like this girl's dream come true." Claire finished eating and yelled over her shoulder. "Come on, Alec, let's go! I got a tan to work on."

I giggled and grabbed her arm, pulling her over to the car. "Well, let's get ready, then." I pulled open the rear hatch and grabbed our bags, tossing Claire Alec's small bag and her own stuff. I hefted my snowboard under my arm and left the keys to Sacagawea behind the visor up front.

"If it's so warm in Aeden, what gives with the gear?" Claire eyed my board suspiciously as we walked back toward the cabin.

"Sand-boarding. Once I strip the wax off this thing, it'll ride just like it's on snow. Or so I hear."

"Cool. Now that, you can teach me. I don't mind moving fast, as long as it's not my own feet doing the work," she laughed.

"Deal," I grinned. "Maybe we can find someone in Valhalla to copy the board and make more. You're not going to believe some of the tech they have. And some of the tech they don't."

"I know, I know. I'm missing the internet already," she moaned. "Don't remind me."

I laughed. "It's not so bad, you'll see. I bet you won't even notice it's gone."

"Ha!" she snorted in disbelief. "Sure I won't."

Alec emerged from inside and took his bag from Claire, handing us a couple bottles of hard cider.

"Okay, ladies, ready to head out?"

"Isn't it a little early in the day to be hitting the bottle?" I asked.

"We keep these in a double cooler under the cots. Between the insulation and low alcohol content, they don't freeze through all the way. It beats going thirsty. I learned the hard way that water doesn't do so well here in the Canadian winters."

Claire shrugged at me and cracked open her bottle. "Cheers!"

I followed suit, taking a few sips and then handing my bottle to Alec. "I better not finish it. Don't want to drink and drive," I winked.

"Good point," he nodded, finishing the bottle for me and stowing his own unopened cider back in his pack. "We can't all fit on one gravicycle, especially with that board and our bags. I'll take Claire, and there should be some rope with the cycles to strap down your board."

"Sweet," I grinned as we set off into the woods. The birds were singing, the sun was shining. It was a beautiful day.

For a moment, I felt a pang of sadness in my chest, watching a gray squirrel scamper through the woods. It was the first in a string of moments I'd never share with Miko.

Alec must have sensed my sadness because he reached over and grabbed my free hand, holding it casually as we walked through the woods. On my other side, Claire smiled at me over her cider, clearly excited about our destination.

We walked on, the leaves crunching under our feet, puffs of vapor trailing away from us. Finally, the cave that led to the tunnel loomed ahead of us. Alec passed out flashlights and Claire shook her head, igniting a small blue ball of fire in the palm of her hand.

"No thanks, I got my own light," she said.

"That is so cool. I am totally jealous," I said, staring at the dancing flames.

Alec nudged me. "Who needs fire when you can see in the dark?" he reminded me of our heightened earth senses.

The fire in Claire's hand flickered as she looked up. "Can you really?"

"Yeah, not as good as this guy, but I'm working on it."

"Awesome. I guess we're all set then. Let's rock this tunnel!" She surprised me, striding fearlessly into the opening in the rocks without knowing where she was going.

Alec took my hand and we followed her into the darkness.

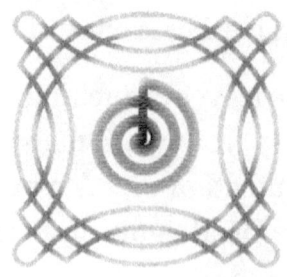

CHAPTER 33

The flight to Valhalla was exactly what I'd needed. Watching Claire's excitement when she climbed on the gravicycle and Alec helped her strap on the safety harness, following as we navigated the inky black tunnels lit with vivid fluorescing rocks, hearing her cry of shock and triumph when we'd burst out of the tunnel in the skies above Aeden, it was like watching myself all those months ago.

We dipped down through the low clouds and skimmed the trees, their purple and blue foliage glimmering below. Two massive ravens flew nearby, their black wings throwing off the warm sunlight in a flush of iridescent violet.

They cawed at us and showed off, diving and swooping in welcome. I stood up on the gold rails of the gravicycle and cawed back, feeling an immense sense of freedom and relief. It was strange, but I hadn't realized how much I had missed the underworld. I felt home.

We flew on, passing mountains, silvery streams and cerulean fields. I could see Alec pointing out various landmarks to Claire as we passed by, showing her the sights.

Finally, a giant sequoia pierced the distant horizon. As we grew closer, the seven golden spires of Valhalla became evident, circling the tree of life like children begging for candy from their mother. Above them all, the brilliant red sun of Aeden shown, casting its undying light upon the realm. As we passed over more fields and smaller buildings, Alec gradually slowed his speed from a breakneck 170 miles per hour to a sedate highway speed. He pointed at the cycle deck of tower three and started his descent.

We settled down at the far end of the deck in line with a dozen other gravicycles. While I removed my harness and started untying my gear, Claire hopped off their bike and jumped up in the air with a victory fist pump.

"That. Was. AWESOME!" She yelled. "Yes!"

I laughed. "I know, right?!"

"Please tell me we can do that again," she danced over to me and begged.

"Oh, most definitely," I agreed. "Hey Alec, where are those dunes you were mentioning?"

"There are some smaller ones near the sea here, but I was thinking we could go down the coast. The further south we go, the stronger the currents are on the sea that fuel the winds. The dunes there are huge, perfect for boarding. I don't know why I never thought of it before. And with a few gravicycles at our disposal, who needs a ski lift?"

"I'm in," Claire grinned.

"First though, we're going to need to check in with Bran and debrief." I groaned, and Alec continued, barely hiding his amusement. "And, of course, we need to check on your mother, and get Claire settled in."

"Right, of course," I sobered up. How could I have forgotten about my mom, even for a moment? Suddenly, I felt like the worst daughter ever. My feelings must have been clear on my face, because Claire wrapped an arm around me.

"Hey, it's okay. I bet she's dancing circles around the other patients by now. She'd be happy to see you smiling, you know."

"I know. It just feels weird sometimes to be doing things without her. She's been there every day of my life, you know? And now I've seen things I never even dreamed of, I have a whole new life, new friends, new home – and she's missed everything."

"I know. And I know she'd be so proud of you, too." She hugged me.

"Hello Alec, ladies." I looked up and saw Mireia striding gracefully toward us across the balcony.

"Mireia, hi! This is my friend, Claire Brucie. Claire, meet Mireia Yamuun. She can basically answer any question you could possibly have about Aeden."

"Such glowing praise," Mireia smiled, lifting an eyebrow. "Welcome, Claire. Jade informed you would be coming. We have prepared a room for you right next to Siri, so you will feel more at home during your visit."

"Thank you, Mireia. That's so great."

"Alec, Bran is waiting for you in his quarters. He requested that you head straight there when you arrive for debriefing."

"In his quarters?" Alec sounded surprised.

"Yes." Mireia ignored the question in his voice and turned to me. "Siri, if you and Claire will come with me, we can get you settled in and freshened up before you head to see Bran."

"Do I have to see Bran first? I'd really like to go see my mother. Is she awake?"

"Yes, she is, and yes, you do. Patience, faeling. Alec, did you need something, or have you forgotten how much your Commander hates to be kept waiting?"

"Um, no. Of course not." He blushed and ran his hand along the back of his neck looking at me and clearly still not wanting to leave. "I'll see you soon, Siri. Claire." He nodded at us both and stalked away. I really hoped that he wasn't going to be sent off on another mission right away. In just a few short days, I'd gotten used to having him around again.

Mireia waited as we hefted our bags, then led the way to the shady entrance to the tower. "We'll have to remove our shoes," I explained to Claire, dropping my stuff again and removing my sneakers. "They're not good for the cala."

301

"Cala?" Claire asked, slipping off her boots.

"Yeah, most of the floors here are covered in cala. It's this amazing blue grass that helps fae bodies stay energized and healthy. Something about the mega-negative ions it gives off, helps keep us young and hot," I winked.

Mireia laughed. "Not the most scientific explanation, but it'll do."

Claire ran her toes through the cala and sighed. "That's amazing. Shag carpeting has nothing on this. Why is it blue? I haven't seen a single green plant since I got here."

"The red sun triggers a different response in the plants for chlorophyll production," Mireia answered, "and the light waves slightly alter how the eyes see color, too. When exposed to the yellow sun above below, plants quickly turn green in a matter of days. The same goes for the plants from your part of the world. Within a week of exposure, they change to blue or violet."

We followed Mireia through the tower to our rooms. I left Claire with Mireia at hers and opened the door to mine. As soon as I was through the door, I was tackled by a blur of white.

"You're back!" Auroreis squeezed the life out of me. I hugged the fourteen year old back, brushing her wild platinum hair out of my face and laughed.

"I sure am."

"Oh! You need to take a bath right away, your grandmother said so. But you mustn't delay, your father is waiting in his rooms." She started taking my things from me and prodded me towards the bedroom. "I will set out some clean clothes. Your bath is waiting, I ran it as soon as Mireia sent word you were arriving."

"Okay, okay!" I laughed. "Geez. I missed you, too."

She paused, eyes wide. "Did you really?"

"Of course I did," I smiled. "And to prove it, I have some things for you."

"Really?" She clapped her hands and bounced up and down on the balls of her feet.

"Yes, really. But, I couldn't find any jeans, we didn't wind up having time to hit any stores. However, I was able to get you a pretty sweet collection of my favorite Midgard candies." I started pulling the small packages out of my bag and handing them to Auroreis. "Skittles, Mars, Nerds, Mentos, and oh, my absolute favorite, Reese's Peanut Butter Cups."

"These are really all for me?" Auroreis looked up at me with wide eyes.

"Yes," I laughed. "Try not to eat them all in one sitting."

She rushed forward, hugging me again, and then plopped down in the armchair by the closet to look through her new stash.

While she was safely distracted, I hurried into the bathroom and eagerly stripped off my clothes. There was nothing better than a bath in Valhalla. The water here was amazing, with a life force all its own. After a quick soak and thorough wash, I felt like I'd had a full night's rest.

When I came out, Auroreis was gone, but she'd left an outfit on my bed: loose, wide legged linen capris and a form fitting midriff tank in a dappled grey with white trim. The best part, in my opinion? The tank top had seamless support built in, so I never had to wear a bra, not even for glima training. The fae in Aeden had the comfort market totally cornered.

I left my rooms and knocked on Claire's door, which was opened for me by Auroreis.

"Mireia has assigned me to look after your friend, as well. I hope you do not mind. It's so exciting to meet another mid-worlder!"

"Of course I don't mind," I laughed.

"Auroreis," my grandmother called from one of the couches by the window, "please do let Claire know it is time to get out of the bath. I fear she may have fallen asleep."

"Blissed out, more likely," I giggled, watching Auroreis rush to the bedroom doors. I walked over and sat with my grandmother. "How are you? Did everything go smoothly? Did you have any problems getting here? What about my mom? Is she okay?"

"Easy now," Jade patted my leg. "Everything went fine. No one gave us the least bit of trouble. Your mother is awake, they spent all night running tests on her and the other patients and released her this morning. She's still supposed to rest, of course, although she's never been one to follow doctor's orders."

"Where are your rooms?" I asked, assuming they were sharing a suite.

"I'm right across the hall from you. Given your connection with Alec, I thought it best to be nearby.

Someone in this family needs to show some restraint," she muttered.

"Excuse me?" I asked.

"Oh, not you dear," she said absentmindedly, patting my knee. "It's your mother. She's...well, you'll see."

Worried, I started to ask what she meant but was interrupted by Claire bouncing out of her bedroom. She wore mauve linen pants and a cream ballet-style wrap shirt.

"These clothes are amazing. Siri, aren't they the softest? And that water! Wow. My parents are going to have to come to Valhalla themselves and drag me home."

"I hardly think that will be necessary," Jade said drily. "You'll return with me after Siri's choosing. The only reason your father even agreed to this trip is because I vouched for your safety personally."

"I know, I know." Claire huffed and sat on the arm of the sofa next to me. "So, now what?"

"Now, I am going to take you on a tour of the city while Siri sees her mother with Bran." Jade stood and brushed out the non-existent wrinkles in her pants.

We made our way down the hall to the central tower stairs, where we split up. The two stairs spiraled slowly around each other, one stair rising and the other descending – Jade and Claire went down, while I circled around to enter the upwards stair.

My father's quarters were one floor above mine. It was weird that we were meeting here. I could count the times I'd seen his rooms on one hand. Mostly, we met in the

Command center, where he was always working. My grandmother's words had made me nervous, too. Why couldn't I just go straight to my mom's rooms? Had she woken up different somehow? My grandmother seemed to think her behavior was off. I hoped it wasn't serious, but I was nervous that my father wanted to meet privately with me first.

With that thought, I found myself at his doors. I hesitated, taking a deep breath before I knocked.

Whatever it was, I could handle it. How bad could it be?

Alec opened the door. Looking extremely uncomfortable, he invited me in. I looked at him, questioning, but he avoided my eyes, a muscle twitching in his jaw while he fidgeted. I stepped into the room and looked around.

Oh, it was bad. It was really, really bad.

CHAPTER 34

"Mom?"

She didn't look up from where she was sitting or show any sign of having heard me.

"Um, I'm going to go now. I'm sorry, Siri, but I really can't handle this." Alec apologized, slipping out the door past me. I couldn't believe he was leaving me alone like this, while I stood there in shock.

What I was seeing just did not compute.

My mother sat wrapped around Bran on his lap, giggling like a schoolgirl while he nibbled her ear and held her close. One of her hands was fisted in his hair, and the other was under his shirt.

"Mom!" I practically shouted.

She looked up with a huge grin on her face. The look on her face was so bright and cheery, I thought she might actually combust.

"Siri!" She jumped off of my father's lap and rushed over to me, smothering me in a huge hug and kisses.

"It is so good to see you! I can't tell you how worried I was when you ran off and the Shades took me. They wouldn't tell me if they had found you, or if you'd made it away. They wouldn't tell me anything until I cooperated, but I refused to negotiate with them. Bran has been telling me everything, and Alec just caught us up to speed with your most recent troubles."

"Trying anyway," Bran grinned as my mother sat down next to him again and curled into his side.

"Um, right." I watched my mom as she absentmindedly ran her hand up and down my father's arm, the one that was gripping her possessively. "So, I see you guys remember each other," I said, pointing out the obvious.

"I know, isn't it amazing? All this time, he's been right here in Valhalla. Honestly, I never thought I'd see him again. I'd given up." She gazed up at him adoringly and I almost gagged as they kissed again. If Alec and I ever acted even half as gooey as these two, I really hoped someone would put us out of our misery. I mean, come on. Embarrassing much?

I remembered watching Ewan and Amber when they first got together, and there was just no comparison. Being in the same room with anyone like this would have been a trial, but these were my parents. It was too gross to contemplate.

It made me wonder how they'd even managed to complete their missions the first time they'd met.

I had to get out of there.

"So, ah, was there anything else you wanted to talk about, mom?" I spoke up, fidgeting with a loose thread on the couch. "I think maybe I should leave you to get some more, um, rest, maybe?"

Bran let out a bark of laughter and lifted his head from my mother's.

"I think we are embarrassing the faeling, love."

"No, not at all, it's just..."

My mom giggled again.

Giggled. Who was this woman?

"I think you're right, darling" she agreed, smoothing his hair away from his face before she sat up and beamed at me. "I'm sorry, Siri, I promise we will behave better, really."

"No, really, it's okay, just if there's nothing else at the moment I should probably go and grab some lunch. I haven't had anything to eat since yesterday."

"Oh dear, you must be starving. Run along then, we'll see you for dinner in your grandmother's quarters at six, all right?"

"Great, I can't wait." I got up, gave them both hugs, and retreated from the room as fast as I could.

I could hear them murmuring to each other and the creak of the sofa as the door slid shut behind me. I squeezed my eyes shut and did not turn around. No, I liked my eyes, just fine, thank you very much. I saw no need to develop sudden blindness or require burning them out of my head.

I leaned against the door and groaned. Someone started laughing and I opened my eyes to see Alec watching me as he leaned against the wall next to the door.

"You suck," I said without meaning it.

That was it. He lost it, cracking up.

I pushed away from the door and started walking away, wanting to get as much distance between me and my parents as possible.

Still laughing, Alec chased after me and caught up. "I'm so sorry, I was just coming out to try and warn you away when you showed up. At least you got out of there quickly. I was stuck in there for a whole half hour, debriefing Bran while they cuddled and made eyes at each other. No one should ever have to see their boss like that." He winced, "Not ever."

"Ugh, don't remind me. How about we agree to never speak of this again? Maybe they will have mellowed out by the time we eat dinner."

"Dinner with them?" Alec groaned. "No, please, I am not ready to see Bran again today. Or tomorrow. Or this month."

"No way. You are not leaving me alone with them. Nuh-uh. If I have to suffer, so do you." I sidled up to him suggestively. "Don't you know, that's what relationships are all about?"

Alec looked at me, the violet ring within his emerald eyes flaring. "Oh yeah? I don't know. Maybe I need some convincing."

I leaned in, smiling, and hooked my leg around his. He came forward, expecting a kiss, and I dropped him to the ground, straddling his hips with lightning speed.

"That was too easy, Mr. Ward. A Guard must never let himself be distracted."

"Oh, I don't know," he said, rubbing his thumbs over the exposed skin at my waist. "Who's to say I don't have you right where I want you?"

He reached up and put a hand behind my neck, pulling me down for a long kiss. Someone cleared their throat noisily as they approached us in the corridor, and I looked up at Dorian.

"Well, hello Dorian, so nice to see you," I greeted him with a grin.

"Has your entire family succumbed to the surge, then, Ms. Alvarsson?" he asked drily.

"I'm afraid so," I shrugged, looking up at him innocently.

Alec laughed and I stood up, giving him a helping hand. He peeked at the report in Dorian's arm and shook his head.

"If you're heading to see the Commander, I'd wait an hour. Maybe a day. Seriously, you do not want to go in there right now."

Dorian looked horrified. "But I was told by Tower Four to get these papers to him immediately."

"Trust me," I said. "He will not thank you if you interrupt them right now."

I shuddered. Just thinking about it skeeved me out.

"Wait, did you say Tower Four?" I asked. "Is it about the cure?"

I leaned over, trying to get a look at the papers but Dorian swatted me away.

"I don't know, and even if I did, I certainly wouldn't be telling you, faeling."

"Fine, whatever, Dor. I'm sure he'll tell us all about it at dinner, anyway. Have fun with your 'debriefing'," I laughed, taking Alec by the hand and dragging him away.

CHAPTER 35

Several hours later I was sitting between my mother and father at my grandmother's table. Alec was on my grandmother's right, across from my mother, and Claire sat next to him, across from me. My grandmother had made us all place cards, much to my own relief, and my mother and Bran's disappointment. Separated by several feet, their ardor seemed to have cooled somewhat.

At least they wouldn't be making out at the dinner table. I wasn't sure how much more my eyes (or ears) could have taken.

My grandmother finished blessing the food and placed her napkin in her lap. The rest of us followed suit. Auroreis and another young girl carried in steaming bowls of a brilliant azure blue slurry – some sort of pureed leaf soup, as far as I could tell. A rich dollop of cream floated in the middle, softening the fresh spicy flavor of the soup.

"This is wonderful, mother, my first real sit-down meal in longer than I can remember. Thank you for having us," my mom smiled at Jade.

"You make it sound as if I haven't fed you, Frederika," my father chided.

"Well, I did say sit-down, didn't I?" my mother said off-handedly.

I almost choked on my water, imagining how and where my father had been feeding her. My grandmother, too, apparently had the same thought, because she chimed in over-brightly.

"I'm so glad you have been resting, dear." My mother opened her mouth, looking as if she might correct that statement, but Jade plowed on. "Have we had any news about the rest of the affected patients, Bran? How are they all faring? Can Tower Four synthesize more of the cure?"

My father laid down his spoon, frowning. "Actually, Tower Four has sent me some worrying news. There was barely enough Lux essence to counteract the anti-serum in the patients they had. The scientists were only able to reserve a few drops for analysis. Unfortunately, their tests concluded that it is not something we can synthesize. If any new patients come in, we'll need to get more of the Lux essence from Airmed."

"But Airmed doesn't have any more," Claire said in dismay. "She said that she can only make a limited supply each year from the one flower she has."

"I know," Bran sighed. "Mialloch explained the process to me already. Tower Four has a team working on creating

314

a vaccine from the blood of those who have been cured, but it's a long shot. Honestly, we just don't understand how the Nelumbo Lux is able to even cure it. The magic of Airmed is beyond our science to replicate. We may just have to wait until this year's bloom is harvested to cure anyone else that gets affected."

"Can we cultivate more of the Lux?" I asked. "Make more?"

"No, apparently Airmed's never been able to reproduce the plant."

"But what if the anti-serum becomes an active virus?" I asked. "What would we do then?"

"Honestly?" Bran looked at me looking defeated. "I have no idea."

"Can that really happen?" my mom asked, looking concerned.

I nodded. "Yeah, at least, Airmed thinks that's what the Morrigan is planning. She thinks there is a way for a healer like me to jumpstart the virus, activate the cells or something. Not that I would, you know that. But she thinks that's what they are trying to do, why they want me so badly. Then they could immobilize the entire Light resistance at once, and turn humans into mindless worker bees."

"Why don't they go after Airmed?" my mother grumbled. "Why do they have to go after my baby girl?"

"Because, dear, they don't know Airmed even exists," Jade spoke up. "Most people think she's dead. She's worked very hard to stay off everyone's radar the last several hundred years. Plus, Siri's power is growing every day. After her Choosing, who knows what she'll be able to do?"

"Well, I don't like it," my mom pouted.

"I don't think anybody does," Alec agreed.

"So, what do we do about it? What's our plan?" She looked at my father for an answer.

"Right now? We prepare for anything and everything we can think of. Siri has been training for months with Amber learning glima, and is ready to start practicing lasair next. She should begin training with Alec, he's one of our best Lasrach warriors, and now that you and the others are better, I can cut back on his missions for a while."

"Actually, Siri's already up to speed on the fundamentals," Alec interrupted.

"What, since when?" Bran looked surprised. "Amber didn't tell me she'd started training you."

I shrugged, swallowing the last of my soup. "She didn't."

"I did," said Alec, smiling at me across the table. "We practiced in Montreal. She's a natural, even without knowing the actual forms. She picked it up right away."

I leaned back in my chair, arching my back and stretching. "Ewan thinks it's because of the surge. He says when he taught Amber she learned really quickly, too."

"Maybe," Alec said, waving his spoon. "But she wasn't able to match him for weeks. You picked it up in one hour."

"What do you mean, because of the surge?" My mom was staring at me. "Who's Ewan?"

I looked at Bran. "You didn't tell her?"

He flushed. "Honestly? We haven't spent that much time talking. I figured I'd leave the honors to you."

My mom crossed her arms across her chest, putting on her best "mom" look. The look she used to give me when I pretended I'd eaten dinner, but really I'd hidden it in my napkin. Yep. That look.

I fidgeted with my bread and took a sip from my glass.

"Yeah, okay. Right. Well, Alec and I met right after you were taken, he brought me here to Aeden actually, and..."

I trailed off, not quite sure how to say it.

"Go on," my mother prompted in a tone that indicated I should probably do the exact the opposite. I could hear her foot tapping under the table and winced.

"The children have a strong connection," my grandmother spoke up, saving me. "Unlike some people, they have shown tremendous wisdom and restraint. Young Alec has even had the decency to ask for my blessing."

"Your blessing?" My mother sounded strangled. "Your blessing? Who are you to give my daughter your blessing? She's only seventeen!"

I reached out and put my hand on her shoulder. "It's okay, mom. It's not like we're getting married or anything." I glanced at Alec, and saw the light go out of his eyes. "Now! I mean, we're not getting married now. Besides, I'm practically eighteen. Come on people. Someday, yeah. That's all I meant to say. We're not even having sex yet." I rolled my eyes at Alec and the humor came back into his face, dimple and all.

"Right," he agreed. "We have all the time in the world. I don't want to rush Siri into anything. I want us both to receive normal human educations, maybe even live normal lives for a while. Who knows? It doesn't matter. Whatever Siri wants, I want to be by her side, making it happen, making her happy."

"Well, I suppose I can live with that plan," my mother conceded, still looking put out.

"You should be grateful," Jade rose an eyebrow at my mother. "I think they are both acting quite responsibly. Why, based on the way some people act, I would have thought it was impossible to have any rational thought in the presence of the surge. I mean, to hear you talk, it's all 'poof', it's the surge, 'poof', it's a baby."

My mother had the decency to blush. "Yes, well...oh, look, what is this we're having now?" The girls had returned with the main course of the meal, mounds of grain salads and poached fruits.

Jade winked at me and I hid a smile behind my napkin.

Everyone served themselves from the colorful platters and returned to the business of eating. Something was bothering me, though.

"So that's it? I just keep training, relaxing and waiting for my Choosing date? Aren't we going to do anything to try and stop Mikael Morrigan?"

"We're not giving up, Siri," my dad said. "I have teams hitting every facility we can think of looking for a cure or a hint of what they're planning. I still find it hard to believe that the Shades would use something so dangerous without creating an antidote. The anti-serum must have some sort of effect on them, too. Not that Mikael is known for always thinking things out. But a few weeks aren't going to make a lot of difference where you are concerned. Enjoy yourself. Enjoy your friends and your family. Who knows what is going to happen once you have your Choosing. Your powers...they are already so strong. I haven't heard of a faeling developing powers like yours so early in generations. Be a faeling for a little bit longer. Enjoy this time."

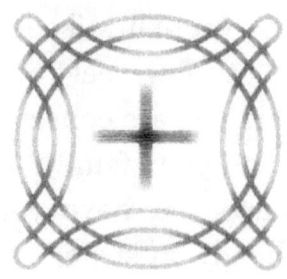

CHAPTER 36

It was a week later, and I'd taken my father's advice to heart. I'd spent part of every day nagging the interns in Tower Seven while they fabricated replicas of my Anu.

Now, here we were, standing on the high dunes of Zerssura ready to ride. We'd left most of the gravicycles at the bottom, tripling up to ride to the top.

The gleaming sandboards were finally ready for their first real run. The artisans in the R&D tower had melded the hardest wood in Aeden with a polished golden base and edges. According to their computations, the boards would practically fly on the dunes. They didn't even need waxing.

Alec, Amber, Claire and Mialloch were all standing ready in a line, waiting for my signal. We'd already spent an hour on one of the smaller, gentler hills so everyone could get the basics of it. Alec had skateboarded as a kid in Boston, so he'd picked it up easily. Amber was a natural with her small, graceful frame, and Claire was dauntless, not caring how many times she fell down.

One of the girls in Tower Four had even copied my goggle designs, creating shock-proof polarized lenses for everyone in the group. So far, they'd come in pretty handy, keeping the dusty sand out of our eyes, and we also had a sand sled, which was basically a large hammered saucer big enough for an adult to sit in cross legged. I'd figured if anyone decided boarding wasn't for them, they could still have fun. Which was a good thing, since after about ten minutes on the board, Ewan had claimed the sled for his own, claiming that his higher center of gravity made boarding impossible.

None of us pointed out that Mialloch was almost the same height as him, and seemed to be doing just fine. He wasn't exactly graceful, but he and Claire had become a sort of tag team, helping each other back up every time the other one fell in the soft warm sand. Everyone was busy laughing and having fun. The fine particles clung to our skin and got in our hair, but no one cared. It was the perfect day.

"Okay everybody! Any last questions?" I looked around at the group. Everybody shook their head. "All right, here we go!"

We all hopped forward, allowing our weight to tip the boards and create momentum. I grinned at Alec and blew him a kiss.

"Last one to the bottom has to bring my parents breakfast tomorrow!" I heckled and shot off down the dune as everybody groaned. I raised up my arm and reveled in the feel of the heated wind on my bare arms, the red sun beating down on my skin. I was free. This was home.

I saw a small lip up ahead in the sand and veered toward it, hoping to gain a good jump. Instead, the metal edge of my board caught on something hard, sending me into a spin, head over heels. I flipped, landing on my face. I could hear my friends calling my name, but I couldn't respond. I was being pulled into a vision, something familiar, dark and terrifying. I watched the scene unfold,

experienced the feelings of loss as I ran, wondering where my friends were. How would I get out of the tunnels? I felt the rocks pummeling my head and back, again. Fell into the wall, bruising my arm, again. And realized that the barrier was failing. Again.

And for the second time, I came to a bitter realization. There was only one thing left to do.

"I have to lead the Shades into Aeden," I whispered numbly.

"What?" Claire pulled up my goggles, peering into my eyes and checking for a concussion. She looked at Amber. "What did she just say?"

"I have to lead the Shades into Aeden. The barrier is going to fall, and...I don't know. I don't know why, and I don't know how," I rambled. "I just know that I was running through the tunnels, and the world was falling all around me, and I knew what I was going to do. What I had to do."

I looked at my friends kneeling around me on their boards, hoping for some sort of answer or explanation, but they all looked as shocked as I felt.

"Why would I do that?" I pleaded.

"I don't know," Alec murmured, stroking my hair. "I'm sure if you were going to do it, you would have a reason."

"Am I going to turn Dark?"

"Did you feel Dark?" he asked.

"No. I felt...desperate. Determined."

"Then don't worry," Amber said. "Look, you've had other visions that didn't pan out, like that one at your school with the tornado. Now that we know the barrier could fail, we'll let Bran and the Council know, and they'll check into any possible weak points. Disaster averted. It'll be okay."

"I don't know. My vision of the school...it didn't come true exactly, but Holly did die, that didn't change. This is the second time I've seen this same vision. I didn't remember before, but I had the same one when Rowan blasted us. And I'm not sure, but I think it's connected to the vision I had before we got on the plane in Dublin, remember, Alec?"

Alec opened his mouth, but he didn't seem to know what to say. Instead, it was Mialloch spoke up, choosing his words slowly.

"I think you should listen to Amber. There isn't anything you can do about it right now. None of us are planning on going near the tunnels in the next few weeks, so even if it's a true vision, it's not going to happen anytime soon."

"Loch's right," Alec said. "This is the happiest I've seen you in days. Don't let the Shades take that away from you. Let's do some more runs, and when we head back I promise I'll go straight to Bran. I'll even go to his quarters."

That got a smile out of me. "You'd risk running into another make-out session?"

"For you, yes." Alec stood up and offered me his hand. "Now, are you ready to conquer this mountain or what?"

I took his hand and pulled myself up. "Ready and willing, team leader," I saluted.

You could feel the tension burning away in the hot sun like water on a skillet.

"Let's do this," I smiled at everyone fit my goggles back over my eyes. I watched the rest of the group set off down the dune, Amber punching the air and shouting joyfully, racing Ewan on the sled, while Claire and Mialloch set off more cautiously. Alec hung back with me.

"You know you got this, right?" he asked, wrapping an arm around my waist. My skin tingled where we made contact, and I gazed into his bright eyes, gleaming behind the shady lenses.

"I know," I said. And I knew we both meant more than just the dune.

Whatever the Shades threw at us, I could handle it. I had the best team of friends a girl could ever ask for. My mom had reunited with the love of her life. Everything was great. Everything was perfect.

The barrier failing? Piece of cake. Shades trying to get into Aeden and dominate humanity? Let them try. The Norns had always told us life was fated. Me, I was going to make my own decisions. My own choosing.

I leaned up and gave Alec a long, deep kiss.

"We got this," I agreed.

I let go of Alec's hand and tipped my board down the hill, picking up speed as I carved my future into the surface of the sands.

ACKNOWLEDGEMENTS

Having never written a multi-book fiction series before, embarking upon the second book in this trilogy was both a daunting and exhilirating proposition. I wanted each book to be an exciting part of the story, not just a means to an end, and cliffhangers be damned. Even before I finished *Shades of Valhalla,* I knew exactly where the story was headed, how it would all end. But how best to get there?

Thankfully, I have had a wonderful, supportive group of people around me while I tackled *Fates*. Perhaps the most important is my family who never once resented the many hours I spent at the keyboard, especially my husband who slept so peacefully beside me into the wee hours of the night when inspiration would strike.

I am deeply grateful to the team at Earth Lodge for creating such luscious book covers and assembling my amazing group of beta readers. To my betas – thank you for your suggestions, and I promise all your questions will be answered in book three! The story only gets bigger and better.

ABOUT THE AUTHOR

Ellis Logan has been writing stories since she was a little girl. She lives a quiet life with her family in New England, where she enjoys skiing, hiking and eating chocolate...always chocolate!

Follow Ellis on Facebook at EllisLoganBooks

and

Join Ellis's mailing list at EllisLogan.com
to stay tuned for new releases, support the movie project, and never miss a giveaway!

Gifts of Aeden
Inner Origins Book Three
Coming Fall 2016

www.ingramcontent.com/pod-product-compliance
Lightning Source LLC
Chambersburg PA
CBHW020217260626
47156CB00002B/426